Night Sweats and Hockey Nets

HOT FLASH HOOKUPS
BOOK THREE

MARIKA RAY

SYLVIE STEWART

Night
Sweats
and
HOCKEY
NETS

Description

When I kissed her in that crowded bar, I had no idea she was my coach's daughter. I know better, believe me. It'll never happen again.

I'm on the cusp of hanging up my hockey skates forever while embroiled in a custody battle for my young daughter. I have no business getting involved with any woman. Least of all the one that's totally off limits.

Chloe, meanwhile, is embarking on a new chapter in life, determined to push aside pesky signs of impending middle age and focus on fun and adventure. Which means she has no problem exercising her flirting skills–or flaunting her impressive hockey moves and sultry good looks. In fact, I think she enjoys torturing me.

When I need a nanny to prove to the judge I have the means to take care of my daughter, Chloe steps in as the perfect solution.

Before I know it, she's moved into my house, filling it with her vibrant energy and charm, and winning over both my daughter and me. It's getting harder and harder to deny I have a crush on my coach's daughter, my kid's nanny. Suddenly, Chloe isn't the only one breaking out into night sweats...

Chapter One

Niko

I pause on my way out of the locker room, raising a finger to tell Coach I need a minute as I stare down at my daughter's text message.

Benny, our first-line center, shuffles by me with a brief, "See you in Toronto, Druggy," but I do not spare him a nod or attempt to correct him about my name. These idiots persist in using the awful nickname despite all my protests that it makes me sound like a corner drug dealer.

Damn. I should have predicted this. Why did I not listen

when Joe told me to make the new puppy a surprise? Probably because he is a sports agent and not a father.

> Me: We only need one dog

A single German Shepherd will be sufficient to protect my house and my daughter. Why would we need two?

> Ayana: You can't have Paul without Prue. It just doesn't work that way.

What is she talking about?

"Ayana?" Coach asks, taking my attention from my phone. When I look up and nod, his expression turns sympathetic. He cocks his head toward the stairs and starts that way. "Come to my office when you're done."

Chatting about dogs with my seven-year-old should not be my top priority while I am at work, but it is always hard setting her aside. Especially since I do not get to see her or talk to her nearly as often as I would like.

Peyton, my ex-wife, was pissed when I bought Ayana a phone, saying no child that age needs one. But Peyton is also the one keeping my daughter from me, so I use every tool I have at my disposal to stay in touch with Ayana. Even if it means she has to hide her phone from her mother.

> Me: The dog's name is Strakh, not Paul. Paul is the name of an actor who never ages. Strakh means terror in Russian. It is the perfect name for a guard dog.

> Ayana: Srsly?

I can read her eye roll in her text. It is one of Peyton's mannerisms, and I do not like that Ayana is picking these things up.

> Ayana: Wait. What do you mean by guard dog? I thought we were getting a little puppy.

Shit. I need to stop splitting my focus here.

I picture my beautiful daughter bent over her phone, her fine blond hair falling forward onto the screen as she frowns down at it. She probably has her lip pulled between her teeth with worry due to my carelessness. I cannot stand even the thought of her being worried or fearful—something that, to my dismay, has been unavoidable as Peyton and I fight for custody.

I drop my bag to the hallway floor and fumble my thumbs over the screen's keyboard. They need to make bigger phones for people with hands the size of mine.

> Me: He will be small and cute. Do not worry, zajushka. And he will love you no matter if his name is Strakh or Paul the Ant-Man. He will not be able to resist you.

> Ayana: K. But who's Ant-Man? Don't you know who Paul Hollywood is? He does Bake Off with Prue!

Right. I should have guessed this had to do with baking. The child is obsessed with television shows about cakes and desserts. She even made me watch some absurd show where contestants guess if something is a real object or a cake made to look like one. Where do all these people find the time for such frivolous pursuits?

> Me: I need to go now. But you can show me this program when I see you tomorrow. I cannot wait.

I silence the phone and tuck it in my bag where I will not feel it vibrate. It is time to focus on work and my meeting with Coach Bowman.

"Drugov," he greets me when I enter his office moments later. "How is Ayana?"

"A tongue without bones," I reply. "The same as always." Coach tilts his head, and I realize my answer did not translate, so I clarify, "She never runs out of things to say."

"Ah." He nods with a half-smile. Coach is excellent at keeping his finger on the pulse of the team and all its members. It is part of his coaching philosophy that hockey is 90 percent a mental game. But I am acutely aware that he has taken a special interest in me over the years, though I cannot imagine why.

I am a private person by nature, but Coach has coaxed more personal details from me than just about anyone. He knows the specifics of my custody battle just like he knows the circumstances surrounding my divorce from Peyton. The man has an uncanny knack for tracking me down when my guard is lifted, when I am most in need of a shoulder to lean on or an ear to bend. From most others, I would decline, but Coach has worked hard over time to push past my defenses without invading my privacy or being pushy.

We are cut from the same cloth, however, so it is no surprise that he generally keeps his own private life under wraps. The man has been my coach for fifteen years, but outside of hockey, I know very little about him–and I respect him too much to pry. In our conversations about Ayana and Peyton, I have learned that he too is divorced and has a daughter. Perhaps that is part of the reason we connect so well.

"How's the case going? You get any visitations recently?" he asks.

I sink into the chair across from his desk and settle my

elbows on the armrests. "I have her for the next three days." I cannot suppress my grin.

He lifts his bushy brown eyebrows. "I can find some All-Star tickets for her and Peyton if you want to fly them both up to Toronto later in the week. I'm sure Ayana would love seeing her dad do what he does best."

"That is kind, sir." I shake my head and shift in my chair. "But I am happy with the three days. I would not like to push it."

"Gotcha. Okay." As always, he knows when to move on. "I wanted to touch base before you take off for the bye week and Toronto. How are things going with Picard and MacDougal?"

I have been tasked with being a mentor to our backup goalies, Hugh "Cappy" Picard and Jack "Mac" MacDougal. "Good. They are joining me for extra workouts each morning now. Repetition is the mother of learning, yes? I am sure you have noticed Picard's left recovery sharpening up."

"I have." Coach nods, clearly pleased.

I am a pragmatist, so I am under no illusion that my hockey career as goalie for the Florida Storm Chasers or any other team will last more than another season. I knew my days were numbered when the doctor put me under the knife three years ago for my second hip surgery. That also happened to be the year we lost two-thirds of our games during my absence.

Cappy was not ready to be a starter at the time, but the team had picked him up as my backup after we lost our previous one. The whole thing was bad timing. Now we have Cappy lined up to take my place as starter and Mac ready to slide into his top backup spot once my contract is up at the end of next season. My job in the meantime is to continue dominating between the pipes and to help make sure these boys are ready when the time comes.

I am no longer twenty-five. Being a goalie is brutal on the

body, and it takes a strong disposition—and a degree of insanity—to repeatedly put yourself in the path of a hundred-mile-per-hour piece of vulcanized rubber coming your way. But I live for it. So do Cappy and Mac.

And Cappy is champing at the bit to become starter. If he is not ready, management will bring in a trade, keep Cappy at backup, and let go of Mac altogether. Coach and I are determined for that not to happen. We believe in Cappy's abilities, especially as he has grown in the last couple years.

We discuss a few ideas for Mac and chat about my performance at last night's game—the team's last one before the bye week, in the middle of which I will be flying to Toronto for the All-Star game. It is my fifth appearance at the elite event, and likely my last. Part of me considered they gave me the spot as a token gesture for all my years dominating in front of the net. But then I remembered my stats as well as all the blood, sweat, and tears I have given this season and dismissed the notion. I deserve that spot, and I intend to be on the winning team.

But all of that comes after Ayana. I have her for the next three days before I leave for Toronto. The Storm Chasers' packed schedule does not allow me to spend much time with her during the season, so I am looking forward to this uninterrupted time with my little girl. She seems to have grown an inch each time I see her. It does not help that Peyton enjoys playing games and using our daughter as her pawn.

It made sense that Peyton got primary custody when Ayana was small and I was working and traveling all the time. Hell, I am the one who paid for Peyton to stay home with her, despite our marriage having fallen apart. I did not want strangers caring for my daughter.

But that was probably my first mistake, because now Peyton flatly refuses to allow me time with Ayana unless the court forces her. And even then, she manufactures excuses to cancel my visitations and weekends whenever she can. Which is why we have been in this nasty custody battle for the past two years. I need joint custody, and I am not resting until I get it.

When I retire from professional hockey, I want my daughter with me, and each time Peyton cancels or evades is another day for Ayana to grow apart from me. She will not want to live with her father if our relationship is allowed to fade in the meantime.

I accept Coach's good wishes for the All-Star game and head out to my Land Rover in the parking lot before retrieving my phone from my bag. Expecting to see a response from Ayana about her baking show, I am blindsided by the message that waits on my screen.

> Peyton: Ayana won't be able to make it tomorrow. We're going to my parents' for a few days.

I drop my phone to my lap to keep myself from throwing it at the windshield. I am done with Peyton's games. It is time to finish this once and for all and secure my future with my daughter.

Chapter Two

Chloe

"This is so dumb," I mumble as I pull the clean fitted sheet over my mattress. At this rate, I'll need to start buying puppy pads to keep from ruining my sheets. "At least it's not a bladder control problem, right?"

I point double finger-guns at my pet fish, Sushi, like she knows anything about bladders. Do fish even have bladders? She flutters her blue fins and swims into the castle in her tank on my dresser, clearly not wanting to discuss my insane night sweats.

"Not very nice, Sushi. The least you can do is sympathize about midlifing with me. Wait, do Betta fish go through menopause?" Seems unfair to expect an animal who only lives four years to spend any of that time in hormonal hell. Sushi still doesn't come out. Which is fine. I've got a bazillion things to do and zero time to do them in.

Agreeing to attend the All-Star hockey games in Toronto just a week after moving my whole life to Tampa, Florida wasn't my smartest move. Then again, I promised myself I'd live life to the fullest, and that means saying yes to things. Including hockey things, even if Dad has warned me away from hockey boys for as long as I can remember.

Thankfully, packing isn't an issue. I still have several boxes in the corner of my new condo that say *Winter Clothes* on the side of them. Having lived in Madison, Wisconsin since college, I accumulated a lot of parkas, scarves, and sweaters. I won't be using any of that here in Tampa.

After packing appropriate clothing, I pull on my favorite leggings and a black-and-white polka-dotted corset top that puts my ample assets on display. Reaching up, I feel my curlers and discover them to be cool to the touch, which means it's the perfect time to take them out and finger comb my bouncing black curls before tying in a red bandanna as a head-band. My image in the mirror is so different from a year ago, but I like it. It shows growth.

For a few years there, I didn't have time to dress nicely or play around with makeup. Every single minute of every day was spent teaching my third graders or taking care of my ailing husband. I wouldn't have wanted to do anything else, but now that it's been some time since Josh passed, it feels like I'm ready to turn my attention to myself for once.

Satisfied with the reflection in the mirror, I step aside to zip up my suitcase and set it on the floor. "Sushi, hold down the fort. Mom said she'd stop by to feed you once a day while I'm gone. Don't let her know about the night sweats. She'll start fretting about my 'advanced age' again. The last thing I need is Mom setting me up with her friends' divorced sons."

Sushi pokes her head out of the castle and opens and closes her mouth several times, which I take as confirmation that her lips are sealed when Mom's around. One can only hope. Mom, with the very best of intentions in her heart, tried to set me up with a man just six months after Josh died. While that wasn't so bad as far as timing goes, the blind date showed up talking about marriage and monogrammed napkins and hyphenated last names. I left after appetizers, claiming a migraine coming on.

It's been over a year now since Josh's passing, and while I'm ready to date again, I need it to be casual. For fun. Something I haven't experienced much over the last few years. Is it wrong for a girl to want some physical contact from a handsome man without the heavy burden of forever hanging over her head? To lose herself in a hot kiss in a dark bar? To get sweaty in my bed from something other than night sweats?

I close the door to my duplex and hustle to the waiting rideshare out on the street. I have a flight to catch and friends waiting for me. If I get lucky, I just might meet a man in Toronto who can show me a good time for the brief few days I'm in town. Then I'll come back to Tampa and start building my new life.

The hotel in downtown Toronto is packed with fans sporting their favorite hockey players' jerseys. The energy is palpable, and it makes me happy I said yes to this trip. I dump my suitcase in my room, finger comb my hair, and run back downstairs with a leather jacket over my thin corset top. Roman LaFontaine and his fiancée, Olivia, are waiting for me at a restaurant just down the street. Roman's known me for two decades now and was even at my wedding. Thankfully, I hit it off with his new fiancée. I met her a few months after Josh's funeral when I was in Tampa scoping out condos and the possibility of moving there. She's reached out regularly to check in on me since then. Being in a better headspace now, I'm looking forward to getting to know her more.

I see them at a table tucked into the far corner of the restaurant. Roman waves and I walk over to give them both a hug before sitting across from Roman. Olivia looks gorgeous as usual, and Roman can't seem to take his hands off her. It would be cute if it wasn't so nauseating. Honestly, I'm happy for them. Everyone deserves a chance at love, no matter their age. Just not me. I don't want any more chances. I only want to have fun, no strings attached.

"You look incredible, Chloe!" Olivia gushes. "We ordered a bottle of cabernet for the table. Would you prefer something else?"

"Thank you. I've been experimenting," I admit. "And yes, cabernet is perfect."

Roman groans. "Please tell me we aren't talking about fashion tonight. I hear about shoes every single day."

Olivia is a famous trendsetter who started a shoe company a few years back. All the celebrities wear her designs, and she shipped me a pair of her most coveted shoes right after we met. She lets go of Roman's hand. "You shush. You love talking fashion."

Roman pouts but doesn't argue with his fiancée. I chuckle, enjoying the changes in him since he's gotten engaged. Roman was the perpetual bachelor for years, being photographed with puck bunnies on his arm in every city his team flew into. It's nice to see that he's settled down and found his person.

"I decided that while blondes might have more fun, I couldn't pull off such a drastic change to my brunette hair so I went jet black." I take a sip of the wine and hum at the smooth finish.

Olivia holds up her glass and swirls the deep red wine. "It's more than that though, isn't it? I know I saw you during a rough patch, but you look vibrant today, Chloe. Luscious and womanly and incredibly sexy. Right, honey?"

Roman holds up his hands, looking alarmed. "I haven't looked at anyone but you, sweetheart."

Olivia and I both roll our eyes, but I see her reach over to hold his hand again. She turns her attention back to me. "You look amazing, let's leave it at that. What have you been up to, other than moving to Tampa?"

The server comes over and tells us the daily specials. I order the shrimp dish on special, Roman gets steak, and Olivia gets a salad with the dressing on the side. She mumbles something about 'damn menopause' but I don't comment. I'm here for fun this weekend, not to rehash all my midlife problems.

"I was actually hoping to talk to you about my plans," I say once the server leaves to place our orders. "Thanks to a generous life insurance policy, I don't need to go back to teaching, but I'm not quite ready to retire yet. I want to get back to my roots."

Roman leans his elbows on the table, a big grin on his face. "Please tell me it's hockey."

Considering he met me when I was a D1 hockey player and he had just signed a huge contract with the NHL, he would know exactly what my passion is. We both used to live for the ice. For me though, a guy, marriage, jobs, and real life ended up distracting me from that passion.

"Fuck, yeah." We share a grin only weirdos would understand. Takes a special person to want to skate across a sheet of ice on razor blades and smash people up against the boards. "I want to coach the younger crowd. Kind of a blend of my two passions: kids and hockey."

Olivia groans this time. "Here I was thinking this dinner would get me away from all the hockey talk."

Roman rubs his hands together. "Okay, so Banks Bennet was just talking to me about looking for a coach for his Little Brother. Wants to get the guy in skates for the first time. You might be the right fit."

I take another sip of wine, already feeling lit up inside. This is what I've been looking for. No more obligations that weigh me down. I just want to chase what makes me feel alive. "I'd love to meet him. But I also want to get a whole league together. For recreation. Too many of these young kids are being pushed into expensive and time-consuming clubs. I want my league to be for fun. For the love of the sport, not to sign a professional contract before middle school."

"Oh, I love that," Olivia sighs. "So many kids are being pressured into the next big thing, when all they want to do is play. We need to let kids be kids sometimes."

"Exactly!" I put my wine down, far too interested in the conversation to take time to sip. "Life is short and not every kid is cut out to play in the NHL, but they should still be able to play for fun. They'll get all the benefits of physical activity and the team aspect. Just without the pressure to impress a high-level coach."

Roman sits back in his chair. "I love that idea, Chloe. If anyone can do it, it would be you. You have a knack for meeting people where they are and working with them to make them better than they were before they met you."

That compliment might be more insightful than any I've ever received. "Thank you, Roman. I just like to help people."

"As long as no one takes advantage of you," Olivia pipes up. "My ex-husband used to rely on my constant offers of help to the point that I was burned out on life."

I suck in a deep breath. Fuck, that sounds all too familiar. My eyes fill with tears before I can will them away. I haven't teared up in public like this in a few months. I thought I was done with that stage of grieving. Olivia grabs my arm in alarm.

"I'm so sorry. I didn't mean to imply . . ."

I wave away the rest of whatever she was going to say. "No, it's okay. That actually hit quite close to home. I don't want to speak ill of the dead, but Josh used to do the same. He didn't even know he was doing it, but it was hard just the same."

Olivia's face is a mask of sympathy. At least she doesn't look revolted that I said something negative about my late husband. "Well, you had to take care of him when he was sick too. That had to have been hard."

I nod, trying not to think about those two straight years of caregiving, on top of my full-time job. He was my husband, though. Of course I stepped up and took care of him. Even if that meant putting myself last every single day.

Our server arrives with our meals, and it ends that line of conversation, which is just as well. I don't need to turn this dinner into a therapy session. We reminisce and talk about the future while we eat. By the time we're all stuffed, we have plans to meet up tomorrow for breakfast before the skills competition. We'll be sitting together, and I'm looking forward to more time with Olivia. She's incredibly insightful and a sympathetic listener. A winning combination for a woman coming off the hardest years of her life and looking for new friends.

As we step outside and the cold breeze hits my heated cheeks, I inhale and look up at the sky. I don't know what my life will look like in Tampa, but right now, in this moment, I'm happy. And that's enough for me.

Chapter Three

Chloe

"Are you sure you don't want to walk back with us?" Olivia looks concerned. While it's dark out and probably not the best time for a single woman to be walking the streets, there's a rush of activity with the All-Star game taking place in the city. I'll be perfectly safe.

Olivia has the same look everyone has had since Josh passed away. I still see it right before someone squeezes my arm and asks me how I'm doing. I always answer with "the best I can right now," when what I really want to say is "I'm grieving, I'm relieved, I'm terrified, I'm ecstatic, and I feel guilty for feeling all of it." I know enough not to answer truthfully these days. No one actually wants to hear the inner workings of my brain. Better to plaster on a sad smile and not rock their world with my deranged thoughts.

"I'm good. Seriously. Just going to grab a drink, people watch, and then head back to the hotel."

Olivia gives me a hug and so does Roman. He doesn't have

that sympathetic look on his face, but he is studying me. "Don't do anything stupid." Then he cocks his head to the side and gets a twinkle in his eye. "Actually, maybe you should."

"Roman," Olivia groans. "Don't be a bad influence."

Roman shrugs but quits examining me so closely. "What? Her husband died, but she didn't."

Olivia backhands his arm with a shocked expression. A laugh explodes out of my mouth. No one back in Wisconsin was brave enough to say something like that to my face, no matter how true the statement is.

"It's been too long since we caught up," I say truthfully, giving them both a smile and a wave as I back up. There's a bar two doors down that I looked up ahead of time. It's known to be the happening place in downtown Toronto. Exactly the type of establishment I wouldn't have dared to enter just a few years ago. Funny how people can change.

My high-heeled boots click on the concrete as I hurry down the sidewalk. The breeze is brisk here and no match for the leather jacket over my lacy top, but soon I'll be ensconced in a busy bar with the body heat of a hundred people to keep me warm. The glass door swings open, and a couple pours out, the man holding the door for me as I enter. It takes me a second to scan the area and take in the loud music and even louder conversation from dozens of beautiful people. I see an open seat at the far end of the bar and move in that direction, wanting a good vantage point for my people watching. Ignoring the hulking man sitting next to me, I haul my short self up into the barstool and grab a leather-bound drink menu. The bartender eventually comes over and I order a glass of champagne.

When the glass slides across the bar top with bubbles streaming upward and the bartender moves away to another patron, I lift my drink in the air in a toast. "To myself," I say out loud. And then I take the first fortifying sip. I close my eyes and hum as the taste explodes in my mouth and slips down my throat like a cooling balm in the middle of summer.

The man next to me snorts and my eyes fly open. His hair is a shaggy sandy brown that looks like he's been running his fingers through it. The thick jacket hides his physique, but with his feet touching the ground even on these sky-high barstools, he must be tall. When he turns his head in my direction, I get my first look at piercing blue eyes, a crooked nose, and slashes of eyebrows that hold annoyance so well.

Holy shit. I'd know that face anywhere. It belongs to Nikolai Drugov, the goalie for the Storm Chasers. That was the one thing my late husband and I had in common: hockey. We met at the University of Wisconsin, both of us ice hockey athletes. It seemed like a match made in heaven. Until it wasn't. Of course, I had a thing for hockey players back then, and based on the way those blue eyes scanning my body feel like a caress, I still have a thing.

I arch an eyebrow, feeling excitement in my gut for the first time in a long while. "Did my toast not agree with you?"

"Very little agrees with me," he answers, his voice so low and gruff I barely make out the words. The accent though, whoa boy, do I hear that accent. It sends a shiver across my skin.

"Hmm. I know what you mean. Hence my toast to myself. At least I can count on myself." I take another sip of my champagne, feeling his gaze trickle down to my ruby red lips. Interesting. Is the elusive, handsome goalie checking me out?

A frisson of nerves hits my stomach. I haven't flirted in so long I'm not sure how to start.

"Only ourselves, eh? Then we have truly reached the handle."

I tilt my head and try to wrap my mind around whatever

the hell he means. The handle? Was that a euphemism for something else? Something dirty? Jesus, I feel old.

"I don't reach for many handles," I say truthfully, downing the rest of my champagne. If we're already talking about dicks, I need to be far less sober. I raise my hand and the bartender notices, nodding his head. My bar companion also raises a thick finger, signaling another drink.

"That is good," he says, his rich accent quite delicious. "None of my friends reach the handle, but I find myself there often."

Oh my. That's more information than I needed to know from a virtual stranger. I squish up my nose, hoping I'm still flirting properly. "Well, I prefer to reach for the handles not belonging to my friends. Better to take that . . . handle holding . . . out of the friend group, you know?"

Nikolai looks at me again, his eyebrows nearly colliding. "You Americans say weird things."

The bartender arrives with an amber-colored liquor for Nikolai and another glass of champagne for me. I take a hefty swig before setting the glass down. Clearly, I'm doing flirting wrong. "I just mean I wouldn't date within my friend group. Better to not mix pleasure with friendship, you know?"

I learned that the hard way, when after Josh's death, our couples friend group fractured. It became painfully obvious that they'd been primarily Josh's friends, and I'd just assimilated into the group. Sure, they were supportive right after his death, but their messages and phone calls dwindled quickly, replaced by a deafening silence. Even my fellow schoolteacher friends fell silent, probably due to feeling uncomfortable with death in general. I lost not only my husband, but all of my friends. While I rebuild the second half of my life, you can bet your ass I'll have a diversified friend group this time. And definitely no handle holding within the friend group to break it up.

Nikolai loses the frown and holds up his glass. I quickly join him, thinking maybe I've turned this sinking ship around, and he clinks the glasses together. "To not being friends."

We both drink to the oddly endearing toast and I rest my elbow on the bar top, leaning in his direction, hoping this position threatens to spill my breasts right out of this top. As predicted, his gaze drops, but he looks away quickly, swallowing hard.

"If I tell you my name, that won't make us friends, right?"

Nikolai grunts and even that's attractive. "I have few friends and do not plan on making more."

"Oh good. Then I'm Chloe." I hold out my hand, glad I took the time to paint my nails bright red before I came on this trip. Look at me go with all this self care. I'm the self-care queen.

Nikolai slides his hand into mine, covering it completely. "Nikolai."

We stay just like that for an extended moment, holding hands and breathing the same air. Being a short, curvy woman in the plus size category, I frequently feel like the shortest one in a group, but I rarely feel like a man could haul me over his shoulder and run us out of a burning building if he had to. Josh had been taller than me, but slight. My inner cavewoman likes that Nikolai looks like he could pick me up and not even be breathing hard. My cheeks heat and it has nothing to do with the champagne. He lets go of my hand and takes all that warmth with him.

"Nice to meet you, Nikolai. I, like you, don't have a lot of friends, but I'm actually looking for some." At his look of alarm, I clarify. "Not you, of course. I'd never be friends with you. You're entirely too tall."

He scoffs. "What is wrong with tall?"

I shrug and take another sip of champagne, then start counting off on my fingers. "Lifelong neck problems from always looking up. These curls can't handle my head being the arm rest for tall people. Oh, and having to ask my tall friends to reach things on top shelves makes me feel so needy, you know?" I shake my head. "Far better to avoid the tall people."

It might just be my imagination, but I could swear Nikolai's thick lips start to curve upward on the ends.

"I would not like to cause you so much pain and hassle, Chloe of the short people. Good we have decided to not be friends."

I won't even try to pretend that hearing my name in that accent isn't doing crazy things to my insides. I've heard about Nikolai, of course, and even seen him play live. Anyone who follows hockey knows he's one of the best at protecting his net. Most people also know he's a recluse, almost never giving interviews nor being seen out socially with the team. And yet, here he is cracking deadpan jokes with me. He's as funny as he is ruggedly handsome. All I want to do is keep him talking.

Okay, that's a lie. That's not all I want from Nikolai Drugov.

"And why don't you want friends, short or otherwise?"

He drains his drink and sets it down on the bar with a solid clink. "I do not like talking, and friends require so much *proklyaty* talking. I prefer to watch."

My eyes open wide. My mind, after absorbing the Russian dripping from those lips, went so far into the gutter I'm no better than a street rat. "You prefer to watch, huh?" I lick my lips, imagining him watching me undress. What it would be like to have all of that high-performance focus on me and only me.

Then I realize his gaze is trained on my mouth and every last drop of sanity slides downward to gather in my gut. Hot, molten desire takes over every sane thought I have left. Maybe it's the champagne. Maybe it's this life unfurling into something I didn't expect. Maybe it's just Nikolai. But I have to shoot my shot or I'll live with regret. And that's one thing I refuse to do. I pull myself up by my designer bootstraps and decide to live boldly.

"Since we've established we're not friends and you prefer to watch, how about you come back to my hotel with me? We can not talk the rest of the night?"

His startled gaze latches onto mine, his icy blue eyes smoldering into something much, much hotter. My palms are sweating, but I reach over to grip the lapels of his jacket and tug him closer. His spicy scent surrounds me while his broad shoulders seem to block out all the other people in the bar, taking those nerves and spinning them into a dangerous liquid pool of desire. His gaze flicks downward to my lips again and my heart pounds. Roman's words echo in my brain and spill out of my mouth.

"Let's do something stupid."

Chapter Four

Niko

I have a rule: no puck bunnies. Not since Peyton set her sights on me and upended my life.

But I cannot tell if this Chloe woman is playing games or not. She somehow managed to lift my spirits when nothing else could touch the foul mood I have been in since the cancellation of my visit with Ayana earlier this week. Instead of annoying, I find her chatter almost charming, something I cannot make sense of. Women do not charm me. I am uncharmable. Some people might label that as coldness—or perhaps grumpiness if they are being kind—but that does not bother me.

I would be lying if I said part of this woman's charm did not lie in her pouty red lips and those full tits pushed up in her top to create the most luscious cleavage I have ever seen. And here she is, so close I can smell her sweet scent and feel her warm breath on my chin as she gazes up at me with challenge in her blue eyes.

It would be so easy to give in and bury myself between her thighs for the night—push my problems from my mind until the sunrise brings them back. But that is not how I operate. I should not even be here at this bar, not with the skills competition tomorrow afternoon.

I open my mouth to tell the raven-haired beauty she has chosen the wrong mark, but that is when I notice the slight tremble of her lips and the quickness of her breathing that has her breasts rising and falling in a rapid rhythm. What I mistook for aggressive, lust-fueled game playing is tinged with . . . nervousness.

Chloe is no puck bunny.

This does not mean she is not still off limits, but it does compel me to act with more care than I otherwise might have.

Instead of rebuffing her advances outright, I find myself softening my tone and saying, "You do not strike me as stupid, Chloe of the short people."

Her mouth falls open in barely disguised dismay before her tongue darts out to swipe across her bottom lip. Not a puck bunny at all. "Oh," is her eventual response. My cock swells in my pants at the mental image of that tongue licking my cock from root to tip.

Her grip loosens and her chin begins to dip. Soon, she will turn from me and dismount her barstool, embarrassed by the failure of her charms to capture my interest. I want to tell her she is wrong. If anyone could tempt me, it would be someone like her.

My eyes drop to her red lips again, and I make a split-second decision. My hand comes to the underside of her chin and I use my index finger to lift it. Her surprised expression makes her eyes go wide and her lips part again, and I take advantage by ducking my head and capturing them with mine.

The first brush of our lips is electric, and I feel the hairs on my arms stand on end under my shirt and coat. It must have to do with the cold, dry March air in Toronto, no matter that we are indoors. When I go in for another taste, Chloe's fingers tighten once again on my lapels, and she leans fully into me. I worry she will tumble from her barstool, so I lower a hand to her hip to hold her steady. My fingers dig into the soft curve and I inwardly groan, my mind imagining driving my cock into her from behind as my hands brace her lush hips.

But that will not happen. I will keep this encounter to one kiss with a stranger who will never be anything more.

Chloe tests my resolve when she whimpers into my mouth and swipes the tip of her tongue over my lip. The hand that was at her chin curls upward to hold her jaw so I can further explore her hot mouth as I part my lips and take over the kiss. My tongue forces hers back in her mouth as I delve in for a thorough taste. Bright champagne hits my taste buds, but it is the velvety, sweet softness of her mouth that does me in.

Our kiss rapidly turns hot and wet, all the sounds of the lively bar and its patrons fading to a dull buzz as my senses focus their attention on the suppleness of Chloe's body, the sound of her low moan, the sweetness of her hot tongue, and the scent of her honeyed skin.

Maybe taking her up on her offer would not be such a bad move. When one of her hands leaves my coat to skim up the side of my neck and delve into my hair, I am convinced of it. I tear my lips from hers, intent on flagging down the bartender for our bill when my phone rattles on the bar top next to me.

At the name on the screen, my hard-on instantly deflates.

Jane: Can you talk?

Shit.

My eyes flick back to Chloe who is blinking at my chest now, clearly not having her wits about her yet. I do not blame her. If Jane's name had not just jarred me back to reality, I would still be lost in whatever spell Chloe cast on me.

"My lawyer," I say, my voice coming out hoarse. It is a mystery to me why I feel the need to explain. We owe each other nothing.

Chloe's hand falls from my hair as her head tilts back, and I almost smile at her still-dazed expression as she continues to blink, this time at my face. "Wh—what?"

I take my phone in one hand, turning the screen her way while my other hand finally releases her hip. "I need to call her. Right away." This is about Ayana, and nothing comes before my daughter—certainly not a random sexual encounter with a stranger, no matter how unexpectedly she has piqued my interest.

"Oh." Chloe gives her head a quick shake and straightens on her stool. "Of course." She sends me a smile, and I cannot tell if it is forced or genuine. She leans forward once more, bringing a hand to my face. I intercept it, thinking she is ignoring my wishes, but it only makes her laugh.

"You've got red lipstick all over your mouth, Nikolai of the tall people. I'd hate for you to walk around the rest of the night getting funny looks."

I release her hand, allowing her to swipe her thumb over my lips to remove the stain, not understanding why I didn't just do it myself. The touch is somehow even more intimate than the kiss we just shared.

"There," she says before settling back again, her lips still curved in amusement.

Rising from my stool, I dig into my pocket for my wallet. I drop a hundred dollars on the bar top, nodding my chin at her half-empty champagne flute so she knows I have her drinks as well.

But instead of making a quick retreat to find a bit of

silence to call Jane like I should, I hesitate. "Would you like me to see you back to your hotel? For safety," I quickly add.

She smiles again and shakes her head. "I'm good." Her fingers wrap around the stem of her glass and she raises it toward me. "To strangers," she offers.

I nod, intent on simply saying goodnight as I know I should. But my tongue betrays me with the truth instead. "I wish tonight had gone differently so I could see what else your mouth can do, Chloe." I don't wait for her reaction to my words before turning to pick my way through the crowd and exit into the cold night.

"You're lucky I'm playing with a bum wrist, Drugov, or you never would have won that hundred grand last night," the keeper for the Pittsburgh Fury says as he skates by me two days later.

My only response is a glare paired with a smug grin. I excelled at the skills competition, winning first place among the goalies and earning myself enough prize money to pay my sister's rent for the foreseeable future.

But I credit anger as the driving force behind my win. When I left the bar the other night to call Jane, her news was both good and bad. Our request for a new hearing in front of a judge had been granted, but the court date isn't for another two months. Which means at least two more months of Peyton's bullshit and likely two more months without Ayana.

The wall of my hotel room took the brunt of my frustration, necessitating a call to the front desk and a two-hundred-dollar tip to the unlucky housekeeper who vacuumed the remains of my broken glass at ten at night.

As I lay in bed staring at the ceiling, I had a strong pang of regret that I had not asked for Chloe's phone number. But it was for the best.

My eyes drop to the ice beneath my skates as I push toward the net on the other end of the rink for warm-ups. My team won its first game earlier today, so we are now competing in the final All-Star matchup. Benny is on the opposing team, so I will enjoy the opportunity to meet up with him at the net and show him who the dominant player is.

It is time to center my focus on the game and leave all else behind. Just as I tighten my resolve, however, I hear a voice bellow my name. I lift my head to see Roman LaFontaine, my former teammate and captain, waving from the stands a few rows back from the glass. I lift my chin in greeting as my eyes shift next to his fiancée, a lovely woman named Olivia, and then to Kaitlyn Philips, Benny's current agent and the object of his not-so-subtle lust.

When I bring my right skate forward to continue on my way, however, my gaze catches on a fourth in their party. A curvy, raven-haired beauty who is all too familiar to me, despite the fact that I was never meant to lay eyes on her ever again. Chloe, the stranger, is clearly not a stranger at all.

I open my mouth to say something—anything—finally settling on, "I did not know! I give you a tooth!" Because I *am* telling the truth. I had no idea Chloe was friends with people in both my professional and personal circles. How did I not realize? How did she not tell me? Especially after our discussion of not mixing friends with . . . benefits.

My racing thoughts have me narrowly missing the boards, prompting one of our team's wingers to laugh up at me from where he is stretching on the ice. "A ghost walk over your grave, Drugov?" he asks. Although I have no understanding of his meaning, I simply nod. It is far preferable to explaining my current frustration.

His comment does have the effect of bringing me back to the ice. To the game. To my fucking job. It is time to focus again, and not on a pair of pretty tits and a woman who might have a knack for distracting me for a moment or two but will never figure in the long game.

It's time to win a game, for Christ's sake. And that is the only thing on my mind.

Chapter Five

Chloe

Not gonna lie, that kiss with Nikolai has had me walking on billowy puffs of clouds the last forty-eight hours. I can still feel the thick, soft scruff of his overly long hair. Just enough length to grasp in my fist. Dammit, I wanted to have enough time to run my fingers through it and maybe even roughly pull his head between my legs.

Well, not in the bar. In my hotel room. Not even this new lease on life and promise to say yes to things is enough to have me adding public indecency to my list of new experiences.

But I got shut down by a lawyer instead. It's true what they say: lawyers are killjoys.

So I went back to my hotel room alone, my body keyed up and my brain looping through all the scenarios in which I could have reached new heights of sexual empowerment by keeping Nikolai up all night. But it's fine. Sometimes one needs to dip their toe into the pool before cannonballing their way into the deep end. And that kiss was certainly the type of toe dip that had my heart fluttering.

Not that I should be comparing–but fuck, it's only natural to do so, so I'll cut myself some slack–I never experienced that kind of kiss with Josh. We'd been inexperienced college kids when we first started dating, and then we were old married people with mortgages to pay, gym memberships to ignore, and then serious health problems to face. Josh and I had slipped into being friends without the benefits somewhere in our marriage. If I am being honest, our sex life was never super fulfilling for me. Josh was a neat freak and all about the end goal, not the process. Where I wanted cuddling and foreplay and maybe a lubed-up toy or two, he wanted sterile conditions and missionary for the three and a half minutes–five if it was our anniversary–needed to seal the deal.

Based on his last comment about my mouth, I have a feeling Nikolai doesn't mind getting dirty . . .

"What's with Niko?" Kaitlyn's voice brings me out of my sex-starved thoughts.

"Huh?" I blink and refocus on the packed arena around me. A loud buzzer sounds, and I catch the backside of Nikolai barreling his way off the ice.

"Ew. Why's he offering you a tooth, ice bath king?" Olivia asks Roman.

Kaitlyn barks out a laugh. "That's just Niko. He's got a thousand Russian phrases and not one of them makes any sense."

"Wait, what?" If they're talking about Nikolai, I have a sudden burning desire to know exactly what they're saying.

Olivia looks at me funny. "We said hi to Niko but he just shouted about not knowing and giving Roman a tooth." She looks over at Kaitlyn. "They drug test, don't they?"

"He's not on drugs," I say quickly and confidently. When both women turn to look at me, I realize my error. According to their knowledge, I've never met Nikolai. "I mean, he'd be stupid to risk his entire career on drugs right before the All-Star game when millions of eyes will be on him. Right?"

Kaitlyn nods. "He's not my client, but I'd kick his ass if he tried anything like that. Banks says he's fighting to get custody of his daughter. Drugs would be a serious problem for the judge."

My breath catches in my throat. The call from the lawyer who interrupted our kiss. It might have been about his daughter. I curl a lock of hair around my finger and twist it over and over. Shit, I was pouting over a spoiled sexcapade, and the quiet goalie was fighting to be part of his daughter's life. I see over a hundred third-grade girl faces in my mind, my prior students and little girls who deserved to have a present father figure in their lives. All that pitter-pattering of my heart turns into a puddle of sympathy.

Another loud buzzer makes me jump and we all take our seats for the start of the game. The announcers are practically screaming with excitement, and though I've been to a lot of hockey games in my life, my breath is pumping in and out of my lungs like I'm out there on the ice myself. Mostly because Nikolai comes skating out to take his place in front of the net and now I can't rip my gaze from him, even when Kaitlyn and Olivia keep up a steady chatter.

His focus is intense. He never takes his eyes off the puck, always moving this way and that, positioning himself in the crease like it's some kind of fluid dance. Two opposing players break away and race down the ice toward him. I hold my breath. Nikolai moves lightning fast and deflects the puck with such grace I'm officially staring. Half the crowd cheers and the other half boos their disappointment. Just for reference, I'm part of the cheering crowd. We may have agreed to stay strangers, even after the best kiss of my life, but I will always cheer for that huge man to win.

But also? I realize we have to remain strangers, despite my daydreaming fantasies. He's in a legal battle for his daughter and being seen with a random woman on his arm would not help his case. Not that he has a bad reputation, it's just hockey players in general have a bit of a stereotype. Hence, why my father always warned me to stay away from them. Little kids have always held a special spot in my heart. I wasn't blessed with children, but I've spent my life teaching them instead. I would never come between a dad and his daughter.

"He's staring over here again. I swear. Are you sure he's not on drugs?" Olivia asks Kaitlyn, chuckling.

I realize with a start that we've reached the intermission of the All-Star game and Nikolai has skated off the ice with his teammates. I push all my thoughts aside and enter the conversation, steering it toward Kaitlyn and Banks Bennet, her boyfriend. They've been dating quietly, being that she's his agent, but she's here to tell him she's ready to make it public. She looks like a woman in love. Her cheeks have color and her eyes are practically sparkling. Hell, even her hair looks amazing and shiny like a shampoo ad. What I wouldn't have given for Kaitlyn's physique back when I was a teenager. She's tall and thin and looks like she has more confidence than all these hockey players combined.

"So, I hear you're moving to Tampa?" Kaitlyn asks, turning her attention to me.

I nod, all that excitement from the kiss now deflated. "Yeah, already moved into my duplex. Just putting together plans to start my own youth hockey rec league."

Kaitlyn grabs my arm. "Oh my god, yes! I come across so many kids who just want to play but have burned out on all the travel teams and trying to get the attention of scouts."

We exchange numbers, and I promise to call her next week to discuss my league further. A buzzer sounds again, and players stream out onto the ice. I turn my attention to Nikolai, who doesn't have his face mask on yet. He flicks a glance my way and just the brief moment of eye contact sears into my skin. His jaw is locked tight and those eyes are so focused I can barely breathe. I remember what it felt like to have those full lips on mine. He breaks the eye contact by jamming his face mask on and skating in the opposite direction.

"Wow," Olivia breathes. "He looks pissed about something."

"Seriously, honey, you gotta stop checking out the hockey players," Roman whines.

Kaitlyn snorts and Olivia snuggles into Roman's side, proclaiming there isn't a woman in the arena who didn't feel that look from Niko. I stand so quickly I almost kick the box of popcorn the person next to me set on the ground. All heads turn my direction.

"I'm not feeling so great. I think I'll head back to the hotel," I tell my friends. Olivia and Kaitlyn give me a hug and Roman studies me before offering to walk me out. "I'll be fine, thank you. Just need some more sleep," I reassure him.

I actually need out of this arena where I can finally take a deep breath and forget about Nikolai Drugov. He's in a custody battle, and I'm just looking for some harmless fun. We're so incompatible it's funny. He wants us to remain strangers and strangers we shall be.

I get a rideshare to take me back to the hotel, not wanting to spend any more time in these heels that are damn cute but cutting off circulation to my toes. I wash all the makeup off my face and slide into silky pajamas, another indulgence I'm trying out. My phone pings, and I pick it up off the bed to see a text.

Dad: Do you have plans the first weekend in April? I'd like to host a barbecue.

My calendar has been wide open for months and, sadly, I don't see that changing by April.

Me: Um, sure. Can I bring anything?

Dad: Just yourself, sweetie! I'll be making an announcement.

Me: Well, jeez, Dad. Now I won't be able to sleep all week! What's the big news?

Dad: It's really not that interesting but an old man needs any excitement he can get.

Me: Sure. But if this is about you moving to The Villages, I gotta stop you right there. I'm not on board with that.

Dad: It's not that. But out of curiosity, why not?

Me: Google The Villages and shower loofahs.

He doesn't answer for a while, which I hope means he moved on to something else. My phone pings just as I'm settling into a good romantasy book on my Kindle.

Dad: Jesus, Chloe! I can never unsee that. Can never use a shower loofah again either. Thanks a lot.

I crack up and return to reading, determined to put loofahs, announcements, and hot, grumpy goalies out of my mind.

Niko

"Still not speaking to me, Druggy?"

I turn to see Bobby Rhodes, our second-line center, standing on the lawn a few feet from me, flanked by Pete Fornier and Alexi Barinov. All three of the younger players look to be on their third or fourth beers.

When I don't immediately respond, Roadie pleads, "Oh, come on. It was just a joke."

A tired joke, indeed. It is not the first time a teammate has played this particular prank on me at practice.

"Cutting my glove laces is the only way you can get a puck past me, is it?" I finally respond, causing Forns and Barzee to double over laughing at Roadie's expense. He deserves it for making me re-lace my gloves and miss valuable practice time. "If you are afraid of wolves, don't go to the woods, Roadie."

"Hey, asshats!" Monkowski shouts in their direction from the other side of Coach's expansive backyard. "Coach wants everyone to gather 'round." He gestures to the built-in outdoor seating area behind the large house where Coach Bowman stands with his back to us.

Coach does not often invite the team to his home, but I have been here a handful of times, on my own or with LaFontaine. When the invitation for players and significant others arrived in our mailboxes, it was a given that we would all drop everything to attend this barbecue.

Luckily—or unluckily, depending on how you look at it— I do not have Ayana today. Although, I did get her for an unusual overnight visit earlier this week. I have to conclude Peyton had a date or some other obligation that night.

I ordered Ayana's favorite Mexican takeout, and we worked on the same one-thousand-piece puzzle we have been toiling over for the past six months. I leave it on my coffee table at all times, even when weeks pass between our visits.

The breeder called yesterday to inform me Strakh-slash-Paul will be weaned and ready to come home with us in two weeks, so I am focusing my efforts on keeping Peyton from cancelling Ayana's visit that week. Having learned my lesson, however, I have not told Ayana about his arrival date yet. I will not have her tears on my conscience.

We make our way closer to the house where Kaitlyn Philips waves at me from her spot on the lawn next to Benny. I am glad those two finally worked things out between them, especially after what transpired with Ed Presley, the now-ruined hockey agent who had been causing them both a great deal of trouble.

Coach raises his hand to draw our attention. "Thank you all for coming." But he surprises me by reaching his other arm out and pulling a short, black-haired woman into his side. It takes a moment for me to recognize her, and when I do, my shock is so great I almost miss Coach's next words. "For those of you who've never met her, this is my daughter, Chloe. She's finally decided to make Tampa her home after all my years of nagging." He smiles down at his daughter with pride.

I swallow hard and try focusing only on my coach, but it is impossible not to stare at Chloe. She looks much the same as the last time I saw her in the stands at the All-Star game, except today she is wearing a sundress fastened behind her neck in a way that shows off her breasts to their best advantage. How did I not see this coming?

Ever since Toronto, she has crept into my thoughts, catching me off guard each time. The memory of her soft lips under mine and her even softer hip against my fingers has woken me up from a dead sleep more than once. But I have refused any temptation to reach out to her through our mutual friends or colleagues. Which was clearly the wise choice now that I find out she is the daughter of Coach Bowman! I rack my brain trying to recall a photo of her on his desk in his office or on his mantel inside, but I draw a blank, only conjuring a vague image of a lighter-haired, rather plain-looking woman from Wisconsin. A woman I cannot imagine ever mistaking for the Chloe standing before me now.

Just the thought of crossing that line with Coach's daughter has my skin itching. I suppose I have my sense of discipline to thank for saving me from such a disrespectful course of action—even if it surely would have been an explosive encounter to remember.

I force my attention back to Coach's words as he begins to explain his reason for inviting us all here this afternoon.

"And I'm glad she's here with me today while I make this announcement. I wanted you all to hear it from me first because I hold each of you in high esteem and value my relationships with you and the Storm Chasers franchise." He takes a deep breath before continuing, "This will be my last year serving as head coach." A few gasps sound in the crowd, but Coach only raises his voice to be heard over them. "It's been a hell of a ride, but it's time for this old man to hand over the baton and go back to being a regular old hockey fan."

Chloe turns into her father to give him a hug as she smiles up at him. He returns her expression, and for a moment, the scene makes me think of Ayana and me.

My teammates descend on Coach, offering handshakes and hugs, but I stay where I am and watch. I am not as surprised as I imagine some might be at Coach Bowman's news. I, too, would crave a change after all the time he has spent at the helm of the Storm Chasers. A wise man knows when it is time to say goodbye.

I drop my eyes to my shoes and shove my hands in the pockets of my shorts as I attempt to guess who will replace Coach. He leaves big shoes to be filled. But my thoughts are interrupted by a familiar voice.

"Hello, Nikolai."

When my eyes flash to Chloe's face, the first thing I notice is that she is wearing the same red lipstick as the night we kissed. My cock twitches, and I silently curse myself.

"Chloe," I acknowledge as I glance around the yard to see if anyone is paying attention.

Any wishes I might have had that she intended only to greet me as she passed by are dashed when she steps closer and continues, "I take it you're surprised. Sorry about that."

Instead of directly responding, I mentally dig into my memory banks. "We have met before. Before Toronto, I mean." Why did I have to bring up Toronto? "You do not look the same." The words come out almost as an accusation.

Her lips spread in a smile at my words. "No. I don't. I'm surprised you remember. That was a long time ago, and I don't think we were ever even properly introduced."

She is right, from what I recall. She attended a Stanley Cup championship game years ago and was in the locker room with her father during our celebration. But she was nothing like the stunning siren in front of me now.

"It is for the best," I declare, straightening my spine as I look down at her.

"Which part?" She is still grinning, which I find frustrating. Does she not understand how precarious this situation is that we have put ourselves in?

"All of it. We cannot be seen together."

This makes her laugh for some reason, a sound that sets my blood simmering—both from frustration and lingering lust. Damn the woman.

"You need to lighten up, Drugov."

I have no response to this, so I tighten my jaw and remain silent.

The woman then has the nerve to wink at me before waggling her fingers and turning to show the exposed skin of her back. "Don't worry. My lips are sealed. See you around, Nikolai." She struts toward Benny and Kaitlyn, leaving me with a racing heart rate and a cock at half-staff.

Maybe Roadie and the boys had the right idea after all. I take myself directly to the large cooler filled with beer and crack one open before tipping it back to let half its contents spill down my throat.

See you around? The words echo in my head like an omen.

Chapter Seven

Chloe

"Why are men so dumb?" Sushi doesn't answer me, but she does swim around and around in a circle, against the perimeter of her tank. Maybe she's getting in her daily exercise like I did this morning with the new treadmill that takes up half my bedroom. While I'm not looking to drop any weight–I'm fucking perfect the way I am, thank you very much–I do want to be my healthiest self. And that means working out. Just not in the hot Florida sun.

Nikolai's words echo in my brain at the most inopportune times. "Can't be seen together? Even as colleagues? What am I? A dirty little secret?" I smirk and lean closer to the mirror over my dresser to swipe on more mascara. "Although, I kind of like the idea of that."

After a very vanilla marriage with Josh, I might like the idea of being someone's dirty little secret. Even just the thought of it, and especially being *Nikolai's* secret, has my skin flushing. I twist the cap on the mascara and toss it in my makeup bag.

"I'm off to consult with Dad. Don't get into any trouble." Sushi stops her circles long enough to swish a long, turquoise tail at me.

With the sun fading into the Gulf, I swing my duffle bag onto my shoulder and hop in my car to drive to the practice arena to speak with Dad about my rec league. He should be about to head home for the evening. It's taken me several weeks just to research the do's and don'ts, and to come up with the proper documentation to get this thing going. Apparently, lawyers like to be involved so no one can sue the league if there are injuries. I think I have everything in place and can now start to reach out for donors. That's where Dad comes in. He knows everyone in hockey, and he knows who has the deep pockets. Even with retirement on the horizon, he still has the clout to help me negotiate renting the practice facility at a steal.

I hold out the name tag Dad made for me the day I moved back to Tampa and flash it at security. They wave me through, and I head straight for Dad's office. As predicted, he's packing up his bag and straightening up his desk. Dad has always been meticulous about his office space, the complete opposite of Mom's chaotic mess. One of the many reasons those two weren't compatible over the long run.

"Hey, pumpkin." Dad immediately comes over to give me a hug. "Have I told you how glad I am you're back in Tampa?"

"Only several dozen times," I drawl.

He has a seat in one of the two club chairs in front of his desk and waves me to the other one. "What's on your mind?"

I pull out the worn notebook from my duffle bag where I keep all the notes about my league. I go over the recent developments and ask for possible donors to hit up. Dad lists off almost twenty names which is more than I hoped for. I'm feverishly writing down the names when I realize he's looked at his watch twice.

"Got a hot date?"

Dad makes a choking noise and tugs at the collar of his pristine deep blue polo shirt. "No, no. Just getting hungry. Forgot to eat lunch."

Interesting. I study his face and the way he's no longer looking at me. Dad may be retirement age, but even I can see he's a handsome man. He's kept fit over the years and the silver threading through the temples of his dark brown hair only makes him look like George Clooney. I decide to put him out of his misery. I snap the notebook closed and drop it into my duffle.

"Hey, any chance I can take a spin out on the ice before I leave?"

Dad stands, looking relieved. "Sure, sure. There's a junior league that's just about finished. You can skate once they clear out. Fred won't be by with the Zamboni until eight."

I give him a hug and lug my bag out of his office. He rushes off and I watch him go, mind tumbling with this new reality. Dad's dating? I'm not sure how I feel about that, but if it makes him happy, then I guess I need to get used to it.

The second I step through those doors and feel the blast of cold air, I feel like I'm stepping back in time. So much of my youth was spent on the ice. Hell, even the smell brings back memories, some good, some that make my ribs ache. Once upon a time, I fell in love with a man in one of these rinks. Shouts from the junior league fill the air and I plop down on a bench to pull out my old skates. God, I haven't worn these in years. Probably not since Josh got sick. I figure if I'm going to be running a youth hockey league, I have to practice so I don't fall on my face the first time I take the ice in front of the little kids. I'm hoping it's like riding a bicycle.

My hands go through the motions, lacing my skates from

muscle memory. The junior league barrels off the ice, making so much noise I almost feel the need to plug my ears. Instead, I sigh and wait, wondering when I got so old that teens being rambunctious became annoying instead of funny. Once they've cleared out of the rink, I stand up and get my bearings. My forty-two-year-old ankles let out a warning, but I silently tell them to buck up. I grab one of the loaner sticks off the bench and try to ignore how much tape is wrapped around it. Back in my day, I had the newest, most expensive equipment money could buy, thanks to Dad.

Taking a few tentative steps, I grab the wall and look down at the ice. So many memories flash before my eyes, but I shove them all away and glide out onto the icy sheet like I'm a new woman.

The wind ruffles my hair, and my thighs tremble a bit as I pick up speed, my body inherently knowing what to do without my brain having to engage. I get close to the end of the rink and I slow, leaning a bit and pushing off, effortlessly gliding into an arching turn. As I hit the straight away, I close my eyes for a moment, letting all the emotions flood through me, ending with a triumphant return to a part of myself I'd stuffed away in favor of dealing with the heavy responsibilities of life.

I fucking love hockey. My heart rate seems to pump out that simple sentence over and over until I'm screaming it in my head, elated to be back out on the ice. A smile stretches across my face and I feel more like me than I have in decades.

"Blind hockey is a thing in America, yes?"

A deep baritone has my eyes flying open and my skates catching on a ridge of ice left over from the teenagers. Nikolai stands there in a pair of sweatpants, a Tampa Bay Rays sweatshirt, and black skates, his hockey stick slung casually against his shoulder. His hair is artfully rumpled and the short beard covering his jawline is worthy of a cologne ad. I do a quick double step on my skates and wobble more than I'd like to admit, but I'm able to stay on my feet. "She is beauty, she is grace" does not apply to me in any way right now. Nikolai reaches one hand out and grabs hold of my elbow as I come to a pathetic stop right in front of his skates. Pretty sure I spray ice onto his sweatpants and I hit him in the chest with my stick, but I don't dare look down to confirm.

"Didn't know anyone else was here," I say lamely.

"It helps to have one's eyes open to know if someone is there," Nikolai drawls in that accent that gets under my skin. "I come for extra practice most days of the week."

His hand is still on my arm, and I try to ignore how much I like his hands on me. "I'll keep that in mind next time."

"I did not know you skate."

My smirk is more flirt than snark. My stomach swoops with nervous energy when his gaze drops to my mouth. "Daughter of a hockey coach? You better believe I can skate. That and the D1 scholarship for hockey."

His blue eyes widen just enough to let me know he's surprised. Most people are when they find out that girls can play hockey too. Who would have guessed owning a uterus doesn't preclude one from swinging a stick across the ice?

"What?" I challenge when he still doesn't respond and his thumb starts to sweep across my bicep. I deeply regret the long sleeve shirt that keeps our skin from actually touching.

He swallows hard, and when he speaks, his voice is rockier than this sheet of ice after a herd of teen boys. "That is fucking hot."

Every cell in my body warms and preens under his gaze. "Want to play?"

I'm surprised the ice doesn't crack and liquefy under the heat pumping between us. Nikolai's hand grips me tighter. "I most definitely want to play with you, Chloe."

Why does that feel like a promise that'll have my toes curling? "You gotta let go of me first, brick house."

Sadly, he does, surprise written all over his face, like he isn't even aware that he stayed connected to me long after social graces suggest letting go. I dig in my blades, skating backward away from him. I'm grateful beyond belief when I don't wobble or completely bite it. He pulls a puck out of the pocket of his sweatpants and throws it at my feet once I'm ten yards away.

"Would you like to score, Chloe?" His lips quirk up at one side, and I nearly die right on the spot. This is a man of few words, but when he decides to flirt, those words are fucking potent.

I casually swipe a gloved hand across my mouth, just to make sure I'm not actually drooling. "I don't know. I was always taught not to play with strangers." Referring, of course, to his stupid insistence on acting like we don't know each other when we've already shared a kiss.

Nikolai says nothing and I spring into action, swiping my stick and sending the puck toward the net. I miss by over three feet, but he's gracious enough not to taunt me about it. He flicks the puck back and nods at me to go again.

We go like that for half an hour, me rusty as hell and trying to get a puck past a world class professional goalie. Not a single one goes in, but by the time I race across the ice with the puck zig-zagging left and right before I flick my wrist, I feel like I've dusted off the cobwebs of my skills. Nikolai deflects the puck so seamlessly, even without his pads and gloves, that I forget to stop, crashing into him at full speed. I hear the audible "oof" from his mouth, but he drops his stick and twists so it's his body that hits the ice as we go down. Even so, every bone in my body is jarred.

A few seconds later, I blink my eyes open and assess whether I'm still alive. I'm laying across Nikolai's warm chest, my thick legs tangled with his long limbs. I huff some hair that had fallen across my face and gawk downward at the most handsome man I've ever met. *Good grief, Chloe, you could have maimed the man.*

"You should have let me take the fall. Dad would kill me if you got injured."

His smile is slow to bloom, and I have a front row seat to it. Hopefully the smile means he's not injured. Or maybe the smile is the after effect of a concussion. I should really read up on first aid before I open my league.

"How would he even know? We are strangers still, yes? You were never here."

A man who would literally take the fall for me? Fuck, I can't tell you how much I love that. I lick my lips and realize belatedly that might not be the best thing to do when laying on top of the man you dream about when you're all alone at night. His smile falters and his gaze follows my tongue.

"What if I don't want to be strangers?" I ask, suddenly breathless.

His icy blue eyes grow impossibly warm. "I will not blow at the whisker. You are in my mind constantly, Chloe Cooper, which means you could never be a stranger."

Chapter Eight

Niko

Chloe's breath comes out in a cloud of condensation over me, and everything in me wants to close the distance and crush my lips to hers. But I have already let things go too far.

She caught me off guard by showing up out of nowhere in what I consider to be my domain. And now I learn she is a hockey player as well? It should not be a surprise, I suppose, given her father's profession, yet it is. She is so . . . feminine, so soft. It is difficult to imagine her delivering slapshots and checking opponents. Such a juxtaposition, and one that unfortunately makes her that much more intriguing.

I was finished for the day but hoped to catch Mac for a few late day drills when I spotted Chloe on the ice. Her serene expression as she glided across the rink drew me, and before I could think better of it, I was intercepting her and putting my hands on her as I know I should not.

It is clear it has been some time since she played, but her raw talent is evident, as is her determination. I imagine she is the kind of woman who puts everything into each endeavor she under-takes. Even the way she trapped her tongue between her teeth while delivering a decent backhand shot had me wanting to smile. I am impressed. And it is no secret I am turned on as well.

There is no use denying it, despite the fact that I plan to do nothing about it.

To that end, I disentangle my legs from Chloe and sit, pulling her up with me. When we have both reached our feet, I release her arm, confident she has her footing now. If she is disappointed or surprised, she does not show it.

"Nice matchup," she says, offering me a smile that reaches all the way to her eyes. I steadfastly ignore the ice clinging to her ass as she skates away to the boards, twig in hand, and disappears. I remain on the ice a few minutes longer, wondering why I enjoy torturing myself so much.

Mac has obviously left, so it is time for me to get on with my evening. I change into shorts and pack up my gear before heading out to my vehicle. I pause beside it when my phone rings, a reluctant grin curving my lips as I see who is calling.

"*Privet*, Safiya," I greet in my native Russian.

"I ran into Katya this afternoon," my sister says without preamble.

My response is immediate. "Tell me," I demand, dread slithering through my gut.

Safiya does not make me wait. "She tried to play it off, but she looked unwell. Tired."

I curse under my breath. It would be just like Katya to fall out of remission and lie to me about it. When Ivan was alive, there was never a doubt she would be taken care of, but since my old coach and mentor passed away, his widow has no one. Except me–and Safiya.

I made Ivan a promise before he passed away that I would care for her, but there is only so much I can do from halfway across the world. Still, I owe Ivan more than I can say. It has been five years, and the world continues to feel wrong without him in it. Sometimes, I begin dialing Ivan's number only to remember partway through that he is gone.

"The cancer is back," I speculate, hoping I am mistaken.

"You do not know that, Niko." My sister makes a tutting noise. "I should not have called."

"Yes, you should. I need to know these things. I will phone her doctor tomorrow and make an appointment for you to take her." I check my watch, calculating the time difference in my head. If I stay up late tonight, I can reach the office first thing in the morning in Kazahkstan.

"Let me do it," Safiya offers.

"No, I have all of her information. And I am hoping to speak to a nurse or doctor myself." I open the driver's door and climb into the Rover, phone still to my ear.

"Fine, but do not schedule it for Wednesday. I have an interview." When I do not immediately respond, she continues, "Do not act so surprised, Brother."

I would lie and say I was not surprised, but my sister would spot it instantly. Her employment record does little to inspire confidence, unless a prospective employer is specifically seeking a nocturnal artist specializing in lifelike depictions of drag queens.

"Not Wednesday. Understood. Do you still have money left from what I sent last month?" I ask as I start the vehicle, needing a task for my hands.

"A little." Her response is timid. Safiya does not like appearing needy or weak, preferring to lead with confidence and defiance. It is a family trait.

Not in any mood to judge or lecture, I say, "I will send more. You take Katya for lunch and get her to talk to you, yes?"

"I can do that." My sister pauses before adding, "Ivan would be proud of that shutout yesterday."

I close my eyes and grip the steering wheel. Last night's game went particularly well with me delivering a shutout against the Golden Eagles and furthering our playoff chances. The end of the regular season is drawing near, and we are in a precarious position. But now is not the time to talk about me. Or Ivan.

"How are Mother and Father?"

It has been a year since I have been back to Kazakhstan, and neither of our parents like flying, so they rarely come to the States. Ivan, on the other hand, used to enjoy any excuse to come check on me, while Safiya simply enjoys any opportunity for a vacation.

"They are fine . . . Father still will not drive the car you gave him, though." This is no surprise to either of us. Our parents are very set in their ways. Despite the excellent living I make, they do not believe in good things lasting. I am certain my father keeps the BMW in new condition with a mind to selling it when my career or the world falls apart—either one likely to happen at any time, according to him.

"Did you take them to that new restaurant?" I ask. Safiya makes sure to treat them—and Katya—to nice things now and then at my behest. Nothing too extravagant that they can refuse, but nice little escapes from the every day. They are used to a quiet farm life on their land outside of the city, so it is not always easy to convince them.

"Mother ate two desserts."

"Excellent." My lips twitch.

"I will let you go. Message me about the appointment, yes?"

"I will."

"And if it is not too much trouble, I would like to see more shutouts before the season is finished." She is trying to make me smile, and it almost works.

"I will do my best," I promise before we say our goodbyes.

I stare out into the parking lot, thinking about my family and about Katya and Ivan.

We had an understanding, Ivan and me. I would never take anything for granted in my career and life, and always —*always*—give my best and act in a way that would bring pride to him and to my family. If it were not for Ivan, I would be working on my parents' farm, scraping for pennies and only dreaming of hockey. He risked everything for me, and I owe him my life. The very least I can do is live up to my promises.

"I will take care of her," I vow to the empty car. "Do not worry, my friend."

I put the vehicle in drive and look up into the blue Florida sky. Family. Ayana. Hockey. That is my duty. My only duty. Nothing else matters.

"You wanted to see–oh, sorry." I stop just inside the doorway of the training room, where Coach Bowman summoned me, to find Chloe standing beside a bench talking to him. It is as if the universe has it in for me, putting her in my path everywhere I turn these days. First at the barbecue, then the practice rink, and now Flagler Arena. I even spotted her pulling out of my bank's parking lot in her bright red Bronco with the top off last week, her dark hair tied in a red kerchief, the ends blowing in the wind like she was on the set of an old Hollywood movie. I remained in my vehicle to avoid her.

"Niko. You remember Chloe," Coach gestures to his daughter as he smiles my way.

"No." My immediate response is denial—until I realize how that sounds. "Yes. It is nice to see you again, Ms. Cooper."

It is clear she is biting back a laugh. A woman who enjoys my pain is one to be avoided at all costs.

"Mr. Drugov," she responds with a nod. Coach looks between us, and I find myself without words, so I attempt a smile. It does not appear to work.

"Everything . . . okay?" Coach asks, brows drawn together. This time I see Chloe roll her lips between her teeth to keep from laughing. I am glad she finds this so funny.

"Fine," I manage. "I will come speak to you after the game."

I turn and exit before he can protest, long strides taking me down the hall and toward the tunnel. That was way too close. Coach Bowman deserves as much of my respect as Ivan for how he has nurtured and supported my career, not to mention how understanding he has been about time I have needed to take for my personal troubles with Peyton and Ayana. The way to pay him back is not by lusting after his only daughter like some cocky rookie with no regard for ethics and honor.

By the time I exit the locker room, dressed for warm-ups, I believe I am being tested by god himself because there stands Chloe, chatting with Roadie, of all people. I feel my jaw lock. The boy isn't even thirty, yet his eye always strays to more mature women—women who I hope know better.

He says something that has her throwing her head back with a laugh, exposing the long column of her throat and making my fists clench. He watches her laughing with a look in his eye I do not like. Perhaps he needs a reminder of his place, something I might effectively communicate by slamming his body into the boards during tomorrow's practice.

"It is not time to socialize, Roadie," I bite out as I pass, not daring to look Chloe's way. "You twirl your tongue like a cow twirls its tail."

"Lighten up, Druggy!" he responds, using the same words Chloe used with me at the barbecue. The part of me that is not frustrated by the similarity wishes I had been the one making Chloe Cooper laugh.

Chapter Nine

Chloe

"You've been back for two months and I've barely seen you!" Mom sinks onto my couch with her usual flair for dramatics. She crosses one leg over the other, bejeweled sandals catching the light streaming in from the expansive windows in my duplex. "Please tell me it's because you've been out on so many dates recently you can't even find time for your own mother."

I put down the overflowing notebook that's basically my brain in written format. Perimenopausal brain fog can't win when the thoughts are in black and white. "Mom, I'm starting a new business. I don't have time for dates or casual lunches."

She slaps a hand to her chest, outraged over my statement. "There's always time for love, honey!"

I shake my head and have a seat on the couch next to her. The woman would know. She's remarried three times since she and Dad divorced, collecting spousal support each time. The last one only lasted two months. "You sound like those mamas on Bridgerton, trying to marry me off. I'm a widow, and I'm okay with it."

"No one's okay being a widow," she scoffs.

I roll my eyes. "I don't mean it like that. Of course, I'm not happy Josh died, but I'm happy being on my own right now. I'm focused on my business and on me. And it feels good."

She eyes my outfit, an admittedly skimpy black shirt that shows more of my stomach than usual, paired with cut-off jean shorts. To be fair, I wasn't expecting company and therefore hadn't gotten dressed beyond what the excessive May heat in Florida called for.

"Yes, I see that. I just don't understand the youth's need to show everything. Clothes are made to cover." Mom's eyebrows are furrowed, but not creased. She'd never allow the Botox to run out enough to cause a wrinkle. "You are a gorgeous girl, Chloe, but you don't dress to your advantage."

In Mom-speak, that means I'm showing off the fact I'm not a size two. Or any size in the single digits. Thank god for Dad and his unwavering support of my athleticism over the years. I learned to view my body as a machine, capable of Olympic feats, not window dressing for a man's gaze. Although I wouldn't mind a man's gaze either. A girl can have both, right?

"Can I ask you a question?" I blurt out.

"Always," Mom answers, tilting her head curiously.

"I know we've talked about the night sweats, but did you also experience issues with word recall when you went through menopause?"

Mom lifts her nose in the air. She hates when I bring up any subject that reminds her she's aging. "I did not. Just night sweats and weight gain. The plastic surgeon took care of the latter, but the former plagued me for years. Why? Are you having some issues?"

"Yeah, I was on the phone with a possible donor the other day and couldn't remember the name of my company. I wasn't sure if dementia was setting in already or if this was yet another perimenopausal symptom."

Mom leans over and pats my hand. "Go get checked by a doctor, honey. And while you're at it, make sure they check your thyroid. I think they're missing something there."

I barely refrain from rolling my eyes at her subtle dig about my weight. "What brings you by?" I ask, quickly changing the subject to less turbulent topics.

"We texted yesterday about it!" Mom shakes her head like I've lost it.

And maybe I have. I completely forgot we agreed for her to come by and visit. Oh well. Since she's here, I can show her all the new plants I added to the condo. She'll be coming by every day to feed Sushi and water my plants while I'm in the Bahamas for Roman and Olivia's wedding next month. With all the league planning, and wining and dining of donors, our little get-together had completely slipped my mind.

"Right!" I rush to stand, tugging on the bottom hem of my crop top. It's no use. The little shirt won't cover my stomach no matter how much I tug on it. Instead I straighten my spine and take comfort in having gorgeous, voluptuous boobs. "Come on back and I'll show you all the new plant babies."

Mom sighs as she stands, probably ready to launch into her usual monologue about wanting to be a glamorous Gigi to real grandchildren, not plants, but I don't let her. I lived with Mom for eighteen long years and learned how to deliver my own monologues. She's about to be educated on the proper care and feeding of Monsteras, snake plants, and peace lilies. I must do a compelling job because she doesn't get a word in edgewise until we're back at the front door and I have her handbag held out.

"Oh, I meant to tell you I have another eligible bachelor who would love this little hockey thing you're putting together."

I grit my teeth over the "little" adjective. "Oh, yeah?"

"He's not a hockey player, don't worry," Mom says, tittering over her joke. She and Dad have only agreed on one thing in life and that is keeping me away from hockey players. While they both came to love Josh after the initial shock, they weren't too happy about his career aspirations. When he gave up hockey after college and got a "real job," they were both relieved. "He's a stock broker. Or maybe it's a financial adviser. I can't remember."

Either one sounds like boring fundraiser dinners and fancy vacations. "I'm not in the market, Mom."

"Honey." Mom puts her hand on my arm and levels a serious glare at me that would have had my pre-teen self shaking in her Birkenstocks. "You need to make time for love or time will pass you by. One dinner. That's all I ask."

I sigh. I'm not getting anywhere with Nikolai and no one else has caught my eye. That itch I wanted scratched is like poison ivy now. "Fine. One date. And he better be good looking."

Mom's face lights up with approval. "Oh, he is! No kids, one divorce, makes good money, and he's handsome. He's quite the catch, Chloe." She looks me up and down. "Make sure you go buy a new dress, okay? And no black. Men love a sundress. Maybe pink or baby blue?"

I'd rather throw myself into the gator infested waters of Florida than wear a baby blue sundress, but what Mom doesn't know won't hurt her. "You got it. Just send me his contact info."

She leaves happy, and I instantly put the date out of my mind. I have flyers to send off to the printers and a reporter to email back. The first open house will take place right after I get back from the Bahamas and I have a million things left to do to make sure it goes off without a hitch. But first, I need to get dressed and head to the arena to talk to Banks Bennet. Roman indicated his Little would be interested, and I feel like word of mouth among the kids is the best way to advertise the new rec league. And if I can rope Banks into coming out for the first open house to impress the parents? Double bonus.

Thirty minutes later, I'm dressed to kill and heading to the rink. Probably not dressed in the way Mom would have preferred, but I'm feeling like a million bucks and that's all that matters. My ripped black jeans are hugging my curves, and my bright red top is a welcome splash of color. And boobs. These badass bitches are on display in this top, but I figure you gotta flaunt your assets or everyone will focus on your flaws.

And Nikolai will be there.

I let out an evil laugh as I find a space in the parking lot and walk to the building that houses the practice rink. I had every intention of staying away, but then Nikolai flirted with me on the ice, and I can't seem to help myself for wanting a bit of payback. Security waves me in, recognizing me right away now. I sit in the chill air and wait for practice to end, all the while eyeing Nikolai from behind. He hasn't seen me yet and I kind of like that I can just observe him in his natural habitat. He's so damn talented. I'm starting to think I have a competence fetish.

"Hey, Chloe!" Bobby calls out, startling me. Practice is now over, and the boys are starting to stream off the ice. Out of the corner of my eye, I see Nikolai's head pop up. I can feel the weight of his stare on the side of my face.

I smile and wave at the young kid. I'm not dumb. I know that he flirts with me every chance he gets, and I eat it up like Ben & Jerry's after a breakup. Men aren't the only ones who like to have their egos stroked.

Plus, it pisses off Nikolai.

"Hey, Bobby," I call back. "Did you get ten years older overnight?"

He sends me a wink that must make women's knees wobble. He rocks those innocent brown eyes paired with a sculpted jaw and muscled body that makes you want to see if he'll turn naughty or nice in the bedroom. "Nah. You still won't date me, baby."

A hand comes out of nowhere and slaps the backside of Bobby's head. The kid turns a frown on Nikolai, who skates past with a grunt I can just barely hear.

"Have some fucking respect."

"Dude. What's your issue? You've been in a bad mood all day," Bobby whines to the backside of Nikolai as he skates off the ice.

I bite back a smile. "I'm actually here to speak to Banks."

Bobby whistles and then shouts. "Yo, Benny. Hottie wants to talk to you!"

Nikolai grinds to a halt right next to me and turns to glare at Bobby. I can feel the anger pulsing off him. I can also smell a healthy sweat from a long practice. Somehow, it's like my own personal pheromone blend because my insides turn to jelly.

Banks glides over and steps off the ice to give me a hug. "Hey, Chloe. Nice to see you again." Nikolai doesn't move, staying by my side like some kind of watchdog. Banks slides his gaze over to Nikolai, but then refocuses on me. "Kaitlyn told me all about your rec league. I talked to Eli and he's in. He thinks hockey is for losers, but I have a feeling you'll change his mind pretty quickly."

I rub my hands together. "Nothing I love more than hotshot kids who get their asses handed to them and walk away with a new level of respect."

Banks laughs. "God, I almost want to be there for the first

practice, just to see him flounder. Good blackmail material, you know?"

I lift an eyebrow. "All practices will be recorded . . ."

Banks shoots me a single finger gun. "Name your price."

"Chocolate. Not the shit kind from the grocery store. I'm talking quality from Belgium."

Nikolai grunts. Banks and I turn to look at him. "Switzerland has the best chocolate."

Banks pats Nikolai on the shoulder. "You're always looking out for me, Druggy."

I reach into my satchel and pull out some of the flyers I stopped to pick up. I hand a few to Banks and shoot my shot. "Might be fun to swing by the open house. Hopeful parents always love to see a pro."

Banks confirms he'll be there, then gives me another hug before marching down the hallway to the locker room. Nikolai holds his hand out and I look down at it. Calluses line his palm. My whole body shivers, thinking about those hands touching my skin.

"What?"

"Do I get a . . . what do you call it . . . paper too?"

I put a hand on my hip and revel in the way his gaze dips down to take in my body before flicking back up to my face. "A flyer about my league? Do you have a youth hockey player in mind?"

He nods, a lock of his golden brown hair falling over his forehead. "Flyer. Yes. My daughter, Ayana, might want to take a few lessons."

My heart warms and my smile shows it. Nikolai trusts me with his daughter. I hand him a couple flyers. "She's welcome any time."

We stand there, flyers between us, gazes locked as we breathe the same cold air. He doesn't break the stare down and neither do I. My heart rate starts coming faster and I remember every vivid detail of that kiss at the bar. The way he took control of my mouth and made everything around us disappear. His blue eyes heat and if I'm not mistaken, he's remembering that kiss also. Too bad Mom couldn't fix me up on a blind date with this man.

"Chloe?" Dad's voice behind me breaks the moment.

Nikolai steps back and waves the flyers in the air, nearly clipping me in the face with them. "Thank you for the flyers," he says comically loud. Then he marches off to the locker room, leaving me with Dad.

He watches Nikolai for a moment. "That boy all right?"

I let out a nervous laugh. "He's fine. You know all goalies are odd." Except he's not odd. Not really. He's a lot of things all wrapped up in a proud, loyal package that most people don't understand. I want to understand him even better, but he'll never allow it.

I inhale sharply and turn my focus back to my priorities. "Want some flyers?"

Chapter Ten

Niko

"*Blyat'!*" I hiss in a breath as the razor nicks my skin and blood beads to the surface in my reflection. These fucking porkchop sideburns. Shaving these down is the one and only benefit of losing in the conference finals this past week. It feels like I have been wearing earmuffs on my face.

All hockey players have superstitions, some more than others. Dan-O, our captain, wears the same underwear every game day–much to his wife Sara's horror. Monkowski, known to all as Money, kisses his skates before putting them on. I tap my stick on the ice in sets of three and talk to my posts before each game. I also have an entire gameday routine that never changes. I get out of bed on the left side, both feet touching the floor at the exact same time. Then I do one hundred pushups and one hundred sit-ups before leaving the bedroom. Next is a breakfast of black coffee, three hard-boiled eggs, whole-grain toast with peanut butter, and a banana. It never varies, no matter what. On the road, I even make certain the night before that the hotel can accommodate my breakfast order.

So, I understand superstitions more than anyone. That does not mean I enjoy looking like a nineteen seventies television cop with these bushy sideburns Benny declared we had to grow during playoffs. It messed with the beard style I usually wear.

I wipe my face with a towel, inspecting my trim job. I would have gladly kept the awful style through the finals, but it was not meant to be this year. Since next season is my last, I must impress upon my teammates the importance of another Stanley Cup win at every practice. But, for now, it is time to breathe—and switch my entire focus to Ayana.

With that in mind, I exit the bathroom, grabbing my phone as I go to the kitchen for coffee. Strakh opens one eye from a dead sleep next to his food bowl. I tired him out with a run earlier, and he has been dead to the world since. My assistant walks him when I am out of town, but she is not a runner like me.

"Rest up, little one. We see Ayana today," I tell him as I put in my earbuds to call my lawyer. He doesn't move, apart from a quirk of his eyebrows.

Before I can place the call, a new text alert pops up from Safiya.

> Safiya: Did Katya call you?

I quickly type out my reply.

> Me: Of course not. I called her.

As it turns out, Katya's cancer did not return; she was just running herself ragged and not eating enough, something she eventually confessed to her doctor. Since then, I have arranged for a weekly delivery service of fresh food to keep her stocked up and save her the errand.

> Safiya: [laughing face emoji] Not even sure why I asked.

> Me: The doctor is pleased.

Katya's bi-annual blood tests came back yesterday showing healthy numbers, something I found out when I called her earlier–after waiting fruitlessly for her promised call all night.

> Safiya: Just wanted to make sure you heard. Talk to you later!

I scroll to my lawyer's contact and press it.

"Niko," Jane greets me once her assistant puts me through. Her tone is upbeat, which I hope spells good things.

I do not mess with pleasantries. "Any news?" I pull the coffee canister from the cupboard and set it by the machine.

"As a matter of fact, I just got off the phone with Peyton's lawyer. Since the court date has been bumped *again*, they've agreed to a two-week visitation in the meantime."

I freeze in place. "Two weeks?" I am unsure I trust my ears. The most extended stretches I have ever had with Ayana were one week, which is very seldom. It is usually the odd weekend or weekday here and there.

"Two weeks, big guy." I can hear the smile in my lawyer's voice.

"When? When can she come? My calendar is empty . . ." I begin to pace the tile floor of my kitchen, coffee forgotten. Two weeks with my Ayana. It is a dream.

"You and Peyton can discuss it and come up with some dates."

I jab my fingers through my hair, mind racing. "I am

picking Ayana up in an hour for the afternoon, so I will speak with Peyton then." This is fantastic news.

"Sounds good. Continue keeping good records like you have been, and stay the course as the choir boy so we don't give them anything to use against us. Chin up, Niko. I'm confident the judge will see things our way."

"If we are ever allowed to see him." My voice does not carry its normal despair this time.

Jane does not directly respond to my comment, instead saying, "Give your girl a squeeze from me, and I'll be in touch."

I quickly make coffee and inhale a sandwich before packing supplies in a backpack and hustling Strakh to my Land Rover. The puppy seems to prefer car rides to anything else, and Ayana insisted I buy him a seatbelt harness to keep him safe. So, of course, I did. The drive to Peyton's Mediterranean-style home is thirty minutes, but I know the route so well, I hardly pay attention. I am lucky she remained in the Tampa area after our divorce, but she has a vast network of friends nearby—even if she lacks a job keeping her local.

That is not to say she does not work. But she appears to change jobs more often than Benny changes sticks. I believe she currently works as a model and actress in local advertisements. I saw her in an ad for a car dealership last week.

I pull into the driveway, noticing the grass needs a trim. I will have to hire a new company to take care of it since it is clear Peyton is not tending to it, as she promised. Ayana needs grass to play on—not weeds to carry mosquitoes.

But the grass is forgotten when Ayana bursts out the front door and down the two steps, her gorgeous bright smile aimed at me. "Dad!"

Strakh barks, straining against his seatbelt and pawing at one of the back doors, but I am claiming my daughter's first hug. *Too bad, furry one.*

I round the hood of the vehicle and lift Ayana into the air. "Ms. Drugov, you have grown two inches!"

"I've been eating tofu," she announces, circling her little arms around my neck. "And I lost another tooth. See." She widens her mouth in a grimace, showing off a new gap along her bottom gums.

"You will have to leave it for the tooth mouse so you will grow a strong tooth in its place."

"Mom says it's the tooth *fairy*, not the tooth *mouse*." She eyes me earnestly. "I'm going with the fairy since she deals in cash."

I have no chance to respond since Strakh has reached his limit as his barking escalates. Ayana drops from my arms and races to the backseat to greet her dog.

"So, that's the famous Paul, huh?"

I turn to see Peyton in her front doorway. She looks beautiful, as always, her wavy blond hair catching the sun, and her body encased in form fitting workout gear that leaves very little to the imagination.

I step closer so we can speak without Ayana overhearing. "We are still working on the name," I tell her before getting down to business. "My lawyer says you are giving me two weeks."

She nods, her eyes still on our daughter. "I have some plans, so I thought you could take her while I'm busy."

"I am always happy to take her. You know this."

Her gaze finally shifts to me, and she does a quick sweep of my body and face. "You look good, Niko."

I cannot discern her tone, but I am automatically on alert. It is not like her to hand out compliments, much less make it easy for me to see Ayana. I can only hope she is turning over a new leaf and not hatching a new scheme.

I settle on, "You too," as my response, keeping my eyes only on her face. "I was thinking . . . there is a wedding in the

Bahamas in a few weeks. Roman's." She knows my former teammate and captain from the old days. "I thought Ayana might like to come. You know how she loves the beach."

Peyton's eyebrows spike. "The Bahamas?" But she does not immediately shoot me down, instead bobbing her head from side to side for a few moments. "Let me think about it, okay?"

I nod, pleased enough that she will consider it. "So, when are these plans you have?" My entire summer is clear, so it matters little to me.

"The last two weeks of this month."

"Done." I nod again. "And I will send a new lawn crew over to start caring for the lawn." I do not understand why she fired the last crew I hired. Then again, I do not understand most of what Peyton does.

I am surprised again when she agrees. "Okay. I meant to get to it. I've just been . . . busy."

"Bye, Mom!" Ayana yells from the backseat. I turn to see Strakh sitting on her lap and licking her chin.

"Bye, baby!" Peyton waves, and I turn to go. "Back before five, Niko. She has dance," she instructs me, her tone returning to a more familiar one. This Peyton, I know how to deal with.

"No problem," I respond before jogging to the driver's side, anxious to squeeze in as much time with my kid as possible. But I have two weeks on the horizon, and I cannot wait.

Chapter Eleven

Chloe

The warm, damp air of the Bahamas feels a lot like Florida in the summer. Thankfully, I had a few months to adjust to it before coming here for Roman and Olivia's wedding. I knew enough to pack multiple swimsuits, the lightest of sundresses, and all the sweat-proof makeup a girl can find at Sephora. I spent yesterday at the pool working on my tan, which ended in a full body pink burn that will probably just fade away into my normal pale color the day after I return to Florida. I saw a few people from the team floating around the hotel, but I did not see Nikolai.

Not that I'm looking.

I snort and sip the iced coffee I got in the lobby, staring out at the bluest water imaginable from the balcony of my third-floor hotel room. I am *so* looking. I can't seem to help myself. The man delivered the best kiss of my life, then pushed me away, all the while giving me longing glances and frowns like he has some opinion about how I live my life. He's taking up space in my brain and I don't appreciate it. I need that space to juggle all the details of my league.

Glancing at my phone for the hundredth time today, I refresh the screen to see that I now have twenty-two kids registered for the first open house. It's a scary number. If all of them want to join my league, I'll be looking at hiring another coach to assist me as soon as we get started.

I nearly choke, seeing the time in the corner of my phone screen. I slam my coffee cup down on the side table and rush back into my room to buckle my feet into the tall wedge sandals that take me all the way up to five-foot-seven. A slick of bright red lip gloss over the carefully painted lip liner and I'm off, tucking the tube into the tiny handbag I bought to match the red hibiscus flowers splashed all over my tea-length sundress. The straps around my neck leave my back bare and my breasts lovingly pressed together for impressive cleavage. I may or may not have had torturing Nikolai in mind when I bought this dress . . .

The wedding ceremony takes place outside in a stunning white gazebo in front of the backdrop of the ocean. White chairs break up the expansive green lawn. Flowers are positively bursting from every surface, making me feel like I'm on a secluded tropical island getaway. I slip into a chair next to Kaitlyn and compliment her dress. She's got that pregnancy glow, making a gorgeous couple with Banks. So much so, a little crackle of jealousy threatens to bring down my mood. They're clearly in love and planning for a future that I'll never have.

The hairs on the back of my neck rise and I shift in my seat to see Nikolai sitting down directly behind me with a few of the other players on the team. They all say hello to Banks, Kaitlyn, and me, but I'm only acutely aware of one of them.

"Hello," I say quietly, letting my gaze trail down his long body. Damn. The man can clean up, that's for sure. He's in linen pants, brown leather loafers, and a white button-down shirt that's open at the collar. The shaggy hair I once had my fingers in is styled like he just stepped away from a photo shoot.

"Chloe," he answers quietly. His gaze dips down to my cleavage and then darts to the side, studying the flowers tied to the chairs on the end of the row.

Soft music plays from hidden speakers as people continue taking their seats. I swivel back to the front and try to control my breathing. Why does this man do this to me? He just says my name and suddenly I'm about to hyperventilate? *Get your shit together, Chloe.*

The music changes and Roman and Olivia's three kids each come down the aisle and then stand up at the front by the gazebo. Roman steps through the back side of the gazebo where he's been waiting and hugs each of the kids before standing next to the officiant, looking like a million bucks in his tan suit. There's a moment of silence and then a haunting instrumental love song plays. The whole audience stands as one and looks toward Olivia's entrance. And this time, my attention isn't pulled away by the frustrating goalie. Olivia is stunning in a fitted white lace dress, the height of fashion and yet looking so at ease in her skin. I sneak a look at Roman to find his jaw locked tight and his hands wiping his eyes as he tries to hold it together. That's my favorite part of weddings; seeing the groom react to seeing his bride. Josh had smiled and nodded at me, but no tears. I'll always wonder if that was my first sign that we would have been better off staying friends.

"Welcome to the wedding of Roman LaFontaine and Olivia Wylder. You may be seated."

I go to sit down and nearly jump out of my skin when a single finger slides across my exposed back like a lover's caress. As quickly as it's there, it's gone. I glance back to see Nikolai clear his throat as he sits behind me and stares straight ahead. I turn my eyes forward again and try to grapple with the knowledge that he touched me slyly right there in the open. For the last few months, he's been doing his best to avoid touching me at all.

My brain, now officially hijacked by the man behind me, doesn't hear half of what's said, but I do manage to stand and clap when my newly married friends make their way back down the aisle with broad smiles. Nikolai gets lost in the sea of people as we all exit the lawn and make our way to the outdoor dance floor surrounded by round dinner tables and twinkle lights overhead. It's probably for the best because I see Dad at one of the tables, his hand over his head, waving at me.

"Hey, pumpkin. I saved you a seat. Gorgeous place for a wedding, huh?" He gives me a hug and we both sit.

"Most definitely. Then again, Olivia is always on point with trends and fashion. I would expect nothing less from her wedding." My gaze darts around the space, still not finding Nikolai.

Several players and their spouses fill in our table, and soon the conversation turns to hockey. The first course is served, and Dad decides now is the time to turn his attention to my business. He gives each of his players a stern glance.

"Did you all spread the word about Chloe's youth hockey league? First open house is next week, you know."

Heads nod and I smile graciously. "It's all good, Dad. I have plenty signed up already."

His phone rings, cutting off his reply. He looks at the screen and fumbles over his words. "I, um, gotta take this. Excuse me." He scrapes his chair back and rushes off, phone pressed to his ear.

I narrow my eyes, salad forgotten. Conversation continues to flow around me. Danny's wife, Sara, leans over and whispers to me. "Your dad's been getting a lot of phone calls he's been secretive about. I don't want to start trouble, but the guys have been talking about it. Is everything okay with him?"

I dab a napkin at my lips as the waiters whisk away our salad plates and replace them with our main meal. "Interesting you should say that. I was wondering what's going on too. What do the guys think the phone calls are about?"

Sara looks uncomfortable. "They think he's dating someone."

I nod thoughtfully as I sip my champagne. That's it. I'm going to corner Dad tonight and make him spill the beans. If people are already talking, as his daughter, I have a right to know what's going on in my father's life. My rock lobster and fried plantains don't taste like much, not with my head spinning about Dad.

And Nikolai. I finally see the hot-and-cold goalie when the waiters slide miniature slices of rum cake in front of us. He's got a phone pressed to his ear as he leaves the area too. With regret, I push away the cake and stand up, letting Sara know I'm running to the bathroom. Dad's still not back and now Nikolai has left. What's going on with these guys? Don't they know it's rude to leave a wedding reception early?

The quick trip to the bathroom doesn't yield either of the men, so I head back to the reception, seeing that a band has begun playing, and Roman and Olivia are out on the dance floor, taking their first dance as husband and wife. It's adorable the way they look at each other like no one else exists. What must it feel like to be the center of someone's attention like that? The song changes to another and more couples take to the dance floor.

"You have to dance with me, beautiful." Bobby materializes next to me and holds out his hand, his youthful face sporting a wide grin.

I roll my eyes but let him tug me onto the dance floor. He takes liberties, his hands coming around my waist and dipping low enough I kick him in the shin until he moves them upward a few inches. He howls with laughter, and I join in, finding him a breath of fresh air. He's harmless fun. We dance through two songs, chatting away the whole time before I beg for a break and more champagne. He moves away to grab me a glass at one of the bars, leaving me at the side of the dance floor.

A harsh voice in the distance has me turning around and squinting. Out there in the dark by a lit tiki torch is a tall figure on the phone. The man turns and the fire dances across his features. Nikolai. And he looks angry.

I turn on my heel without giving it much thought, striding across the grass toward him. He hangs up and looks up at the dark sky like he's biting back some creative Russian curse words.

"Did you break a nail? I hate when I do that. So annoying."

His head drops and his eyes burn into my already heated skin. "You should not be here."

I twirl my finger in the air. "Like, the Bahamas? Or here on this pathway with you? You'll have to be more specific."

"Chloe," he growls. The man actually growled my name and now I don't want to hear my name said any other way.

I step closer, tilting my head back to stare up at him. The bobbing fire makes his cheekbones look like they've been carved from granite. "Nikolai," I purr.

He reaches out and for one intoxicating moment, I think he's going to bestow another one of those mind-bending kisses on me. Instead, he puts his hand on my back and spins me around. The feel of his palm against my bare skin sends a shiver down my body. He pushes, forcing me to walk back to the reception. I go along peacefully, hoping for . . . something . . . anything from Nikolai that's not shutting me down.

I'm disappointed when he gets right to the edge of the

light from the party and gives me another push, taking his hand from my back. "Go back to the party and dance with your little boys."

My mouth drops open, but Nikolai has already spun back around, his phone jammed to his ear, barking out Russian words I do not understand. He walks away and I watch him go, heart thumping sadly in my chest. Anger replaces the humiliation of him pushing me away again. I stiffen my spine, forget the way his single hand covered the entire width of my back, and make a beeline for the bartender. I do what he says. I drink, have fun, and dance with all the boys I can find, all the while flipping off Nikolai Drugov in my mind.

Chapter Twelve

Niko

"I have had enough of this, Jane!" I bark into the phone before drawing in a deep breath to attempt calming my temper. "I am sorry. I know it is not your fault. I am breaking my head." I run a frustrated hand through my hair and step farther from the wedding festivities so I can hear Jane more clearly.

"I'm as mad as you are, Niko," she responds. "And don't apologize. I've got Teflon skin. If I had a dime for every time I've been yelled at, I'd be retired in Aruba with my own personal team of pool boys."

My only response is a grunt. I am beyond pissed at this point, having just hung up with Peyton before phoning my lawyer. Peyton actually hid Ayana from me when I came to pick her up for the airport yesterday.

It turns out my ex *did* have a reason for her less combative behavior last month. A man. And one richer than me, from what I can gather. I know why she did not tell me, too; she knows I hate Ayana being left alone with strangers, especially strange men. Peyton's last boyfriend went through an extensive background check as well as one week on a private investigator's timesheet. Not that I ever told Peyton that, since the guy turned out to be tolerable.

But guess who got dumped and decided to return to despising me?

My two weeks spent with Ayana was the happiest I have been in longer than I can remember. We hit the beach, took a day trip to that Harry Potter place, flew kites in the park, took long walks with Paul (fine, I gave in), and watched enough baking shows to give me diabetes just from osmosis. We were all set to redecorate her room at my house when Peyton showed up at my front door two days early and announced Ayana's visit was over. I have not seen my daughter since.

"Look, she doesn't have a leg to stand on," Jane continues. "My best guess is that her lawyer will argue two things: the same old song and dance about you traveling too much during the season, and some load of BS that you're not equipped to care for her since you have less experience."

"I would have more experience if I could be allowed to see my daughter!" I shout before remembering where I am and glancing toward the party where music plays as guests chat and laugh. It is like another world. "I am sorry. Again."

"I know. The judge isn't stupid, Niko. You'll see. But we need to nail down the childcare details for the season before we set foot in that courtroom. It's the first thing he'll ask for."

I sigh and sweep palm fibers from my shirt. I must have brushed against some branches in all my pacing. "Right. I will."

"Niko." Her tone is scolding, and I know she is right.

But finding a good nanny to begin working at an undefined point in the future is harder than it sounds. I have interviewed dozens over the past year, and only two met my standards. Of course, they were both in high demand and could not wait around for Peyton to come to her senses or for the courts to force her hand.

"I understand the importance of this, Jane. It will happen. I just need you to make sure Peyton is done with her . . ." I search for the word, finally finding it. ". . . manipulations."

"I'm on it. Try to enjoy your vacation, and we'll talk later. You've got two weeks to find that nanny, Niko. Two weeks."

Two weeks to find someone I trust with my daughter's life and wellbeing. That is a tall order, to say the least. But I must do it.

"We will talk soon. Goodnight, Jane."

I pull the phone from my ear and drop my hand to my side as exhaustion sets in. I stare ahead, my eyes unfocused. I should take up meditation to deal with my stress or I will be dead before the year is out. But meditation is bullshit. Exercise is more practical.

Laughter breaks through my thoughts, and I turn toward the gathered party to see Chloe in that sexy-as-fuck dress, laughing at something Roadie said. Again. She pats his bicep, and I feel it like a punch to my solar plexus.

What is wrong with me? First, I lose my mind and run a finger across her skin at the ceremony, and now I am feeling a physical blow from her flirting with Bobby Rhodes, of all people. He is a child. She could not possibly take him seriously. She would never let him caress her silky skin or brush his lips against her impossibly pouty ones. Would she?

Fuck! It is none of my business. I sent her away tonight, despite my cock telling me to carry her to my hotel room and tie her to my bed until her voice went hoarse from screaming out her pleasure—and my name. My fingers flex at my sides at the mere thought of fisting her hair and fucking her pretty mouth before bending her over to fuck her sweet pussy.

And now my cock is too hard to return to the party without drawing attention. Linen pants were a poor choice.

My phone vibrates and I glance at the screen to see a text from Jane.

> Jane: Here's the number for that nanny service my client recommended.

That is enough to kill my boner.

A flash of red catches my eye in my peripheral vision, and I glance over again to see Chloe on the dance floor now as the band switches to an upbeat song I do not recognize. However, it must be a favorite of Chloe's because she begins dancing in perfect rhythm to the tune. Her movements are fluid, mesmerizing, as she moves her body with the beat. When she drops almost to a squat and rolls her hips on the rise, I have had enough. I tear my eyes from her and stalk to the bar.

"Vodka. Double. Neat."

"Sorry, sir. No vodka. Can I offer you a Rum Runner?" the young bartender asks with a polite smile. My scowl is reflexive. "No vodka?" What is Roman thinking? When the bartender shakes her head again, I wave a dismissive hand. "Fine." She hands over the vile cocktail and I shove a ten in her tip jar to make up for my rudeness.

Sick of myself, I join a small gathering of other guests, including a couple of my teammates. I purposely position myself with my back to the dance floor. Benny and Kaitlyn attempt to draw me into the conversation, but I am shitty company tonight. I am relieved when Forns and Roadie take over, yet I hardly hear a word they say. Every one of my senses is on alert for any sign of Chloe, despite my most earnest wishes. The one benefit is that I am so distracted, I hardly taste the cocktail as I drain my glass.

Roman approaches the group saying something about a flower toss. I pay no attention until Chloe's name comes up.

"There's only a couple women out there and Chloe is uncomfortable."

He is speaking to Kaitlyn, who appears right at home where she is–her pregnant belly being groped by Benny like a rabid dog protecting a stolen shoe.

The scoffing sound is out of my mouth before I can stop it, drawing Kaitlyn's attention, along with a glare I know I deserve. I could not help it, though. Of any woman here at the wedding–or in the Bahamas as a whole–there is no one more comfortable in her own skin than Chloe Cooper. She needs Kaitlyn at her side for a flower toss like I need Roadie to give me lessons on how to get a woman off.

I escape further rebuke when Kaitlyn follows Roman to the dance floor. I take it as a sign and head for the bar again.

Two drinks later–this time a nice whiskey the bartender failed to previously mention–and my head is light and my outlook improved. So much so that I manage to neither throw Chloe over my shoulder and abscond with her to my room or shoo her away like a misbehaving dog when she approaches this time.

"Well, that was romantic," she says with a sigh.

I assume she is speaking of Benny proposing to Kaitlyn on the dance floor just now. The man does love to show off his woman. Ever since the pregnancy was announced, he has been strutting around like a peacock. It is as if he is unaware that any fifteen-year-old boy in the world could accomplish the same deed in less time than it takes him to tie his skates.

"I suppose. If you believe in such things."

I feel Chloe's gaze swing to me, despite my eyes being trained on a flowering tree in the distance. "Nice attitude, Sunshine." She laughs, but it's slightly caustic.

"*Blin.*" I rub my bearded chin. "I am sorry, Chloe." I am an asshole.

"Apology accepted. Now, you want to tell me about the bug that obviously crawled up your ass this afternoon?"

I glare down at her, not failing to notice the new amusement in her eyes. Fuck, she is delightful. I wish I were the kind of man to appreciate such things. Or deserve them.

The least I can do after my rudeness is offer some explanation. "The bug's name is Peyton. My ex-wife. A particularly nasty species that enjoys keeping my daughter from me–and from a Bahamian vacation."

"Ouch." Her brow furrows, compassion shining from her wide blue eyes.

"Most certainly."

She puts a hand on my arm, and it is as if she has licked me with fire. "I'm sorry, Nikolai. That must be painful."

I watch her for a few seconds, my head swimming with whiskey and my heart pounding more loudly in my chest than it should be. "You are very kind, Chloe Cooper. Much too kind. You should go back and enjoy the party." I cock my head to the dance floor where she moved so seductively and freely earlier. "I am not good company tonight. Or any night, really," I tack on. She deserves to know she is dodging a bullet by staying away from me.

Chloe shrugs and wrinkles her nose. "See, I'm not really good at that."

"At what?"

"Leaving a sad guy wallowing in his whiskey? Believing lies? Doing what I'm told?" Her lips quirk. "You pick."

I shake my head and sigh, feeling my own lips curve for the first time since I boarded the plane without Ayana last night.

<h1 style="text-align:center">Chapter Thirteen</h1>

Chloe

There's plenty of hot, single hockey players here tonight and yet not one of them makes my heart pump and my skin tingle like Nikolai. Which is unfortunate because he has some shit on his plate and has made it clear he's not going to take my bait. And yeah, I'll admit I've been baiting him. It's just so damn fun to see his jaw clench and his face turn stony even as a little bead of sweat dots his brow.

Those thick, sensuous lips of his curve upward and every molecule inside my body jumps with electricity. I feel a tug toward Nikolai. Have ever since I met him in that bar in Toronto. Something about him just calls to me and I'm done second guessing it.

"Let's take a walk on the beach, Sunshine. I've learned there's nothing a little salt and sand can't fix."

Nikolai's blue eyes practically smolder as he looks down at me. It's not a practiced look, either. He gives off the vibe that he'd snuff out that heat if he could. "I am not sure that is advisable."

I lift a bare shoulder in a shrug. "It's just a walk, Nikolai. I promise not to take advantage of you."

He growls, the rumble coming from his chest and making my breaths come quicker. "That is not what I fear. Far from it."

I tilt my head, not giving up on this tall, grumpy goalie who clearly feels so much below the surface. "I'm going to walk right over there and head for the beach. I'd hate to walk alone in the dark. Who knows what could happen to a single woman all alone on vacation?"

Without a single glance backward, I turn and walk away, making good on my promise after a pit stop at the bar, disappearing from the party and into the night. The sound of the waves draws me in, and it only takes a few more steps before I hear footfalls behind me. I knew he wouldn't be able to stay behind, not when my safety came into question. The man is disagreeable most of the time, but I'm learning he has a raging case of protectiveness toward those he cares about.

And I suddenly yearn for that protectiveness to be directed at me.

"I believe they have rules about alcohol on the beach," comes his deep voice right behind me.

I stop at the water's edge and turn to him, a challenging smile on my face. "You gonna turn me in, big guy?"

His hand darts out and cups my bare shoulder before gliding down my arm, his rough calluses sending a shiver across my skin despite the island heat. He slowly takes the bottles of beer from my hand and holds them, appearing reluctant to no longer be touching me. I'm getting the feeling he delights in touching me. Based on the way I can barely breathe, I delight in it too.

Without looking away from me, he shrugs out of his sport

coat and lays it on the sand. His free hand comes up between us, palm up. I slip my hand into his and wonder how I can feel so much for a man I barely know. He gives me a tug and helps me get seated on his jacket. I tuck the skirt of my dress around my legs and reach down to take off the wedges that have done a number on my feet tonight. Nikolai sits down next to me and pops the top off one of the long neck bottles of beer in his hands, passing it to me and keeping the other for himself. I can feel the heat of him, smell the cologne and something else uniquely Nikolai.

I hold out the bottle and he clinks the necks together. "What are we toasting, short stranger?"

The grin is immediate. He remembers our conversation back in Toronto as clearly as I do. "To island getaways? To friends getting married? To alcohol being readily available?" I tilt my head and observe the tension that is still visible around his eyes. "To a redo tropical vacation next year with your daughter?"

His eyes close for a moment and when he opens them again, I know I've said the right thing. He must love his daughter very much. "To a redo," he says, clinking the necks again and taking a long pull from the bottle.

I watch his Adam's apple bob, wanting to reach out and trace the thickly muscled neck. I quickly take a sip when his gaze comes back to mine.

"Want to tell me about it?" I ask softly, thumbnail picking at the label on the bottle.

He sighs, hooking his elbows on his knees and dangling the beer between his legs. "I am in a custody battle with my ex. She pulls stunts to keep my daughter away from me and I am tired of it. My lawyer thinks we have a strong case." His gaze darts back out to the ocean. "Well, mostly a strong case."

I frown, wondering what in the world a judge would see and not approve of. Nikolai clearly cares deeply for his daughter and has all the money in the world to provide for her. "What's holding you back?"

He sighs again and I can hear the frustration in his tone. "I travel too much and I do not have a dedicated nanny to watch her when I am working. But how can I have a dedicated nanny when I never know when I will be allowed to see her?" He shakes his head, jaw locking tight. "I will simply have to give onto the paw to get a nanny to stay when there is no actual nannying to be done."

I blink a few times, trying to decipher all of that, especially the paw part. My heart aches for him. He should have the right to see his daughter regularly. Josh and I never had kids, mostly because it wasn't a priority, time got away from us, and then he got sick. But if we had, I know I wouldn't have let anything stop me from seeing them. An idea forms in my head, gaining momentum as Nikolai takes another long swig of beer. His profile is as strong as his muscles, a stoic man with a heart of gold.

I turn toward him, tucking one leg underneath me and leaning so far over my arm wedges against his. His head swivels slowly and he looks down at me. The moonlight casts half his face in shadow and yet he's still the most handsome man I've ever seen.

"My husband died last year."

"Chloe," he starts, but I interrupt him.

"No. I don't say that for sympathy. He was diagnosed a couple years before his death. Cancer. The kind that doesn't have a good chemotherapy drug yet. He fought it, even when the therapy that was supposed to save his life ended up draining the life from him. I eventually had to take a sabbatical from my job, spending every minute of the day and night caring for him. At the end there, it was like taking care of a small child. He couldn't do anything on his own."

I trail off, stuck in the memories of that difficult time. My gaze flies back to Nikolai's when he tucks a lock of hair behind my shoulder, his finger tracing the shell of my ear. My teeth snag on my bottom lip.

"You loved him greatly, yes?"

I hum a noncommittal answer. "I loved him, yes."

Nikolai's eyes narrow. "But?"

My gaze drops to the sand at our feet. I've tucked away the truth, too terrified of peoples' reactions to express it. Too terrified to say it out loud. If I keep it a simple thought in my head, maybe then it won't actually be true. But there's something in the way Nikolai blocks the wind with his big body. He seems like the type to absorb a blow and not even grunt with the effort. He seems like the sort of man to understand and accept the harsher side of life.

I lift my gaze to his and will myself to be brave. "But I wasn't *in* love with him, if you know what I mean." I lick my lips, feeling like I need to fully explain now that I put that out there. "We started out in love, but over time and going in different directions with our careers and interests, it turned into a friendship. I loved him and I honored our wedding vows. I believe he did the same, but by the time I realized what had happened to us, he was diagnosed with cancer. I couldn't leave him then. I wouldn't do that to him. As my friend, I owed him more than that. I took care of him until the very end."

The waves lap softly onto the sand and the faint beat of the music from the wedding reception is a welcome back-drop to the silence that falls between us. I'm not sure if I'm horrified or relieved to have given voice to my thoughts about Josh. Nikolai doesn't say anything for a long while and when I can't take the silence any longer, I blurt out my idea.

"I guess what I'm getting at is that I know how to take care of another human. I can be your nanny, Nikolai."

His head whips in my direction, eyes wide, jaw clenched. "My nanny? You? Why would you offer that?"

I'm not sure if I'm hurt or indifferent to him not believing I could be his daughter's nanny. "Why not me?"

He shakes his head slowly, studying me. "You have your league. Your own life. Why help me?"

I take a chance and put my hand on his knee. His gaze drops to where I touch him, but he doesn't remove my hand. "Because I'm a daddy's girl myself and I happen to believe every girl deserves time with her father."

Nikolai makes a sound like he's choking. "*Zhizn' yebet menya*," he mutters under his breath.

I don't know any Russian, but that didn't sound like a yes.

<h1 style="text-align:center">Chapter Fourteen</h1>

Niko

This is a worse idea than the porkchop sideburns. Chloe as Ayana's nanny? Impossible.

"You are kind." I force the words through gritted teeth as her touch burns through the linen covering my leg.

Her brow furrows, and the breeze off the ocean sends wisps of her hair floating across her face. She tucks them behind her ear and my fingers twitch to reach out and touch it again. I take a sip of my beer instead. The cold liquid does nothing to cool me down, though. "That's the second time you've said that tonight. I might start getting a complex," Chloe responds, her lips quirking as she removes her hand.

I cock my head. "What do you mean?"

"That's like being called 'nice.'" She wrinkles her nose at the word, and I find it charming.

"And what is wrong with that?"

She dips her chin and wedges the bottom of her beer bottle into the sand until it stands on its own. "*Nice?* That's what you call someone when you can't think of any other redeeming qualities. It would be like me calling you an *adequate* goalie."

I scowl. "Swallow your tongue."

Chloe drops her head back and laughs, exposing the silky skin of her throat. "I think you meant '*bite* your tongue.'"

"All these sayings. I prefer Russian."

"I take it you think in Russian? Dream in Russian?"

"Always." I nod. "It frustrates me when I cannot find the right English words to say what I mean."

Chloe barks out a laugh. "You're not the only one."

"What do you mean?"

"Nothing." She waves a dismissive hand. "Does Ayana speak Russian? Wait. How old is she?"

"Seven." I shake my head and set my own beer in the sand. "No. But I hope to teach her one day. It is easier to learn a new language when one is a child. I did not learn English until I moved to Canada for hockey when I was twenty years old."

"I've always thought English would be difficult to learn. So many rules that are regularly broken."

"Yes!" I agree, shifting my position to face her more directly "Tell me why the B at the beginning of 'bomb' is spoken but the one at the end is silent. And what is the point of this 'I before E' rule if there are so many exceptions? And why do you park on a driveway and drive on a parkway?"

She is outright grinning at me now. "All excellent questions." Her back straightens, and she throws an index finger in the air. "And why is a vegetarian someone who eats vegetables but a humanitarian doesn't eat humans?"

I laugh at that, realizing that I am enjoying chatting with Chloe more than I have enjoyed any other interaction in recent memory–aside from my time with Ayana. But that is very different.

"Well," Chloe continues. "It sounds like Russian might be

a breeze in comparison. Maybe when you win your custody battle, you can teach Ayana."

"Perhaps."

She smiles again and then drops her eyes to the sand, a brief silence settling between us. "You don't have to accept my offer, Nikolai, but you should know I'm happy to do it. I have the time, and I love kids."

I should not even entertain the thought, but I cannot seem to help myself. Instead of refusing her offer outright, I say, "The witch from Hansel and Gretel loved kids too."

Her eyes sparkle with amusement as they flash to mine. "Are you insinuating I plan to eat your daughter?"

I shrug, basking in her attention, though I know I am playing with fire.

"I'll have you know I taught third grade for fifteen years and never once baked a child in my oven," she says with a lift of her chin that's almost smug.

My eyes widen. "You are a teacher?" God is certainly toying with me now. He delivers the perfect nanny candidate in the form of my most dangerous temptation.

Chloe nods. "I told you I love kids. And I'm certified in CPR and first aid–and I can make a mean papier mâché Ruth Bader Ginsburg too."

"I have no idea what that means."

She makes another shooing gesture and turns her eyes back to the lapping waves. "Not important."

I watch her for a few beats before asking, "Do you not understand why this is a bad idea?"

When she turns to me this time, it is not amusement I find in her eyes. It is challenge. "Because you're attracted to me?"

No. She does not understand. It seems I must explain. "Because I want to fuck you breathless. I want to take you every way a man can take a woman." My cock stiffens in my pants as her breath quickens in the rise and fall of her chest. I can even see the rush of blood in her veins at the pulse point of her throat. But I continue because she needs to understand. "I want to ruin you for other men, and I would not be the least bit sorry for it."

She tries to speak, but her voice catches in her throat. I know her cheeks are flushed, despite the darkness, and it only has my cock going harder.

I continue as she visibly swallows. "But I cannot. I will not." This time, I cannot help myself. I brush my knuckles along the underside of her jaw, and she shivers at my touch. She wants the same thing I do, and she does not try to deny it. "Every part of my life is under a . . . what is the word? Microscope–by the judge and by Peyton. I will not risk Ayana for anything–or anyone. Having you in my house would be a temptation I am not sure I could withstand."

"I . . ." Chloe begins before swallowing again. "I understand." She rises to her feet and brushes the sand from her legs. I don't follow suit, knowing my cock will make himself the center of attention if I do. "I'm . . . um . . . going to head back."

Lights from the hotel catch her face now that she is standing, and I see that I was right. She is flushed from her gorgeous cleavage to her hairline. My pulse quickens at the sight, but I force myself to stay where I am. "Goodnight, Chloe." She turns, shoes in hand, to walk through the sand. "And thank you." I am not sure if she hears the last part, but either way, this is for the best.

"If she's available, ask if she'll come to the hearing," Jane says from across her impressive glass and steel desk. She does not embody the traditional stodgy lawyer vibe in either her appearance or her decorating style. Instead, Jane leans more toward edgy, something that threw me off when we initially met. But she has proven to be the shrewd asset I need in this conflict with Peyton.

Instead of responding immediately to her comment, I cough into my hand. Jane may be under the impression that I have succeeded in securing a nanny for Ayana in the last two weeks. I have not.

To be fair, I thought I had. Sienna, the candidate, had an impeccable resume and was available to start immediately. But when she showed up at my front door for her interview, she was chewing a piece of gum—with her mouth open! There was no possible way I was hiring a nanny to teach Ayana such bad manners. All I could picture was my sweet daughter sitting on the couch next to this Sienna woman, both of them chomping on wads of gum like cows chewing their cud. I dismissed her on sight, a decision I cannot bring myself to regret. However, it does put me in a bind. One that I fear there is only one solution to.

"I will ask," I respond to Jane, who is now scribbling on her tablet with a smart pencil, her dark brows pulled together in concentration.

"Judge Lopez won't be able to deny you if he meets the perfect nanny in person."

An image of Chloe sitting on the beach in the moonlight immediately springs to mind. "Right."

Shit.

"Okay." Jane drops her pencil and pats her desktop with both hands, her eyes returning to me and a bright smile lighting her face. "I think we're ready, Niko. Next time I see you, you'll be walking out of court with Ayana at your side."

Her tone is eerily close to one I have heard from Dracula right before the "Mwa-ha-ha" evil laugh. I am glad she is on my side.

"That is my greatest wish," I respond, taking her cue and standing from my chair. "I will see you tomorrow." I reach a hand across the desk and Jane takes it, giving me a firm shake.

"Stop worrying," she commands.

I force a smile before turning to leave her office. I spend the elevator ride to the lobby pretending there is another solution to my problem, and I just need another night to think it over. But I am fooling myself. When the elevator doors open, I step out and find a quiet corner before pulling out my phone.

With each unanswered ring, I am tempted to hang up, but this is too important. The call goes to voicemail. "Hi! You've reached Chloe Cooper. You know what to do!" Even her outgoing message is charming and effervescent. This is the right decision. Chloe Cooper would never chew gum with her mouth open.

I take a deep breath as the beep sounds. "Chloe, this is Nikolai. Nikolai Drugov." Fuck. How many Nikolais could she possibly know? Sweat beads at the small of my back as I force myself to finally say the three words that set my heart beating faster than any puck I have ever stopped. "I need you."

Chapter Fifteen

Chloe

The excited chatter of twenty-two kids all attempting to put on skates, some for the first time, echoes around the arena. Most have at least one parent with them, all of whom keep throwing glances my way, gauging my ability to handle a group of rowdy kids balancing on thin blades. I'm used to it, having been a schoolteacher for years, but this feels different. This feels like reconnecting with who I used to be. Hockey was my entire life growing up and it only feels right to return to it now. I'll wow the parents and hook the kids on the sport by the end of today's open house, I'm sure of it.

My phone buzzes in my back pocket, but I ignore it. My entire focus is on giving the most value of any club sport out there. These kids deserve to fall in love with the feeling of accomplishing something they didn't think they could do. As a curvy girl who didn't look like an athlete, hockey gave me the confidence I have today, and it's my goal to pay that forward to another generation.

"This is actually scarier than facing Denver's enforcer," Banks whispers in my ear as he skates up next to me.

I chuckle, knowing the player he's referring to. He's got a crooked nose and two missing teeth you only see when he grins evilly at you right before he slams you up against the boards.

"Stay calm, Banks. They're just kids."

He shudders, making me laugh more. "Exactly."

He's the perfect guy to help me today. Despite his antics, he's amazing with his Little, Eli. I've seen the two of them together and nearly melted into a puddle over their adorableness.

I skate forward and address the line of kids sitting on the bleachers ringing the rink. "Okay, folks! Thanks for coming today. I'm Chloe Cooper, former D1 hockey player for Wisconsin, and head coach of Bring Your B-Game. Banks Bennet is here to assist today, and I doubt he needs any introduction." Several of the kids are wearing his jersey with glazed smiles as they stare at him.

"By show of hands, how many of you already know how to skate?" I raise my hand and see almost the entire group raise their hands. One little girl off to the side looks like she's about to cry when she doesn't join the group. My heart lurches and I make a mental note to keep an eye on her. "Okay, that's great, but no problem whatsoever if you can't skate. We'll start with simple skills out there on the ice, but remember, this is rec league. That means any and all levels are welcome. The only mistake you can make is making fun of someone else. Got it?"

I hear a smattering of yeses and keep going. "Let's have everyone stand up." It sounds like a herd of elephants have arrived, but they all make it to their feet. "Contrary to what you might think, the first lesson is getting used to your skates, and that happens on dry land."

Banks gets off the ice and goes down the line, helping the

kids follow my directions as we move through some movements to get used to blades strapped to their feet. There's lots of giggles, some spills, and also clapping when someone gets back up. Hopefully, I make it very clear that the culture here is not competitive and that we celebrate each other's wins. By the time we finally make it onto the ice, Banks is holding hands with the little girl who was almost in tears earlier. I take the front of the line with the more experienced skaters and teach them how to stop on the ice.

Two hours pass in the blink of an eye. By the time the last potential player files out of the arena, I collapse onto the bench next to Banks and close my eyes. "I think I owe you a whole case of beer."

Banks laughs. "Nah. That was fun. So different from the competitive leagues." He nudges me and my eyes fly open. "Plus, no one got hurt and most left with big smiles. I think you'll have a full roster before you know it, Chloe. Eli already told me he wants to sign up."

Warmth floods through my body. I inhale deeply and then exhale the stress I've been holding onto. "You're right. They did look like they were having fun. Gosh, it feels amazing to do what I love."

Banks takes off his skates and I do the same in companionable silence. "So . . ." he starts. "What's up with you and Druggy?"

My head whips in his direction. "What do you mean?"

He lifts a dark eyebrow. "It was interesting to note you both left the wedding around the same time. Was that coincidence?"

My jaw drops, and I wonder how many other people may have noticed that little detail. "Absolutely coincidence. There's nothing going on there."

Banks studies me, but then shrugs and stands up. "His loss then. See you around, Cooper."

"Thanks again for your help!" I shout after him. He lifts a hand and smiles before disappearing into the locker room.

I sit there for a few minutes longer, just staring at the ice and absorbing everything that happened at my first open house. I feel energized, buzzed, hopped up on the energy of knowing I'm living my dream. Then I pull out my phone with the intention of calling the coach Dad sent me, saying he might be a good fit for an assistant coach. Based on today's attendance, I'm going to need help ASAP.

But there's a voicemail from earlier. I put it to my ear and nearly choke when the deep gravelly tone of Nikolai caresses my ear.

"I need you."

My fingers are shaking as I call him back. There's no hesitation. No second guessing what he could mean. Nikolai needs me enough to leave that message, you're damn right I'm going to call him back. And not just because everything he said to me on that beach lives rent free in my brain every single night as I try to get to sleep.

I want to take you every way a man can take a woman.

I squeeze my eyes shut as the phone rings on his end. That's hands down the sexiest thing a man has ever said to me, and I'm not ashamed to admit I've replayed that moment innumerable times with the help of my trusty vibrator. I've stayed away from him since the wedding, knowing he needs to focus on his custody battle, but that doesn't mean I don't think about him every single day and wish for a world in which he could do exactly what he described on that beach.

"Chloe," he says by way of answering.

My breath whooshes out in a cloud in the cold arena. "Nikolai."

"You got my message."

It's a statement, not a question, but I agree nonetheless.

There's silence for a moment and then words rush from his mouth, agony and shame coating each one.

"I have failed. There is no nanny for Ayana, and we are due at court tomorrow. I will surely lose her if I do not prove I have childcare."

My brain scrambles, running through my to-do list and casting every single item in the long list aside as I make way to help him. "What time?"

"Nine."

"I'll be there." There's no hesitation. No negotiation.

"Chloe," he breathes, the intimate way he says my name twisting my insides and making me burn with heat. "You do not understand what you are agreeing to."

"I do," I say instantly. "You need a nanny and I can be her until you find someone else permanently."

"But what about your league? Surely you need time to work on that, not babysit my daughter."

I stand and grab my skates, jamming my phone between my ear and my shoulder. "Easy. I'll take Ayana with me to practice." When Nikolai makes a sound like he's going to argue with me further, I cut him off, my voice more harsh than I intended. "Quit sabotaging your own case, Nikolai. You're a great dad and deserve to have your daughter with you. Let me help."

There's silence. So much so, I check my phone to make sure the call didn't drop.

"You are a goddess, Chloe Cooper."

I smile as I reach the locker rooms. "I know."

I hang up and collect my things before leaving for the evening. My brain is whirling with everything I'm undertaking all at once. I'm stressed, but in a good way. Sleep evades me as I toss and turn over all the tasks I need to get done, along with another night sweat that requires a complete change of pajamas and sheets, but I finally get a few hours of sleep. I wake up with enough time to dress like a freaking nun and show up at the courthouse address Nikolai texted me.

The black pants, red silk blouse, and black suit jacket are fit for a boardroom, but the stiletto heels that show a peep of my bright red toenails is enough style for me to still feel like myself. I see Nikolai before he sees me. He's pacing at the top of the stairs outside the courthouse, dressed in a suit that probably cost as much as my car. He looks like he stepped off a *GQ Magazine* cover. Even his shaggy hair is carefully styled, and the scruff on his cheeks is shaved clean. The moment he sees me, he stops pacing.

"You are here." He sounds incredulous, which is a bit insulting. If I say I'll be here, I'll be here.

I stop in front of him and pull myself up to my full height, which is a bit more impressive in these gorgeous heels. "I said I would."

He blinks, his gaze dropping to take in my whole outfit before snagging on my feet. He stares so long I get nervous.

"Something wrong, big guy?"

His head whips up and there's confusion in his blue eyes. "I did not know toes could be sexy," he says under his breath.

I grin, thankful my toes have him as off balance as his suit has me. "You know you can't afford me, right?"

He dips his head and takes me by the elbow, steering me into the courthouse. The blast of air conditioning is a welcome change from Florida's steamy morning. "I will owe you my life, Chloe. Name your price."

I think of all the things I want from this man that have nothing to do with money. "Let me think on it."

He opens another door, and I sweep past him into the courtroom with a devilish grin, finding a seat in the front row behind his lawyer. It takes him a moment longer, but he walks up the aisle finally and has a seat in front of me and doesn't look back. Which is a good thing because if the judge asks me questions later on, I'll need my wits about me. I also try not to stare at his ex-wife sitting on the other side of the aisle with her own lawyer because she is the epitome of blond beauty and model perfection.

Pretty much the opposite of me.

Chapter Sixteen

Niko

"As you can see from my client's impeccable record-keeping, he was denied scheduled visitation on numerous occasions, and other visitations were cut short by Ms. Drugov without proper notice–or any plausible reason." Jane points her glare Peyton's way.

My lawyer plays the part of Doberman Pinscher very convincingly, and it has my confidence growing as the hearing progresses. My nerves were a mess until the moment I laid eyes on Chloe on the courthouse steps outside. Something about her manner did the impossible and calmed my anxiety. I still cannot believe she has agreed to help me. I will need to find a replacement as soon as possible so as not to put her out any more than is necessary.

"Your Honor," Peyton's lawyer interrupts. "Conflicts sometimes arise. That is part of life with a young child. There is nothing malicious or underhanded going on here. Synching the schedules of three people, especially when one of them travels for work on a weekly basis, is inherently difficult."

"Okay. Enough." Judge Lopez looks up from the detailed document Jane and I put together and raises a hand before turning his gaze my way. "Mr. Drugov, your job does require a good amount of travel, correct?"

Before I can answer, Jane interjects, "Plenty of parents travel for work. In fact, it's this very job that has provided both Ms. Drugov and Ayana with the lifestyle they both enjoy. It hardly seems fair to punish a man for making a living."

The judge extends his hand again. "Yes, I understand."

"Your Honor," I say, unable to remain silent. "This coming season will be my last before I retire. It is October through May or June. Yes, I do travel during that time, but I am in town more than out of it—and I hardly have a job at all in the offseason. I have hired a nanny for any time I cannot be with Ayana. All I want is my share of time with my precious daughter."

"I propose we keep things as they are and we can revisit next summer *if* Mr. Drugov does, in fact, retire," Peyton's lawyer demands.

"That is preposterous," Jane bites out. "Ms. Drugov has a job as well, yet she isn't being denied time with Ayana. It is not in the best interests of the child to be kept from a father who adores her and is perfectly capable of taking care of her."

When Peyton's lawyer attempts a rebuttal this time, Judge Lopez cuts him off before turning his attention back to Jane. "I tend to agree with you, Ms. Ashford. Now, may I see some documentation on this nanny?"

"Of course," Jane responds, unable to hide the hint of satisfaction in her tone as she sifts through her stack of folders to find the documentation Chloe sent last night. "And we can do better than that. She is here in the courtroom today."

I turn to see Chloe rise to her feet behind me. She looks

like a perfect combination of business mogul and elementary school teacher, even if I prefer seeing her in tight dresses that show off her figure.

"Your name?" the judge asks, and I turn back around to avoid making Chloe nervous. I did not need to bother, though.

"I'm Chloe Cooper," she says in a friendly, confident voice. "I am a semi-retired third-grade teacher turned children's hockey coach with over fifteen years of experience with young children," she says as Jane approaches the bench with Chloe's records. "My schedule is extremely flexible, and, as you can see, I am current on all my CPR and first aid certifications. I love kids, and I'm very much looking forward to caring for Ayana when her father is working."

"I see." Judge Lopez scans the papers before him.

I glance over at Peyton's table to see her sending daggers my way. She needs to grow up; it is that simple. She jabs her lawyer with an elbow and he leaps to his feet.

"Your Honor, we were not notified of this . . . nanny person. Why should my client's child be cared for by some stranger while Ms. Drugov is perfectly able to care for her?"

Jane stands up as well. "Ms. Drugov gets plenty of time with Ayana—more than is stipulated by the current custody order, in fact. And of course, it makes sense to arrange schedules so that childcare is needed as little as possible. But everyone in this situation has lives and jobs. Childcare is necessary at some point in every working parent's life. And Ms. Cooper is more than qualified to fill in on those occasions."

Now Peyton jumps to her feet, and I notice she's wearing a boxy suit that resembles not one other piece of clothing in her closet. She is even wearing reading glasses. "Your Honor, Ayana is all I have. Niko hardly even knows her." She dips a finger behind her glasses to wipe away a tear that is almost certainly not there. "He doesn't know her friends, what music she likes, what time she needs to be at school. He plays a violent sport where aggression is a mandatory personality trait, for god's sake!"

I open my mouth to protest, but Chloe's voice from behind me beats me to it.

"Mr. Drugov is an amazing athlete who takes his job very seriously, and for you to insinuate being good at his job makes him a violent person is preposterous!"

"What are you? His nanny or the president of his fan club?" Peyton scoffs, tears forgotten.

"I'm a former Division One hockey player. And a nanny. It's possible to be both, just like it's possible for a woman to be whatever she sets her mind to. That's a lesson I look forward to teaching Ayana."

"*Damn*," Jane whispers. "I like her."

So do I. Too much to mean anything but trouble.

"My favorite part was when your ex tried faking a heart attack after the ruling," Chloe says, grinning at me from the driver's seat of her Bronco. My knees almost touch the dashboard, but it made sense to get a ride with Chloe instead of Jane. My lawyer drove me to court this morning, wanting to do some last-minute preparations.

I chuckle, feeling like a weight has been lifted from my shoulders. Although the judge did not rule entirely in my favor—yet—he ordered a two-week trial of sorts where Ayana will stay with me, after which a social worker will come and interview Ayana, Chloe, and me. If that goes well, Judge Lopez will grant the shared custody I have been fighting for. Peyton was less than pleased with the outcome.

"It is a good thing she is a model instead of an actress," I reply.

Chloe shakes her head, pulling forward when the light turns green. "Well, that makes perfect sense."

"What does?"

"That she's a model. She's beautiful."

I shrug. "A lot of people are beautiful." *Like you*, I want to say but know I cannot. "There are ugly parts to Peyton as well."

My history with Peyton is a complex one, though it started out simply enough–too many drinks at a bar with some teammates after a tough loss. My carelessness caused Peyton's pregnancy, something I can never regret since Ayana is the light of my life. Through long talks with Ivan, I determined that marrying Peyton was the right thing to do, and maybe it was. But our marriage never stood a chance, not with all my travel and our disparate expectations of the relationship. I sometimes blame myself for Peyton's cheating as well, the straw that broke our marriage's back.

Chloe turns left onto a cross street. We are going to my house so I can show her around, but she wants to stop and change her clothes on the way since we are driving by her place.

"You don't think Peyton will try to pull anything when you go to pick up Ayana tomorrow, do you?"

"Not after the judge's warning." At least I hope not.

"He was *not* happy with her, that's for sure."

Chloe takes another turn into a complex of tidy modern duplexes. When she pulls into a parking spot, she turns to me. "You want to come in while I change? Make sure I don't have bodies hidden under the floorboards before you leave me alone with Ayana?" At my responding frown, she laughs and opens her door. "You should see the look on your face."

I get out too. "Why would you say such a thing? Now I want to inspect your freezer and look under your couch."

She snickers and pulls a set of keys from her purse. "Snoop away. There are no skeletons in my closet." She turns the key in the lock, glancing over her shoulder. "I prefer to keep them elsewhere."

The door swings inward, and Chloe takes a step inside. But as soon as I step forward to follow her, she jumps back, her shoulders colliding with my chest.

"What—" I begin before seeing what made her back up. The entire floor is covered in water, some of it rushing out over the threshold and under our shoes now.

"Oh no!" Chloe exclaims. "What in the world?"

I instinctively bring my hands to her shoulders, gently moving her aside. "You stay here. I will see where it is coming from."

"No! You're going to ruin your shoes. I guarantee they're way more expensive than mine."

"They are just shoes, Chloe." I glance at her feet in those sexy heels. "And I prefer yours anyway. Stay here." I don't wait for her response before stepping inside and trudging through the water. It appears to cover the entire floor, including the carpet. This furniture will all need to be removed.

I finally locate the source when I get to the laundry room off the hallway to find water streaming from the wall. I make my way through the duplex on a search for the main water shutoff. It must be a burst pipe somewhere.

"Do you want the good news first or the bad news?" I ask when I return to Chloe.

"Please tell me I didn't accidentally leave the water running. With the way my brain has been shorting out lately, that's exactly the kind of thing I might have done."

Unsure exactly what she means, I go ahead with my news. "No. You did not cause this. It is a burst pipe. The good news is that I found the valve to shut off the water to your home. The bad news is that your entire floor is soaking wet, and if we do not move your furniture, it will be ruined."

"Great." She lifts her phone, hands shaking. "I need to find a plumber–and somebody to move that furniture. Crap. I guess I need a hotel too."

She grips the phone in both hands, her thumbs working rapidly over the screen as she pulls her bottom lip between her teeth. Deep furrows work into her brow as she types. I do not like seeing her like this, racked with worry and stripped of her usual effervescence.

This is a woman who would give anyone the shirt off her back without question. She does not deserve to suffer in any way, especially over something like this.

Coming to a decision I am certain I will regret, I reach over and pry the phone from her hands, causing her to look up at me with confusion.

"Chloe. Do not worry. I will get Benny or Dan-O over here in twenty minutes to help me with the furniture. In the meantime, go inside and pack a bag. You are staying at my house."

<h1 style="text-align:center">Chapter Seventeen</h1>

Chloe

Before I can even recover from the shock of my home being under water, both Danny and Banks arrive to manhandle my furniture. Nikolai barks out orders, Banks grumbles about him being a tyrant, and the three of them get to work. Nikolai has somehow found a storage unit, rented it, and maneuvered my things to Banks's waiting truck.

"Grab that suitcase and come with me." Nikolai's commanding voice makes me jump. I've been lost in thought in my bedroom, frozen in indecision about just what clothes to bring to his place. I've never lived with a professional hockey player and his seven-year-old daughter before.

Despite being a take-charge kind of woman historically, I am woefully lacking this time around. I've pretty much just thrown everything I own into the suitcase without a plan. On top of the pile? My adorable yellow rubber rain boots. My top lip lifts into a snarl of self-disgust. What was I thinking?

Nikolai must see my indecision because he charges into the

room in his undershirt and slacks from the courthouse, shuts the suitcase, and curses long and low under his breath in Russian when the thing won't close. His suit jacket and shirt are around here somewhere. "Do you have a . . . what do you call it? A bag for clothes?"

I lift my gaze to his, wondering how this giant man is in my space, ordering me around, and pushing me to move into his house. I don't take orders from men. Never have, don't plan to start. And yet, there it is. That ribbon of desire wiggles into my gut at the idea of him ordering me to do . . . *other things*. Dirty things.

I clear my throat and try to stay focused. "A duffle bag?"

Nikolai nods, all serious while my brain is in the gutter. I slip the rain boots out of the suitcase and put them on in place of the heels that are now ruined before spinning around toward my closet. Thankfully, the flooding is minimal on this end of the duplex. I come back out with a duffle bag, which Nikolai takes from my hands and fills with the mound of clothing that won't fit in the suitcase. I nearly swallow my tongue when I see his giant hands close around a red lace bra, but he's all business. He zips up the suitcase, hauls it off the bed that Danny elevated on some bricks in hopes the wood posts would dry, and shoulders the duffle while still having a hand left over to reach for me.

"Come. I have your keys. I will drive."

I frown, leading the way to my front door and grabbing two of my more fragile plants. I'm not sure I need to take them with me, but I can't seem to leave them behind. Nikolai's hand closes in on my back, gently pushing me toward the door and away from any more plants. My peri-menopausal brain can't handle the physical touch of Nikolai apparently. One touch and all trains of thought fizzle into oblivion.

"You will need to call your insurance, but the plumber

came by and confirmed it was a broken pipe," Nikolai tells me as I lock the front door behind us.

I follow him down the walkway toward my Bronco, looking absolutely ridiculous in a pantsuit, yellow rubber boots, and plants in both hands. How the hell does this man move so fast with a suitcase I know for a fact is past the fifty-pound airline limit? Banks and Danny turn the corner and see us, immediately grinning like idiots. Nikolai grunts a greeting and the two part to let us keep walking.

"So," Banks says as they follow behind us, biting back a grin. "You two moving in together?"

I roll my eyes, finally breaking free from the frazzled fog that has held me captive since I stepped into a flooded condo two hours ago. "I'm his temporary nanny, Banks. Don't be starting a rumor."

Banks holds his hands up like he's Mr. Innocent when I know he gossips more than a teen girl. "Just find it curious Druggy needs a live-in nanny. Isn't he old enough to take care of himself?"

"You will shut your mouth, Benny, or I will show you where lobsters spend the winter," Nikolai grouses, stopping in his tracks. I have no idea what that means, but he's giving his teammate a look I know would have Dad stepping in to inter-fere before these hotheads do something they'll regret. Some-thing about the ridiculous threat activates that desire again despite my best intentions.

I take a step between them. "I'm his nanny for *Ayana*, Banks. You know, his daughter? The type of offspring that you and Kaitlyn will soon have? They're small and cute, but they actually take a lot of work." I swing my gaze back to Nikolai. "Which reminds me, I need to call my dad and let him know what's going on so no other pea brains spread rumors about all this."

"Hey," Banks pouts.

Danny laughs, then nearly sprints the rest of the way to Banks's truck, calling over his shoulder. "I don't want to be there for that conversation. Coach might just grab a shotgun. He's been beaming since you moved to Tampa."

My heart melts, then freezes over when I consider what he might have to say about me living with one of his players. I have to phrase this just right or I might damage Nikolai's reputation with my dad.

Nikolai looks like he's trying to incinerate people on the street with his gaze alone. My suitcase lands in the back of my vehicle with a thud. Nikolai takes the plants out of my hands and safely tucks them into the back. Banks heads for the truck, saying they'll unload my stuff at the storage unit and drop by Nikolai's with the key.

"Thank you!" I call out to them, feeling weird about them handling my business like that and not even blinking an eye.

Nikolai spins my keychain around his thick finger, moving to the passenger door and holding it open for me. "We will get lunch and then head to the house to get you settled."

My stomach lets out a growl at the mention of food, so loud even Nikolai hears it based on the way his gaze drops to my midsection. "I didn't eat breakfast today. Too nervous about the court hearing."

His startled blue eyes fly to my face and soften. "Thank you, Chloe. I owe you a lifetime of gratitude."

I walk up to him, doing my best to be saucy in rubber boots squelching against the hot Florida pavement. "A lifetime, huh? I'll have to think of a suitable act of gratitude."

His gaze immediately drops to my mouth and it's all I can do to not lean into his chest and slide my hands over the muscles that I felt under me the night I fell on him on the ice. Doing that would be very bad. Definitely not advisable if we're moving in together. Probably a violation of roommate etiquette or something.

"Chloe," he murmurs to my lips, his hand coming up to cup my elbow.

"Yes?" I sway on my boots, desperate for his touch in a way I don't think I've ever felt before.

His fingers squeeze my elbow and I feel it between my thighs.

"We should call your father on the way to lunch."

And just like that, a proverbial wave of ice-cold water splashes in my face and he's gone, leaving me there between cars in my ridiculous yellow boots and panting like a dog in heat. I blink a few times and then climb into my vehicle, lecturing myself about keeping my hands to myself. He's made it clear over and over again that he can't cross that line with me. I need to respect his wishes. We're on the freeway heading south before I've recovered enough to speak without my voice shaking.

"Hey, maybe we should have some rules about this living situation, roomie."

He swivels his head and looks at me for the first time since we got in the car. "Rules?"

I stare out the windshield, figuring that's safer than looking directly at him. "Yeah, you know. Like, curfews, or sleeping arrangements, or boundaries of some sort? Do you leave dirty dishes in the sink? Or sleepwalk?"

"What is this sleepwalk? And no, I do not leave dirty dishes anywhere." He pauses. "But I do have a dog. Did I tell you this already?"

I clap my hands to my chest and swivel to face him, already forgetting about the not-looking-at-him rule I made up in my head. "Oh my god, you have a dog? I love dogs! What kind? Is he trained? Can he sleep with me?"

The tires hit the rumble strips and Nikolai jerks the wheel so we're back in our lane. He flashes an alarmed glance at me before gripping the steering wheel so tight his knuckles turn white. "No, he cannot sleep with you. He sleeps in a crate. His name is . . . Paul." His lips twist distastefully and I laugh.

"Paul? That's adorable! Okay, so he can't sleep with me, but can I take him and Ayana on walks and stuff?"

Nikolai squeezes his eyes shut for a moment, which is concerning, considering he's the one driving on a freeway in Florida where anything can and usually does happen. "Yes, you can walk him, but in the off season I take him on my run every morning."

I nod, feeling excited about living with Ayana and Paul the doggo. I'm absolutely not thinking about a hot and sweaty Nikolai running around the neighborhood without his shirt on. "Okay, got it. What other things do I need to know? Oh! I know. Do you sleep naked?"

The growl makes me burst out laughing, but when he whips the car to the right at the next exit, I sober quickly. "Sorry," I mutter. And I am sorry. I just can't seem to help myself. He's so fun to tease. One of these days I think my flirting ways might just make his head explode.

He stops abruptly at the red light and turns to me. "First rule. No flirting. Second rule. You must always wear appropriate clothing. Third rule. No bringing men to my house. Fourth rule–"

"Hold up there, big guy. Let me get a notepad and pen. Sounds like you have a long list." I smile wryly at him. "Oh, and the light's green."

He growls again and takes off, throwing me back against the seat. "Call your father."

I salute him. "Yes, sir."

His eyes narrow and he looks like he wants to crack my steering wheel in half. "Fourth rule. Don't say yes sir to me again unless you're naked and ready for me to fill every one of your holes."

I gasp, equally turned on and shocked. When he aims a

smug smile my way, I realize he intentionally went for the shock factor to shut me and my big mouth up. I smile sweetly and pull out my phone. "I think I'll call Daddy. Shall I give him your regards . . . sir?"

Dad answers before Nikolai can come up with a reply. "Hey, pumpkin. What's up?"

"Hi Dad. So hey. I have some news, and before you freak out, I just want you to know this is business only."

"Chloe," he warns. "What did you do?"

"Well, one of your players needed some help, so I offered. You know how I am. Can't not help someone in need, you know?"

"Chloe," Dad interrupts, sounding beleaguered. "Just spit it out."

"I'm moving in with Nikolai so I can nanny his daughter and the courts will give him custody."

There's silence on the other end of the line. Nikolai looks at me with alarm. I shrug. How else was I supposed to tell him?

"Say it all again and start at the beginning this time," Dad finally says. I hear a door slam and there's silence in the background.

"Nikolai needed a temporary nanny so the court would give him joint custody of his daughter. I offered to fill the role. But now my duplex is flooded, and Ayana needs a lot of supervision with you keeping Nikolai so busy, so he offered to have me live with them, considering I'll be there so much anyway. But this is all temporary. Just until my duplex gets fixed and Nikolai finds a permanent nanny. So you don't need to worry."

Dad groans. "Worrying about my daughter is kind of my job. Is Niko there with you?"

I look over at the man who has parked at the curb outside a hole-in-the-wall deli. "Yes."

"Put him on."

I wince and hand the phone to Nikolai. He shoots me a deadly glare but takes the phone. "Sir."

I sink my teeth into my bottom lip and wonder how this is real life. Forty-two years old and Dad is threatening a boy. With his attention diverted, I allow my gaze to trace along Nikolai's broad shoulders, thick biceps and forearms corded with muscle. Not a boy. Definitely all man.

"Yes, sir. Understood. Yes. I swear to you, sir."

Nikolai hits the end call button and hands me my phone. He scrubs his hand across his face and looks a little green around the edges.

I tuck the phone into my purse and worry my lip some more. "That went well, huh?"

He doesn't answer me. He just stares out the windshield for long moments while I squirm. He finally puts his hand on the door handle and sighs. "Let us get lunch. It might be my last meal." And then he slips out the door.

<h1 style="text-align:center">Chapter Eighteen</h1>

Niko

Coach's words echo in my ears even an hour after we spoke.

You know I trust you, Drugov. Don't make me regret it.

I should have driven Chloe directly to his house after sorting her duplex. In fact, I am shocked he did not demand as much over the phone. What was I thinking insisting Chloe stay at my house while her place is being repaired? Clearly, I was not. But she is doing me such an enormous favor, it seemed like the only choice at the time.

Lunch was a quiet affair on my end as I fought thoughts of Coach lopping my balls off with an axe after learning of my fantasies starring his daughter. But Chloe was able to fill the silence with stories about her old teaching job and questions about Ayana. The more I learn about her, the more I am drawn to her—which is going to make the next few days even more tortuous than I already anticipated.

I open my heavy front door, holding it for Chloe to walk through in her curve-hugging suit and ridiculous rain boots.

She enters my foyer, and I follow, lugging her suitcase and bag. Paul's whine from his crate in the kitchen is the first thing I hear. But he can wait.

"Well, this is it. Let me show you your room." I jerk my chin toward the hallway to our left and head that way with her things. My house is a sprawling one-story brick and stucco home on a large lot set away from the street. I was not interested in any of the pretentious gated communities but preferred a large lot with space for Ayana to be a child. The place has four bedrooms and several large living spaces, so maybe having Chloe here will not be as intimate as I fear.

"You will stay in the guest room down here," I say. "Ayana's bedroom and mine are on the opposite side of the house, so you will have plenty of privacy." I look back to reassure her, but she has disappeared. So, I continue to the guest room to drop her things, assuming she went back out to her car to retrieve the plants.

But when I return, the front door is closed, and I hear Chloe's voice coming from the kitchen. I cross the tile floor to see her sprawled out in the center, an excited Paul climbing all over her and licking her face. I have never been jealous of a dog until this moment. My life is officially a clusterfuck.

"Who's the cutest doggo in the whole wide world? That's right. You are, Paul," she coos nonsensically at the German Shepherd while he basks in her attention.

"He will piss all over you if he doesn't go outside right away," I warn her. "He is only four months old, so his bladder is not trustworthy."

Chloe smiles up at me, unfiltered joy in her expression. I thought Ayana was the only person in the world capable of replicating the feel of sunshine on my skin. I was mistaken. Chloe cradles Paul's head in her hands and kisses his nose, laughing when he swipes her nose with his tongue. "You wouldn't pee on me, would you, Paul?"

The words are barely out of her mouth when the puppy finally loses the battle and sends a stream of piss soaking one leg of her pants.

"Paul!" I lunge for his leash, which hangs on a hook nearby, and rush to clip it on his collar. "I am so sor—"

Chloe cuts me off with another laugh. How can being pissed on by a dog ever be a positive experience? "Oh, please. This suit was done for after my duplex swimming pool. It was already destined for the dry cleaner."

"Still. I apologize. Let me take him out." I point toward the guest room hall. "Your bags are down that hall, second door on the left. You should find towels in the restroom where you can clean up." I hurry to the backyard before Paul can demonstrate any more of his bad manners.

Thirty minutes later, Chloe has still not emerged from the guest room, and I am annoyed with myself for keeping track of the time. So I text Mac and Cappy about our offseason training. The timing is unfortunate, since it starts tomorrow—the same day I get Ayana—but training camp is less than two months away and we have much work to do. How was I to know the judge would let me have Ayana so soon after the hearing?

I tell them we must move tomorrow's training to the afternoon because there is no way I will postpone picking up my girl in the morning.

"You have a pool! God bless you." Chloe appears in the entryway to the living room, and Paul races from his spot at my feet to greet her with a vigorously wagging tail. I grit my teeth and do not respond. I'm too busy trying to ignore her new outfit. When she bends to scratch Paul's head, a groan escapes my throat, causing her to eye me curiously.

"What's the matter? Did Paul pee on you too?"

"Rule number two, Chloe!" I bite out as she straightens.

Her amusement is poorly hidden. "There were so many, I can't remember. What was rule number two again?"

"Appropriate clothing at all times!"

She looks down at her outfit, and my eyes follow her gaze before I can stop myself. She is in another of those tops that ties behind her neck and gathers her breasts together like two puppies trying to wrestle themselves out of a sack. There is no possible way she is wearing a bra. The shorts might be even worse, a pair of cutoff jeans with frayed edges that hug her ass and hips and reveal the creamy skin of her thighs.

"What's inappropriate about this?" She appears genuinely baffled. "It's Tampa in July. I'm not going to wear a snowsuit to play with your daughter and your dog."

I rise from the couch, ditching my phone and the magazine I was pretending to read.

"Where are you going?" she asks.

"To turn up the air conditioner."

The sound of her laughter follows me as I go to take what will undoubtedly be the first of many cold showers this week. Afterward, I invent several errands to run so I can put distance between Chloe and me. Being alone in the house with her is not a good idea.

When she texts that she is ordering takeout for dinner, asking if I want something, I tell her to eat without me. It is poor manners to leave her on her first night in my home, and my mother would disown me if she knew. But my hold on my control around her is beyond precarious, so it is best for both of us to avoid alone time. It will be easier when Ayana is near.

It is only when I pull into the driveway and see the guest room light is out that I sigh my relief and return inside. But the joke is apparently on me because I spend the next three hours tossing and turning in my bed. Chloe is on the other end of the house separated by two closed doors, yet she may as well be spread out beside me in my bed for how she dominates my thoughts. I can even smell her shampoo somehow. My cock is too stiff to allow sleep, so I get out of bed and pad into my bathroom.

I dip my head under the hot water pouring from the showerhead and close my eyes, letting the heat suffuse my body. I am simultaneously keyed up and exhausted, thanks to my uncontrollable attraction to my daughter's new nanny. But here, alone in my shower, there are no restrictions on my thoughts—or my behavior.

As steam billows around me, I take my cock in hand and imagine Chloe's painted red lips closing around the head. It takes only seconds for me to get hard enough to pound nails. I want to take my time, so I use slow strokes, but my head still drops back on a groan when I picture Chloe's blue eyes turned up to me as she drops to her knees and takes me deep.

Her small fingers wrap around my base until she has to move them as I thrust my entire length into her mouth, her throat squeezing around the head. She cradles my balls instead, gently kneading them while I pull back and drive deep again. The vibration of her moan around my cock has me going harder still.

"Touch yourself," I demand, and she immediately obeys, one hand diving between her legs and the other cupping one full breast. I enter her mouth slowly this time, letting her tongue rasp against my entire length as I test her gag reflex. But she can take all of me.

I delve my hands into her wet hair to hold her where I want as I continue to fuck her mouth, my pace increasing with each thrust. Her eyes hold mine while she works her clit and nipple and takes everything I give her.

"Good girl," I praise as her eyelids begin to flutter while her hips undulate with her approaching climax. As soon as it hits her, I drive faster into her throat as my own orgasm draws near, until I bury myself deep and come hard down her throat with a guttural shout.

When I pull back to give her air, she milks the last drops of cum from my cock with her tongue and lips, moaning as she does. My fingers wind into her raven hair, my breath coming in gasps as reality slowly filters back in and I feel the hot water pounding onto my back again.

I am alone in the shower once more. If I thought jerking off to fantasies of my houseguest would cure me of my attraction, I was sorely mistaken. And I am beginning to fear nothing will ever do the trick.

"Dad!" Ayana's arms wrap around my waist in a bear-cub hug, and I bend to kiss the top of her head. "Can we watch Tara Swanson's new concert tomorrow?! It's releasing to streaming in the morning!"

"Um . . ." It is never a good idea to commit to something you do not understand, so I go with, "We will see." A streaming concert? Is this a new thing? And I thought Tara Swanson was for teenagers, not seven-year-olds.

When I straighten again, Peyton is coming down the walkway wheeling Ayana's suitcase. Soon, she will have plenty of her things at my house so she will have no need for a suitcase.

Before I can even say hello, Peyton launches into a dissertation. "I'm emailing you the list, but she has dance on Tuesdays and Thursdays at five. I'm assuming you know where the studio is and what she needs to bring. Mackenzie's birthday party is Saturday at noon at the trampoline park in Westchase. Not the one in Carollwood. Make sure she has the right socks, and don't forget to get a gift—not too expensive, but don't be cheap either. Her allergist just recommended some medicine for her ragweed allergy, which I'm sure you know she's allergic to."

It takes a concerted effort not to tighten my grip on Ayana's shoulders as Peyton forges ahead. "And when she flosses at night, you have to watch her or she'll say she's done it even when she hasn't. I've already told her she can watch the Tara Swanson concert, so don't go all overprotective and embarrass her. All her friends will be watching it. Friday is—"

"Enough," I cut her off as I reach over and pry the suitcase handle from her grip. "I get it." It is perfectly clear that Peyton is throwing out a challenge, waiting for me to fail. She will not get her wish, and I will not take the bait she is dangling between us right now. "I am happy to read your email, but we must go now." I transfer my gaze to my daughter. "There is a new friend I want to introduce you to."

Peyton scoffs, but I do not spare her another glance as Ayana's eyes widen. "Another puppy? Is Paul getting his Prue?"

"No." I frown down at her. "This is a human friend—one I promise you will like very much. And one who will teach you to play hockey just like me." Ayana's eyes widen again.

"Hockey?!" Peyton cuts in. "No way. That's too dangerous."

I am forced to look at my ex-wife's scowling face again. "It is a starter recreational league for children, not an NHL team. She will be fine."

Ayana whirls around to face her mother. "Come on, Mom. I can already skate. I won't get hurt." It is true I have used some of my limited time with Ayana over the years to teach her to skate. It would be sacrilege for a hockey player's child not to learn.

"Come give me a hug and then get in the car, Ayana," Peyton instructs our daughter, who does as she is asked, even if it is accompanied by a pout. When the door closes behind Ayana, Peyton steps closer. "You did that on purpose."

"What?"

"Told her about hockey before discussing it with me so I'd be the bad guy if I said no," she accuses.

"I do not see how that is any different from you signing her up for dance classes without my knowledge. Or you telling her she can watch some concert while she is at my house. When have we ever discussed things beforehand?"

Peyton's nostrils flare as she speaks through gritted teeth. "You're enjoying this, aren't you?"

I am finished with this conversation, so I turn to wheel the suitcase to the back of the Rover. "Finally having time with my daughter? Yes." I stow the suitcase and quickly get into the driver's seat before Peyton has a chance to ruin Ayana's and my first day together.

It is time to prove that I have what it takes to be the father Ayana deserves.

Chapter Nineteen

Chloe

Like with every first day of school, I intend to appear cool, calm, and collected when Nikolai comes home with Ayana, but that is too much to hope for, apparently. Paul started whining thirty minutes after Niko left, giving me those puppy dog eyes that are impossible to ignore.

"Seriously, Paul? You just went out." He puts a paw up on my knee and stares into my soul. I begged for a dog years ago, but Josh said we'd make horrible dog parents since we both worked outside the home. He wasn't wrong, but my heart still yearned for a furry best friend.

I close my laptop, where I was supposed to be working on drills to introduce at my second open house next week, but was mostly thinking about how I slept mere feet away from Nikolai last night. He locked himself in his bedroom, hiding out like my cutoff jean shorts held a spell over him. Whatever his reasons, I barely slept. I heave myself to standing. Paul yips and spins in a circle.

"Whoa, there, Paulie, slow your roll." When he's finally still long enough for me to clip on his leash, I take him outside, letting him tug me down the street while he sniffs every single blade of grass before lifting his leg and taking care of business.

It's on the way back to Nikolai's house that things take a turn. First, the neighbor's sprinklers come on and Paul lunges to get in the spray, pulling me with him. He may still be a puppy, but he's stronger than I gave him credit for. His tongue laps the water from one sprinkler and then he's off to the next one, pulling me through the spray with him. I dig my heels into the grass and hope I'm not destroying someone's lawn as I get control of my dog. We finally make it to the sidewalk outside Niko's house, water is dripping in our eyes and one of us is decidedly happier than the other about it. A horn blares as Nikolai's Land Rover pulls into the long driveway.

Paul barks and takes off again, darting around the mailbox and tangling the leash. The pull forward takes me by surprise and the leash trips me up. I tuck and roll while everything happens in slow motion. The pavement makes as hard of a landing as ice.

"Chloe!" Nikolai's concerned voice has me blinking my eyes open. A gorgeous blond girl hovers over me, right before a long, wet tongue swipes across my face.

"Ayana, take Paul inside," Nikolai barks, reaching my side and scooping me up off the ground like I weigh nothing. Ayana must comply because next thing I see is the back of her head as she cajoles the canine back in the house. Frankly, my brain is too preoccupied with the solid chest and steel band of arms around me.

"Does anything hurt?" Nikolai murmurs, the growl somehow still letting concern shine through.

I take stock of my limbs and realize I feel fine, other than being horribly embarrassed. Pretty sure I must have looked ridiculous, ass in the air as I tumbled. "I'm good, actually. You can put me down. Don't hurt yourself."

Nikolai gives me a look so scathing I snap my mouth shut and simply hold on for dear life as he sweeps me into the house and deposits me on the couch. He squats down by my feet and runs his hands along my legs, one at a time. Tingles of awareness shoot straight to my head, making me feel lightheaded.

"What are you doing?" I ask faintly.

"Did you hit your head?" His hands leave my legs and trail over my arms before he cups my face and tilts me this way and that.

A different kind of awareness hits me, and I look past Nikolai's concerned face to see Ayana looking on like she isn't sure if it's safe to come any closer. I bat Nikolai's hands away and jump to my feet, feeling a little creaky, but otherwise okay.

"Hey! You must be Ayana. Did you like my gymnastics out there?" I shoot her a wry grin, which she instantly mirrors, coming into the room with Paul at her heels.

"You got air before you rolled. You cooked out there."

I laugh, and then laugh harder when Nikolai mutters under his breath. "Cooked? Is this English?"

"Did you have lunch?" I ask Ayana, moving away from the couch and the girl's overprotective father.

"Not yet. Dad wanted me to meet you first."

"I am sorry. Ayana, this is Chloe, your temporary nanny. Chloe, this is my daughter, Ayana." Nikolai waves between us. "And this is the dog that will be enrolled in dog training starting tomorrow."

Paul whines, but sits obediently looking up at us. He's cute, but maybe a little training would be a good idea before he gets even bigger.

I clap my hands. "I'll make us sandwiches. Ayana, will you help me?"

She lights up, eagerly following me into the kitchen where

we raid the fridge and make stacked sandwiches with everyone's favorites. Ayana mostly makes a mess, but we get the sandwiches made eventually. I'm cutting them into triangles, Ayana's preferred sandwich shape, when she leans a little closer.

"You know, Mom probably would have made us get rid of Paul if he tripped her." Her voice is so small it makes me want to wrap my arm around her and protect her from the world.

My ribs ache, hearing the hurt in her voice. I don't know much about Nikolai's ex, but my opinion of her gets worse the more I hear. "Mistakes happen and we all deserve second and even third chances. Dogs included."

We plate the sandwiches and head for the dining room, where Nikolai is busy texting on his phone, a furrow to his brow. He glances up when we come in, surprise stealing across his features when he sees we made him a sandwich.

"You did not have to feed me too."

I point to Ayana. "She made it."

Ayana's head snaps in my direction and her cheeks turn pink as she gives me a little smile. We sit down together and eat, Ayana keeping us entertained with her constant chatter. All too soon, Nikolai scrapes his chair back and announces he has to get to training.

"And you have dance tonight, right?" I ask Ayana, knowing the answer before she nods her head. I memorized her schedule immediately after Nikolai forwarded it to me. "Just enough time for us to go shopping for that birthday gift and then we'll head to dance. And then . . ." I give her an exaggerated eyebrow waggle. "It's pizza night. Have you ever tossed a pizza crust like a born and bred Italian?"

Ayana giggles. "No. I'm Kazakhstani, not Italian."

Nikolai hovers in the doorway, his gaze flicking back and forth between us before he finally leaves, a smile softening his face.

My third graders acted older and older each year, but even so, Ayana seems far older than her years. Which isn't necessarily a good thing. I'm a firm believer kids should have time to be kids before they have to take on the responsibilities and stress of the adult world. During her dance class, if she made even the tiniest of mistakes, she would glance out the window toward the hallway where the parents sat watching their kids. I gave her a smile and thumbs up, but that glance kept happening, as if she was expecting reprimand. Makes me wonder what kind of parenting has been going on under her mother's roof.

But at the end of the day, I have no control over that. I only have this limited time with her, and I intend to make the most of it. We head home and have the pizza dough ready to toss when Nikolai returns. Paul scrambles through the house, his nails tick, tick, ticking against the wood floor while he barks his head off.

"Hallo, *zajushka*." Nikolai sticks his head into the kitchen and smiles at Ayana.

She squeaks and runs to him, jumping into his waiting arms. The scene is adorable. Clearly these two love each other and Ayana feels safe with her dad.

"Chloe took me to this place that's all jewelry and we bought this whole set for MacKenzie that she'll love. And then at dance she made Mr. Strabuski laugh, which is, like, impossible, and his laugh sounds like a honking goose. You should have heard it, Dad."

"Whoa, that sounds like a good day," Nikolai answers,

looking around Ayana to me. I can feel his gaze like an actual caress, which is so inappropriate with Ayana in the room. I focus back on my lump of dough.

"Who's ready to toss some pizza?"

"Me!" Ayana shrieks, kicking her legs until Nikolai lets her down. "Dad, you have to do it too!"

"Wash your hands!" I shout when Nikolai reaches for a lump of dough on the counter. He grumbles but does it, returning to follow my directions with Ayana. Before you know it, we all have our pizza crust in the air, though Ayana drops hers several times. Thankfully, we made enough dough to not have to eat hers.

I nudge Nikolai as we put our crusts down and start adding toppings. "You make a fine Italian, Mr. Drugov."

His head lifts and his eyes heat as he looks at me. "I think maybe you should always call me Mr. Drugov."

My face heats, absolutely knowing he's thinking of me naked while I'm saying it. Damn this man and his incredible imagination. My phone pings from the counter by the sink. I step back and let the two of them finish topping the pizzas before I combust. I wash the dough off my hands and grab my phone.

> Unknown Number: Hey, Chloe, this is Tanner Gumphrey. Your mother gave me your number. She insists we'd make gorgeous grandbabies, though I'll be honest, not sure I'm in the market for kids. I am, however, in the market for a nice dinner and conversation. Are you free Saturday?

"Who the fuck is Tanner Gumphrey and why is he talking about babies?" Nikolai barks from over my shoulder. I jump, not realizing he came up behind me.

"Dad! Language!"

I pull the phone to my chest and turn to face a very pissed off Nikolai. "That was a private message."

His huge hands go to his hips. "Tell him no."

My jaw drops. "Excuse me?"

"You heard me. Tell him no. Remember our rules, Chloe?"

I lean in, a bit pissed off that he's trying to tell me what to do, but also knowing Ayana doesn't need to hear all this. "You said no men in the house. This is just dinner out. On my night off."

His eyes narrow and his nostrils flare, but he relents. He steps back and lets me slide the pizzas into the oven.

"Ayana, go take Paul in the backyard before dinner."

"Okay!" Ayana is all too happy to take care of her puppy, talking to him like an actual friend. We listen to her chatter trail off as she finally gets him outside.

I huff my irritation with Nikolai and move to leave the kitchen too, but he snags his arm around my waist and pulls my back into his chest. His scent surrounds me and makes my heart beat double time. I feel his head dip and his breath as it fans across my neck.

"You will not like this Tanner. He does not make you blush like I do." And as if to prove his words, he drops his lips to my neck, a quick kiss followed by the scrape of his teeth and the velvet caress of his tongue. My knees buckle and his arm is the only thing holding me up and we both know it. His soft chuckle brings me back to reality.

My elbow finds its way into his gut and he releases me with an "oof!"

"I do what I want, Mr. Drugov."

And I leave him to get the pizzas out of the oven while I try to get my shit together before dinner.

Chapter Twenty

Niko

I finally understand the English saying, "You are your own worst enemy." Never in my life have I allowed myself to be so careless and undisciplined as I have been around Chloe. I am adamant one moment that she stop flirting, and then the next, I am tasting her skin and teasing her just to see how she reacts.

A familiar panic hit when I watched her tumble to the concrete earlier, one I have only ever felt when Ayana injures herself or gets caught in danger's path. It was . . . unexpected, and I still cannot explain it. I barely know Chloe. Yet my adrenaline refused to recede until I knew for certain she was uninjured.

I blame the lingering residue of that panic for my ensuing reaction to the text on Chloe's phone. Some beast inside me broke free when I saw the message from this Tanner person. *Tanner?* That is a boy's name.

Chloe does not need a boy; she needs a man. A grown man

who can treat her like the most precious jewel while also reminding her what her body was made for–and the array of pleasures it can enjoy in the right hands. She deserves to be the center of a man's world, something I could not give even if I threw common sense and duty out the window. After all that Chloe has been through, she should find someone as generous as she is. But this man named Tanner is *not* that person, I can tell you that.

Much time will have to pass before I can forget the taste of Chloe's skin or the feel of her body pressing into my chest. I fear it has become an addiction.

"*Blyat*!" I curse aloud as I imagine the disappointment on Coach's face had he been standing in the kitchen with us a few moments ago. I am disgusted with myself.

The back door slams and Ayana appears around the corner, her blond hair a tousled mess and her cheeks pink. "Where's Chloe?"

"Restroom," I say, although I do not actually know. Last night, I was the one hiding, and tonight it is Chloe's turn. I should apologize. Later.

"Can we watch the next episode of *Bake Off* after pizza?" Ayana bats her eyelashes like a seasoned professional.

The timer buzzes, and I grab a dish towel to pull the pizzas from the oven. I have learned the hard way that oven mitts are not made for hands my size. "It is already late. You know bedtime is at eight."

"But, Dad, it's summer."

I set the pans on the cooktop, turning to face my daughter again. Her mouth is fixed in a pout. "We both know you will wake up with the roosters no matter what time you go to bed. You need your sleep so you can be a tough hockey player like Chloe and me."

"It's our first night with Chloe too! Come on, please?" She turns my argument back on me, showing a familiar stubborn streak she undoubtedly inherited from me. "I promise I'll sleep until at least eight tomorrow."

Ayana's reminder that I will once again be alone with Chloe after she goes to bed has me reconsidering. What real harm could it do to let the child stay up a little late? It is one night.

"Fine. You win."

"Yes!" She pumps her tiny fist, making me grin despite my consternation.

"What are we celebrating?" Chloe reenters the kitchen, no longer wearing that blush I enjoy so much.

"Dad says I can stay up and watch *Bake Off*." My daughter preens.

"You like *Bake Off*?" Chloe's face lights up. "I love that show! Oh my gosh, is that where Paul got his name?" Her eyes dart around the kitchen, looking for the naughty dog.

"Yes! Dad wanted to name him *Strakh*." She says the name as if it is coated in vinegar.

"*Strakh?*" Chloe mimics Ayana's tone, turning to me. "That's an awful name for a dog. It sounds like you're clearing your throat instead of addressing an adorable furball."

"It means terror in Russian," I explain.

But Chloe's eyes only narrow. "Who hurt you?"

I cannot process her question, so I shake my head in response.

"You need to get another dog and call her Prue!"

I glance at Ayana to see her eyes widen with delight. "That's what *I* said!"

The two females beam at each other as if they have each just discovered their missing soulmate. My heart begins a heavy thrum in my chest, an unfamiliar warmth seeping into my lungs and belly.

But, no, this is not good, regardless of how happy Ayana is right now. Chloe will not be her nanny for more than a couple weeks. I suppose it would be some solace that she will still be her hockey coach, but I may be setting my daughter up for heartbreak, regardless. Fatherhood has a special way of tangling a man into knots.

"We should eat before the pizza gets cold," I say. It comes out harsher than I intended, and Chloe shoots me a questioning glance. I turn my back to retrieve plates from the cabinet and keep my hands busy.

Ayana and Chloe gab like lifelong friends over dinner, and I know Ayana has fallen for her new nanny when she offers to help clean up the kitchen afterward.

"Who are you and what did you do with my Ayana?" I ask as my daughter clears our plates from the table.

"*Dad,*" she leans in and quietly scolds me before turning to Chloe. "I love helping out. After all, if I'm going to be a professional baker, I need to make the kitchen my space."

"I can't wait to taste some of your confections." Chloe grabs an empty pizza stone and follows Ayana to the kitchen. I force my eyes to the table instead of following the sway of her hips as she passes. "I always thought it would be fun to open a dog bakery."

"Oh! They have one of those by the dance studio! We should totally take Paul there."

"It's a plan, then."

The two disappear from sight as they continue to chat. What in the hell is a dog bakery? It cannot be what it sounds like; I doubt there is much of a market for baked canines.

My phone rings and I retrieve it from my pocket to see Coach Bowman's name on the screen. Guilt washes over me.

"Sir," I answer.

"Niko. Just checking in about Picard and MacDougal. I thought I'd stop by the practice rink tomorrow, so I wanted to find out your schedule." With no replacement coach hired yet, Coach Bowman remains committed to our progress with the

Storm Chasers' goalies. I cannot help but think Ivan would have done the same in his shoes.

"Of course. We meet for conditioning at nine. Drills on the ice should be around eleven." I twist my napkin with the restless fingers of my free hand.

"Sounds good." Silence falls between us, and I squeeze my eyes shut. Fuck.

"Coach—" I begin at the same time he says, "Drugov."

I swallow hard. Very little intimidates me. I put myself between the net and hundred-mile-an-hour projectiles on a daily basis, and I can go up against the toughest enforcers in the league. But Coach Bowman is a man who deserves my utmost respect and deference. He has made me the player I am today and believes in me more than anyone. And here I am essentially sneaking around behind his back.

When I don't respond, Coach continues quietly, "My daughter is grieving, and she needs the space to do that."

Fuck! Fuck! Fuck!

"Absolutely. I understand. She is a very thoughtful person to help me with Ayana, but I promise I will not take advantage of her generosity. I will find a replacement nanny as soon as the judge makes his ruling final." *And I will keep my hands off her*, I silently vow.

"I know. I just . . ." he trails off, sounding almost defeated. I need to ease his anxiety.

I let my head drop back, my shoulders falling as I slump against the back of my chair. "You are a father, like me. It is our job to protect and worry."

"Precisely." I hear him inhale before his tone regains its normal gruffness. "Okay, enough of that. I'll see you and the boys tomorrow at eleven. Goodnight, Niko."

"Goodnight, Coach."

I lay my phone on the table and rise from my chair, gathering the last of the utensils from the table. Neither Ayana nor

Chloe notices me where I pause in the entryway to the kitchen. Their heads are pressed together, all of their attention riveted to Chloe's phone screen where some song about a boy emanates from the device.

"This is my favorite part," Chloe says, bringing her hand to her chest while Ayana giggles. My fingers twitch as my eyes zero in on the cleavage under Chloe's hand.

Enough! Never in my life have I allowed a woman to drive me to such distraction. It is time to put an end to this recklessness once and for all.

And I think I know the best way to do it.

Chapter Twenty-One

Chloe

I thought the first day with Ayana went perfectly. The girl is really quite adorable and spending time with her is zero hardship. Her father on the other hand? Major distraction. The man had the audacity to kiss my neck and act like he had the right to tell me what to do about my date. And then he sits on the sofa with Ayana watching *Bake Off*, ignoring me like nothing happened. Meanwhile, I'm sitting in a puddle of inappropriate desire wishing he trailed those lips over more of my skin. While naked. And alone. And maybe with a set of handcuffs. I don't know. I'm open to ideas.

The television show blares and the two Drugovs laugh in unison while I stew on Nikolai's hot-and-cold behavior. They chatter among themselves about the rum cakes that most of the contestants botched as the program ends. The leather chair I'm in squeaks every time I rock back and forth, a metronome that counts away the seconds of my irritation.

"Time for bed, *zajushka*," Nikolai finally whispers,

picking Ayana up from the couch and carrying her to her bedroom while she tries to protest, but it ends in a yawn so big she can't fight it. She smiles sleepily over his shoulder at me, and I wave goodnight.

I follow suit after a few seconds, heading for my own room where I change into a black satin pajama set with spaghetti straps that make a valiant effort at holding in my breasts. The shorts, however, don't even try to contain my ass. I don't normally wear this set, but I have a particular goal in mind. With parts jiggling in what I hope is seduction, I head back out to the kitchen to reach into the upper cabinet for a water glass. I have to go up on tiptoe as it seems Nikolai built this kitchen for his towering height, not the average height of an American.

A choking noise behind me has me grinning like a fool before I school my facial features and turn around with a glass clutched to my bosom. "Oh!" If teaching hadn't worked out, I should have gone into acting.

Nikolai's hands are clenched into fists by his side, but it's the eyebrows drawn together into a straight line over sparking blue eyes that has my heart rate climbing. "What is this?" he spits out from between clenched teeth.

I glance down at the glass sitting on my chest like my breasts made a little shelf just to hold it. "I'm getting water."

"Second rule, Chloe." That growl really is magnificent.

I bite my lip and try to remember all the rules he threw at me. "Sorry, I can't quite remember which one that was. No men in the house? Or was that no flirting?" I lift the glass off my breasts. "Because I'm not flirting. I'm just getting water."

I force my lips into a soft smile and walk over to the sink where a reverse osmosis spout has been built into the counter-top. Another grumble punctures the silence in the kitchen. I ignore him and fill my glass, sure he's getting an eyeful of what doesn't fit into these short shorts. The next thing I know, my hips are pinned to the granite countertop as Nikolai's thick body crowds me in from behind. The glass clanks into the stainless steel sink as it slips from my hands.

His breath is hot against my neck once again while his hands grip my hips before sliding down to my ass cheeks and grabbing more than a handful. Every inch of my skin pebbles into goose bumps at the intimate fondling. I open my mouth to give him more of my trademark sass, but he takes that moment to grind his erection against the flesh he now holds in his hands and all the air is stolen from my lungs. He's long, thick, and so incredibly hard.

"Do you feel what you do to me?" he whispers into my ear.

I grip the counter and focus all my efforts on staying upright instead of spinning and sinking to my knees right there in the kitchen so I can get my mouth on what I know will be the best dick I've ever had the pleasure of seeing. Besides, I'm pretty sure that question is rhetorical. I'd have to be dead and buried not to feel that steel pipe behind me.

"Answer me," he growls louder, gripping me harder. Almost to the point of pain. I know I shouldn't like this manhandling, but I do. Oh, I fucking do.

"Yes," I gasp.

"This is why we have rules, Chloe. Rules to protect you."

I blink, trying to organize rational thought in a brain turned to mush. Protect me? Protect me from whom? Nikolai?

His hands pulse on my ass one more time and then he releases me and steps back with a grunt that sounds a lot like pain. He takes his heat with him and I'm suddenly so cold I'm shaking with it. I don't turn around. I can't turn around. I'm afraid if I do, I'll beg him to forget those silly rules. I've been flirting with him, teasing him, baiting him since day one. It was just some harmless fun, or so I thought. But I heard desperation in his voice just now and I've seen him with his daughter. He's a good dad. One of the great ones who deserves split custody. This isn't harmless fun any longer, and I need to remember that.

I nod, gulping loudly as I stare out the window into his dark backyard. "Understood."

"Go on that date."

Shocked, I look over my shoulder to see him back in the doorway to the kitchen, his jaw still locked tight and his eyes dancing with fire. There's no use arguing with him about the issue, that much I can see.

"Go on your date and forget about me entirely. This," he waves a hand between us. "This can't happen. Ever."

Sadness hits my chest like a thousand knives. "I don't think I can forget about you," I whisper. "Believe me, I wish I could. It would be better for you that way."

Nikolai refuses to meet my eyes now. He takes another step back and his meaning couldn't be any clearer. "I do not care about me. I want to see you happy with a good man. And that is not me."

My lips manage a sad smile. He has no idea how good of a man he truly is. "And that's precisely why I can't forget about you or that kiss we shared."

His chin drops to his chest for a moment, but he quickly inhales, straightens his spine and turns to leave. "Have a good night. I am free Sunday. Would be a good day for you to have off for your date."

And then he's gone, leaving me a shaky mess in the kitchen. I stay there until I get my lungs and limbs under control. Then I tiptoe back to my room and change into baggy sweats, vowing to myself that I won't flirt with Nikolai again. I don't know how I'll manage it when that's how all our interactions have gone, but I know I need to work on it.

I pull out my phone and text Tanner back, agreeing to

dinner and suggesting Sunday night. Nothing about the date excites me, but Nikolai is right. I need to forget him and move on. My whole goal after Josh died was to bring back fun in my life. Pining after a man who's unavailable is not exactly a good time.

Nikolai is already gone the next morning when I wake up. He left a four-word note in the kitchen for Ayana, which neither of us can read because it's in Russian. Looks like Ayana's Russian lessons have already started. I take Paul out back to pee, then feed him breakfast and check the registrations for my second open house this afternoon. Just about the same number as last time, which is good news.

"Can we make rum cake?" Ayana asks, startling me as she walks into the kitchen, rubbing her sleepy eyes.

"How about breakfast first?"

She crosses her eyes and sticks her tongue out. I cross my arms across my chest and give her my best teacher look. She sighs and grumbles, "Okay fine." The teacher look works every time, what can I say?

We make pancakes together, complete with blueberry eyeballs, strawberry smiles, and whip cream for hair. After that, we get dressed, take Paul to the park and play with the neighborhood kids for an hour, and then come home to do some craft projects with whatever Nikolai has at the house. I check my watch and start to clean up the pencils, Crayons, and colored paper.

"Time to get ready for hockey lessons!" I cheer.

Ayana grimaces. My hands still. "Wait. Do you not like hockey?"

"It's not that I don't like it, I just don't know if I'll be any good. What if I suck and everyone makes fun of me?"

I shrug. "Everyone sucks their first time."

Ayana rolls her eyes like she's already a teenager. "Yeah, but not everybody has a pro hockey player for a dad."

I leave the supplies on the table and come over to crouch by her chair. "Hey. That's not the kind of league I'm running. I'm the boss. Nobody's going to make fun of you, or they'll find themselves kicked out. We support each other in my league." I grab her hands and squeeze. "Do you trust me?"

She nods instantly, blond hair flying around her shoulders. "Yeah, you got rizz, Chloe."

I frown, feeling a lot like Nikolai all of a sudden. "Huh?"

She bursts into giggles and slides off the chair. "Come on! You can't be late if you're the boss!"

Chapter Twenty-Two

Niko

"Jesus, Druggy, you're a machine," Mac chokes out as he braces his gloved hands on his knees to catch his breath.

I come to a stop, throwing snow at his skates. "A machine is *built* to excel. I *work* for it. We are adding a four-mile run to your morning routine, MacDougal."

He tilts his head up, cheeks crimson from exertion. "Goalies don't need that kind of endurance training." He pants. "We need flexibility and razer-sharp focus, man."

Cappy skates by and smacks the back of Mac's helmet. "If Druggy says you need it, you need it. This ain't the junior league, dipshit."

Mac straightens and glares at Cap. "Says the guy whose VH sucks worse than my sister's."

"Speaking of your sister and sucking . . ." Cappy taunts.

I manage to catch Mac around the middle as he lunges for his teammate. "Enough! Time for movement drills," I say, lowering my voice as I notice Coach Bowman enter the viewing area. "And if you cannot put all your focus on practice, I am sure management will be happy to trade you."

Both players' eyes drop to their skates. That is what I thought.

Mac has clearly spent too much of the offseason partying instead of working out. He is barely twenty-two and still a rookie, so perhaps it is to be expected. Cap, on the other hand, is looking sharp. He has the focus necessary to be starting goalie after I am gone; now he just needs the confidence.

We run movement drills and then proceed to puck tracking and situational drills. By the time our ice time expires, both men look ready to collapse as they drag themselves off the ice. Good.

Coach does not come over to chat, but I know he was watching with an eagle's eye and will want to discuss Mac's performance soon. The kid is full of attitude, but his instincts are on point. I will continue working on him.

I move to follow Mac and Cappy to the locker room but get sidetracked when I hear a very familiar voice shouting, "Dad!"

Ayana stands behind the glass, knocking on it to get my attention, her gap-toothed smile aimed at me. I forgot one of Chloe's open houses is this afternoon.

I skate toward my daughter, awareness prickling at the back of my neck as I spot Chloe a few feet behind her. She is surrounded by a gaggle of kids and parents, and I do my best to ignore her presence.

"Are you skating with us?" There is so much hope in Ayana's expression, I feel like an asshole when I respond.

"No. I was working."

She bites her lip, eyes dropping to her skates much like Mac's and Cappy's had.

"But I am finished now, so . . . I can stay if you like."

The grin is back. "I'm gonna go get my skates on!" she announces, turning to sprint in Chloe's direction.

"Listen to your coach!" I yell behind her. Ayana is strong-willed and I do not want her causing trouble for Chloe on such a busy day.

My shout draws the attention of the parents, and I curse under my breath when I see recognition dawn in a few faces.

"Oh my god! It's Nikolai Drugov!" one woman yells. It is a domino effect from there as several parents and children swarm the glass like bugs on a windshield. I nod and wave, forcing myself to paste on a polite smile.

"Okay, everybody!" Chloe shouts. "Let's get everyone in skates so we can begin."

I use the distraction to skate to the other end of the rink and exit to the locker room to strip off my gear. I should just change and leave, but I have already promised Ayana I would stay, so I wait fifteen minutes before reemerging in street clothes and my skates.

The rink is crowded with kids, some hanging onto the boards or a grownup for dear life and others gliding easily across the ice. I spot Benny on the other end of the rink and am relieved to see the parents' attention on him now. He is skating backward, holding onto the hands of one of the kids, a feat that has one mom practically swooning for some reason.

I shake my head and skate Chloe's way, coming to a stop behind her.

"Chloe, I am sorry for the intrusion, but I told Ayana I would stay."

She spins around, and instead of her usual saucy grin, her expression is all business. "Hello, Nikolai. That's perfectly fine. Banks and Bobby are here too. The kids love it." She smiles with the same distant politeness I just used with the parents minutes ago. I find myself struggling to form a response, so I say nothing. I simply nod.

As foreign as it feels, this is good. This is exactly what I wanted–to create distance between us and erase the sexual tension. So why do I miss her flirty looks and challenging gaze already? I need to have my head examined.

Ayana approaches on sure feet, executing a perfect two foot inside/outside edge stop when she reaches me.

"Whoa, Ayana! That was great!" Chloe showers her with praise, and my daughter's cheeks heat with delight.

Ayana wraps her arms around my thighs. "Thanks. Dad taught me."

My chest fills with equal parts pride and adoration for this small human who has irrevocably altered my life. "You are a very good student, *zajushka*." I pat the top of her bike helmet. Now that she is interested in hockey, I will have to get her some real gear. The notion of my daughter following in my footsteps has me clearing a knot of emotion from my throat. I am definitely off today.

"Hey, Druggy, try not to eat any of the kids, yeah?" Roadie says as he skates by with a shit-eating grin.

"Behave yourself, Bobby," Chloe calls before skating after him and the three kids on his heels.

I have no idea how Chloe plans to organize such a range of skill levels and ages into a league, but if anyone can do it, she can. I spend most of the next hour lurking in the background or answering questions from curious kids. It is mayhem when Chloe brings out pool noodles to substitute for sticks. Thank god she thought better than to unleash any pucks with this crowd or we surely would be calling an ambulance by the end.

When all participants are off the ice and assembled on the bleachers, she explains what comes next for anyone interested in officially joining. Most of the youngsters look eager to sign on, not that I can fault them. Hockey is my entire life, apart from my family.

Benny and Roadie lean back into the boards beside me while Chloe wraps things up.

"Eli is in," Benny says. "I knew he'd get the bug as soon as he put on a pair of skates."

"He was outskating you by the end," Roadie replies. "Not that that's a difficult task, mind you."

I glance Benny's way. "Who is Eli?"

"Benny's little brother," Roadie answers for him. "Keep up, old man."

"Your brother from Atlanta?" Maybe I really do need my head examined after all. Benny's brother must be close to forty.

But Benny laughs and points out a kid on the bleachers, the same one he was skating with earlier. "No. The kid in the Bucs shirt. I'm in the Big Brothers program–kind of a mentorship thing."

I have heard of this program, but I had no idea Benny participated. It looks like he is more ready for fatherhood than I thought.

"I don't know about you guys, but there are a lot of MILFs giving me the eye today." Roadie waggles his fingers at a brunette on the bleachers. She smiles back as her daughter scowls at both of them.

"Keep it in your pants, Roadie. This is supposed to be about the kids," Benny warns.

The parents and kids file down from the bleachers as Chloe starts gathering completed forms from everyone.

Roadie straightens and shoots us a grin, his signature dimples flashing. "I've always been excellent at multi-tasking." Then he practically trots on his skates to catch up with the brunette.

"That idiot is going to meet his match one day, and I can't wait to see him get taken down," Benny says before patting me on the back. "Later, man. I gotta take Eli for a burger or he'll drop dead from hunger."

I nod my goodbye and stay where I am as I watch Ayana play assistant to Chloe by thanking people for coming and waving farewell. Only when everyone has left do I approach.

"Very impressive," I say before adding, "Both of you."

"I think we might have a winger on our hands here." Chloe smiles warmly at Ayana.

"They score a lot of goals, right?" my daughter asks. When we both nod, Ayana looks up at me. "Now that everyone's gone, can we get some pucks and sticks so I can practice scoring?"

Since I am finished for the day, I nod. "I can take you back out myself and we can give Chloe a break." She has put in enough hours with my chatterbox daughter for one day and could likely use a nap.

"But Chloe loves to play, don't you?" Ayana turns her innocent expression on her coach.

"I do," Chloe responds on a shrug. "Hey, who am I to pass up a chance to put the biscuit in the basket with two generations of hockey royalty?"

"Who's eating biscuits?" Ayana asks, nose wrinkling.

Chloe and I share a chuckle at her confusion, and I feel a new sense of camaraderie that has nothing to do with attraction.

"There is much to teach you," I say with a pointed look.

"I'll grab our skates!" Ayana sprints away and I turn to face Chloe.

"You do not have to stay. Ayana's attention span is like that of a fruit fly. You must have other things you want to do."

She blinks up at me, once again resembling the warm woman that has become so familiar to me. "Nikolai, I'm sorry for teasing you so much, and I understand that nothing can happen here. You need a friend, and I'm happy to help you out with no strings, okay?" She extends a hand. "Friends?"

I hesitate but finally take it, ignoring the frisson of electricity at her touch. "Friends," I agree, hoping I can manage to keep fooling myself.

Since we are not in pads and only Ayana has a helmet, we mostly skate and demonstrate skills for her. It is unsurprising that Chloe's muscle memory kicks in and she maneuvers like a seasoned pro. By the end of an hour, Ayana has scored countless goals on an empty net and is on her way to perfecting her slapshot. Chloe is just as pink-cheeked and joyful as my daughter, and, try as I might, I cannot stop from feeling the effects of her positivity and light.

But friends are *supposed* to make you feel good, right? This friendship thing can work for us. We are not animals, after all. We just have a small case of lust caused by pheromones and brain chemistry. Surely, we can overcome that in no time.

As we exit the facility to the parking lot, however, Chloe makes a groaning sound, and my body's reaction is primal and instantaneous. My cock jumps in my pants and my jaw tightens at the sound.

I barely hear her words as she says, "Remind me to wear gloves next time. I've got blisters already."

I am too busy cursing at myself to hear anything else. In a word, I am screwed.

Chapter Twenty-Three

Chloe

The red wine swirls around the oversized wine glass as I twirl it, leaving legs that Tanner assures me mean the wine is top notch. I have no doubt. Everything about this date has been top notch. The restaurant in downtown Tampa is one that usually takes months to get a reservation. The man across the linen covered table from me looks like a million bucks in his designer suit and fresh shave. The watch he sports on his wrist is certainly Patek Philippe. He screams money and intelligence, which is a good sign, along with the good manners he displayed when he held the door, slid my chair out for me, and let me order what I wanted on the menu instead of what he assumed I'd like.

And yet . . . I feel nothing but a passing fondness for the man.

"Did you leave room for dessert, Chloe?" Tanner asks, leaning forward and putting his elbows on the table and flashing dark, bedroom eyes.

Sadly, I did not, and that's not some vapid female thing about wanting to appear dainty on a first date. I ordered a steak and risotto, not a salad with dressing on the side.

"Not tonight," I say gently, lifting the glass to take the final sip of wine. We finished off a bottle together and it's safe to say I'm feeling good. Relaxed. Not strung out with butterflies in my stomach like when I'm around Nikolai.

His grin turns up a degree, and I can't help but smile back. The man really is handsome. If you like the airbrushed magazine model look.

"Perhaps on our next date?"

I dip my head. "On our next date."

Tanner flags our server and pays for our meal, not even entertaining my argument about paying for my own meal. Then he's by my side, helping me out of the chair and guiding me out of the restaurant with his hand on my lower back. The conversation flows easily as he drives me back to Nikolai's house in his fancy Mercedes. Meanwhile I'm racking my brain to find one fault on this date. One tiny thing that could explain why I don't feel that tug of attraction with a man that should fit every single requirement on a woman's list for a possible mate.

"It's dark. I'll walk you up." Tanner gets out of the car and comes around to help me out of the passenger side, which is fabulous. Between the wine, the skirt and heels, and the low level of the car, I could use a little help getting to my feet. He keeps his arm around my waist as we walk to the front door. His cologne is a bit overpowering at this close of range and I might have just found the one tiny thing wrong with him.

"Thank you again for a truly lovely evening," I say when we reach the wrought-iron front door. Earlier, I explained to Tanner that I live here temporarily while my duplex is being fixed.

We turn to face each other on the welcome mat. "I'll call

you tomorrow. I'm out of town later this week, but if you're available Saturday, I'd love to see you again."

"I'd like that." And I would. Maybe between now and then I can get Nikolai out of my head entirely and enjoy a second date with a perfectly wonderful man.

His hands go to my hips and for a split second I tense, wondering if he's registering the width of my curves and finding me lacking. Then he pulls me closer and dips his head, brushing his lips across mine and I push those stupid thoughts aside. He barely gets a chance to deepen the kiss when the outdoor lights flip on, illuminating the porch in daylight spotlights. We both jump back, startled.

My hand flies to my lips and I laugh breathlessly. "Motion sensors."

Tanner's jaw tightens, but he forces a smile. "I should go anyway. I'll call you."

And then he's gone, striding back down the walkway to his car and waving goodbye as he climbs inside. I put the key in the lock, but the door swings open before I can twist it. Nikolai stands in the shadows of the dark house, his face a mask of anger.

"It is late," he says in a menacing whisper.

I frown right back, shutting the door quietly behind me. I turn and face him, hands on my hips. "I'm sorry, is today not my day off? I thought it was. Silly me."

"Is this sarcasm?"

I throw my hands out to the side, thoroughly exasperated with the man. "Yes, it's sarcasm!" I hiss, trying to keep my voice low in deference to Ayana sleeping. "Why are you up?"

Nikolai drops my gaze and reaches around me to flip off the lights outside. Huh. Not motion sensors after all. My jaw drops open in realization. Nikolai hijacked my date on purpose. I round on him, a long string of complaints ready on my lips, but he beats me to it.

"I just wanted to make sure you got home safe. I do not trust people I do not know and you are . . ." he trails off, looking confused and defeated.

I deflate, losing my train of thought and the righteous anger that flooded me a moment ago. "I'm what?"

He looks up, his blue-eyed gaze finding mine in the dark, and that's when I realize we're standing mere inches apart. "You are special, Chloe."

I narrow my eyes, telling my stupid heart to quit beating so fast. "Because my dad would kill you if any harm came to me while I lived under your roof?"

He shakes his head slowly. His hand comes up and pushes a curtain of my curled hair behind my shoulder. "No. You are special because you are kind and good and talented and a host of other . . . what do you call them? Attributes? You deserve the very best, Chloe Cooper."

My heart melts into a puddle, and even though I want to shake him and make him see that all I want is him, I know he's not mine to have. He's got to focus on Ayana. So I revert to the only way I know of dealing with him: I tease.

"You sure we can't just fuck and call it friends with benefits?"

His eyes widen and then he drops his head. For a second, I think maybe I've ruined things between us. Then he lifts his head and his lips curl up into a smile, right before he lets out a hearty laugh that has me joining in.

Just like that, all the tension between us dissipates. I have no doubt it'll be back, but for tonight, we've sidestepped a ticking bomb of attraction. As his laughter subsides, he pulls me into a hug and then kisses my forehead like I've seen him do with Ayana. My hands land on his waist and it takes everything in me not to let them roam his impressive physique.

"Go to bed, Chloe of the short people. You are talking crazy and clearly need sleep."

I tip my head back and give him a genuine smile. It hits me right there in his foyer right before midnight. I *like* Nikolai. Like, really like him. And even if we can't be anything but friends, I'm going to have to be okay with that because I can't imagine not having him in my life, even after all this nanny business between us is over.

"My neck is already killing me, so to bed it is. Goodnight, Nikolai of the tall people."

We share one more smile and then he releases me. I feel the burn of his stare on my backside until I turn the corner and escape his view. It does absolutely nothing to help me get to sleep.

A mild wine headache blooms just after dawn when Ayana bursts into my room. Nikolai follows right after, averting his gaze when he sees I'm still in bed. Paul shoves past him and jumps on the foot of my bed. Nikolai hovers in the doorway like crossing the threshold would be a crime.

"I am so sorry," he mutters. "Ayana, you cannot go into Chloe's room before eight. I have told you this."

"But," Ayana whines, wrapping her little arms around me. "She said we could make pancakes again, and I love you, Dad, but you make them really dry and healthy."

I chuckle, finding her enthusiasm for cooking adorable. I sit up in bed, thankful I switched to baggy T-shirts and unattractive shorts for pajamas recently. I still have to keep my tabletop fan on high all night to help combat the night sweats, but at least I don't tempt Nikolai with an overabundance of flesh showing.

I give Paul's head a scratch. "Give me thirty minutes and I'll help you with those pancakes. Deal?"

"Deal!" she squeals and runs out of the room. Paul barks and jumps off the bed to follow her.

Nikolai steps back. "Again. I am sorry. Also, there is ibuprofen in the guest bathroom."

I shake my head at him, but quickly stop when that makes the headache worse. "Remind me never to drink wine again. Why does a couple glasses hit you so hard once you turn forty?"

Nikolai tosses me an impish grin. "I would not know. I am still a young man in his thirties."

My pillow narrowly misses his head as he slams the door shut. I hear his deep laughter as he walks down the hallway. I get dressed, swallow the ibuprofen, and head for the kitchen, all the while humming a tune under my breath. Ayana is sitting on a barstool at the counter waiting impatiently for me.

"Dad had to go to practice. He left me another note." She waves a sheet of paper in the air. "I told him I can't read Russian and he told me to use Google translate for now. What's Google translate?"

I pull up the website on my phone and show her how to use it. It takes a few tries, but we're finally able to determine that he wrote *My pancakes are not dry, little bunny.*

Ayana giggles and I get busy plating the unhealthy version of pancakes. Once we're both done eating, I fire up my laptop and click over to a site that teaches various languages.

"Today, we start your Russian lessons." When Ayana gives me a scowl, I hold up my hand. "I will learn with you."

That seems to make her happier about doing schoolwork during the summer. We start the program, and it moves a little faster than I can keep up. I keep having to hit pause and replay so it pronounces the words again. Ayana giggles, already knowing some Russian words. She can even pronounce some of the Cyrillic alphabet, complete with guttural sounds that don't come naturally to me. By the time we finish the first lesson, my headache is back.

"That's enough for today, *zajushka*."

Ayana claps at my attempt to use the nickname her dad uses. Then she slumps back in her chair, all levity gone. "Dad calls me that because of a book he gave me when I was little."

I don't point out that she's still little. Instead, I just listen, glad she's opening up to me.

"He would read it to me every night. Well, every night that I saw him. But then Mom said the book got lost the last time we moved. And then I didn't see Dad as much." She picks at the chipped pink polish on her fingernails. "I wish he still read it to me."

I reach over and hold her tiny hands. "I bet if you asked him, he'd find the book and read it to you now."

Her bright blue eyes hold my gaze earnestly. "I wish he was with me every night, not just sometimes."

My heart aches, knowing how divorce can trickle down and hurt the one innocent party in the whole thing. I squeeze her hands. "I tell you what? Why don't we go down to the rink and bring your dad some lunch? We could have a picnic!"

Her face lights up, even as my heart squeezes hard. While she gets dressed, I call my own father and make sure Nikolai can take a lunch break. He assures me it's fine, but asks me if I'd bring him lunch too. Considering how much dads mean to their daughters, I quickly agree.

As I pack a basket full of sandwiches, chips, and fruit, I remind myself once again to keep things on a friendship level with Nikolai. There's too much on the line for him to be messing around with his live-in nanny. That little girl deserves a father in her life full time.

Chapter Twenty-Four

Niko

"Thank you for telling me about the book," I say to Chloe as I collapse onto the couch after tucking Ayana in. I would bet my bonus money that Peyton threw it in the trash in a moment of anger. "A new copy should arrive tomorrow." Thank you, Prime.

"You know the two of you are adorable enough to make even the deadest heart swoon, right?" she responds from her spot in the recliner where a book rests on the pillow in her lap.

Since I am not sure what she means, I ask, "What are you reading?"

She holds the book up for me, and I read the title aloud, "*Did I Say That Out Loud?* What kind of book is this?" The cover has a broken fork with a deranged face drawn on it. I cannot imagine any situation that would compel me to read such a strange book.

Chloe rests it back on the pillow and tucks a strand of black hair behind her ear. She is wearing another of her tops that ties behind her neck, although this one is more modest than some of her others. And she has paired it with a denim skirt that shows off her legs. Thankfully, the pillow shields much of her from my view. "It's the kind of book that reassures me I'm not crazy." She tilts her head and adds, "At least I'm not the only one."

"Why would you think you are crazy?"

She grins and shakes her head. "I'm not. At least I hope not." She chuckles at the look on my face. "It's just a book about getting older. You know, all the joys."

"Ah." I nod. "Yes. I will be lucky if I make it through next season without requiring a hip replacement." As if I need a reminder, my hip cracks when I shift positions to retrieve my phone from my shorts pocket. My body is exhausted from these practices with Mac and Cappy. I push myself to outperform them even though they are a decade younger than I am and their bodies have not begun to betray them yet. I refuse to show weakness when the team is counting on me to whip them into shape in these short months before I retire.

"Wow. And I thought I was feeling old. I could hear that crack from over here, Grandpa."

I frown at her, which only makes her laugh. Once again, the sound fills me with a lightness I do not often enjoy. Goosebumps sprout on my arms and I wonder for a second if Chloe somehow caused them.

"Is it cold in here?" I ask. Perhaps I am the crazy one. Should it concern me that I have been asking myself that question regularly since Chloe came to stay? Probably.

But Chloe's expression catches my attention. She looks . . . guilty.

"Oh. Um. I may have turned the air conditioning up a tad."

I get to my feet and pad over to the thermostat on the wall.

"Sixty-six degrees?!" I turn back to see Chloe throw the book and pillow aside.

"I get hot sometimes, okay?" She crosses her arms over her chest in defiance, and it props her magnificent breasts up. I try to avert my eyes but fail.

"Is the Short People clan from Alaska?"

"We've been known to visit," she instantly bites back, and something about her obstinate attitude and the seriousness in her tone makes me grin.

Her eyes narrow, which only widens my grin until she finally lets out an exasperated sigh, breaking eye contact and muttering something under her breath about god being so unfair.

It makes little sense to me, so I do not comment, instead returning to the couch and grabbing a throw blanket on my way.

"Oh my god, just turn the air back down, will you?"

"No. I am fine with a blanket." I begin thumbing out a response to an email from Joe, my agent. He is working on an endorsement deal for me.

"*Nikolai*," Chloe says. There is that exasperation again. "I promise I'll live."

"And so will I. Please, read your book, Chloe. I am going to send some emails." I pull the blanket up to cover my torso until I am quite cozy.

"It's *your* house, not to mention *your* electricity bill."

I don't look up from my phone. "And while you are staying here, it is your house too."

If I am not mistaken, she growls in response and then she is striding across the room toward the thermostat. I am too quick for her, jumping to my feet and intercepting her with an arm around her waist. When I open my mouth to speak, I realize our faces are closer than I intended—only inches apart. My voice drops to almost a whisper as I feel her soft breath against my cheek and witness the fire in her eyes. "Why do you insist on arguing with me? Can I not do something nice? Something as simple as wearing a blanket so you can be comfortable?"

Her defiant expression drops at my question and her lips part as her eyes widen—as if she has been struck with a realization. Every bit of fight has fled.

"I . . ." she starts to speak, and my eyes drop to her plump lips. Fuck. Would one kiss really be all that horrible? "I'm not"—her breathing picks up, and my cock responds in his usual manner—"used to people putting me first."

As her words register in my distracted brain, my arm drops from around her and my spine straightens, creating some distance between us. I fear for a second that Chloe might collapse, but she quickly secures her stance.

"Chloe," I begin, my voice coming out hoarse for some reason. But she cuts me off.

"No. That's not . . . I didn't mean . . ." She shakes her head and forces a smile. "That came out wrong. It's totally fine."

My molars grind together as I watch her try to dismiss her own feelings. But I heard the vulnerability in her voice and saw the surprise on her face. As if it never occurred to her that she deserves even casual kindness. But she is so confident and self-assured. Is she not?

Maybe I have not been paying attention. All this time, I assumed Chloe was indestructible, able to easily handle any obstacle that came her way—cheerfully face any adversity and vanquish it with her positivity. It never occurred to me that her fortitude may have grown from necessity rather than choice. It is clear there is much more to this woman than I imagined, and my frustration at knowing I do not have the right to explore those depths sets my molars grinding harder.

"It is not fine, Chloe." The words feel like gravel in my mouth, and my tone clearly shows it, if her wide eyes are any indication. "You, of all people, deserve to be put first." As I say the words, I realize more than ever that I have taken advantage of her kindness, something I am apparently not the first one to do. I am the king of all assholes.

She tries to wave me off, but I do not allow it. I take both of her hands in mine and stare into her stunning blue eyes, eyes that could make a man fall to his knees. "You are so kind and generous and . . . selfless. I am sorry I have taken advantage of your thoughtful nature."

Her head shake is vehement. "No, Nikolai. I'm so happy to help. I love spending time with Ayana. Truly."

I believe her—because it is who she is. But that does not mean she does not deserve more. Better. Chloe Cooper deserves the best of everything. And I may not be the man who can give her everything, but I can certainly give her more than I have been.

She shrugs, breaking our eye contact. "And, hey, you're giving me a free place to stay while those contractors take their sweet-ass time with my duplex."

"Chloe." We both know her father would be more than happy to have her.

But before I can say anything else, she brushes by me with a smile that feels only slightly less forced. "I'm gonna go take a shower and head to bed. You should turn the air back down. The shower will get me plenty cool." She practically sprints from the room and down the hall to her bathroom. The door closes with a thud, and I am left standing alone—and cold—in the living room.

I exhale loudly and scrub a hand through my hair. It is time Chloe Cooper learned what it is like to be appreciated— no, *revered*—for who she is. My stomach churns at the mental image of that Tanner guy kissing her on my porch. He walked her to the door, which says good things about him, and he obviously likes Chloe, which means he is not a moron. And she likes him too. There is no way she would kiss a man she did not like. Or would she? Now I am uncertain of so many things.

Jaw locked tight, I go to the hall closet and pull out two thick blankets. I take one to Ayana's room, stepping quietly across the plush carpet to cover her with it. She is fast asleep, her mouth slightly ajar and her long hair in a mess around her face and pillow. The sight has some of the tension draining from my body. "Sleep well, my little bunny," I whisper before withdrawing from the room.

I stalk to my own room and toss the other blanket on the bed with more force than necessary. Mind still racing with thoughts of Chloe, I strip off my shirt—almost tearing it in the process—and tug on some flannel pajama pants I normally reserve for winter. Then I stalk right back out to the living room to change the thermostat to sixty-four. No! Sixty-three. Whatever she wants.

But before I can, a blood-curdling scream rips through the air from the other hall and has my stomach dropping to the floor. I run on leaden feet to the guest bathroom and fling the door open without a single thought. My mind is solely focused on the terror in that scream and the horrifying notion of anything harming Chloe.

The ensuing scream has an entirely different tone as a completely bare-naked Chloe spins around to face me, shock stamped on her face as her hands futilely attempt to hide all those glorious curves.

Well, that did not go as expected.

Chapter Twenty-Five

Chloe

The Geico gecko stared at me like he had every right to be in my shower, a weird red gizzard thing expanding under his neck as he breathed. I shouldn't have screamed like that, but my mind was focused on escaping the embarrassment of confessing my inner child's deepest wound in front of Nikolai. He turned sweet on me and looked at me with such compassion—and also heat—that I was about two seconds away from begging him to take me to his bedroom. Even though I lectured myself daily—hourly?—about not approaching that subject with the single dad.

And now that look has turned into a raging inferno that threatens to burn us both down if he doesn't get the hell out of this bathroom. Every square inch of me is bared to him and the man doesn't seem intent on leaving anytime soon. His bare chest heaves and his hands are balled into fists at his sides. I know the man is built. Have felt those muscles under my hands the few times we allowed ourselves to touch, but seeing it in person? While naked? This is practically a holy experience. Would it be too weird if I dropped to my knees in supplication? Because they are definitely quivering.

"What is wrong?" he barks.

I toss my head to the side and swallow hard, still rearranging my breasts and arms and hands, trying to cover all the various bits that have no hope of being covered right now. For the life of me, I can't recall the name of the reptile that just scared the crap out of me. "Brown crawling thing."

"Spider or lizard?"

Ah. There it is. "Lizard!"

Nikolai's thick eyebrow hitches upward. "A lizard has you screaming like you are being murdered?"

"Hey," I snap. "How about you save the lecture for later? You know, when I'm not naked?"

His gaze instantly drops, like my mentioning my state of undress is permission to finally look down. I stifle another scream, and he claps his hand over his eyes. The slap is hard enough to echo off the tiled walls and would have made me wince if I wasn't preoccupied with fumbling for the towel on the wall and wrapping it around myself before that hand falls away again.

"Okay," I mutter, holding the towel around me tightly. "Decent."

Nikolai drops his hand and assesses my new outfit. There is zero—and I mean zero—chance of me being able to ignore the fact that the front of his pajama pants have tented with an erection so large it's making my mouth water. Instead of ignoring the elephant in the room, Nikolai just reaches down and adjusts himself and suddenly I've forgotten all the reasons why I can't have a teeny tiny taste of this man.

He steps forward and I think maybe all my dreams have come true, but he sweeps by me, reaching into the shower. He lunges beyond the shower curtain and curses in Russian under his breath. He lunges again and that damn gecko (or lizard, I guess . . . how would one know the difference?) jumps out of the shower and makes a run for it in my direction. I let out another muffled scream and hustle to the other side of Nikolai, hiding behind his back.

The little guy runs right out the bathroom door as I peek around Nikolai in horror. It takes me a minute to realize that Nikolai is shaking, not in fright like me, but in laughter. I look up and up and up, seeing miles of tanned skin covering mounds of muscle. It takes my eyeballs years to make the trek, but they've never been so happy to cover so much ground. Yep, the man is laughing at me.

He spins and reaches for me, cupping my face and pulling me into his warm torso. Dear god, he's thick everywhere, making me feel like a small doll compared to him. I'm acutely aware there's just a flimsy towel between us. The look in his eyes holds humor, but also something else. Something that makes my belly swoop and my heart wish for things I know aren't possible.

"Two things, Chloe Cooper." His voice is a low, sexy grumble that has me leaning all my weight into him. "I will slay dragons for you. A little lizard is not a problem."

I've never had a man make dinner for me, let alone slay dragons. I know it's just a silly phrase and yet I believe Nikolai. He already saved me from a ruined house. "And two?" I whisper.

His eyes lose every ounce of humor, turning stormy as the sea in winter. "You are more beautiful than any woman that has ever existed. You should always be naked."

He flexes his hips, his erection harder than a sledgehammer as it presses into my soft belly. Proof that what he says is true. Before I can gather enough spit in my mouth to even attempt a response, he releases me and steps back. I'm suddenly cold, feeling like I had everything I ever wanted in my grasp one moment and I'm bereft the next. Which is crazy. I literally lost my husband a year ago and didn't feel this gaping sense of missing half of me.

Nikolai spins and leaves the bathroom without another word, closing the door behind him. I stand there, gripping my towel and staring at the space he just occupied, wondering what the hell has happened to me. Have I done the unthinkable? Have I developed *feelings* for this man? Because this all feels suspiciously like feelings that start with the letter L.

The next morning is a frenzy of activity from the second I wake up. The court-appointed guardian ad litem is coming today to assess Ayana's living situation with her father. Nikolai and I don't discuss the events from last night, which is fine by me. I need several more days to wrap my head around my feelings—especially when this year is supposed to be all about having fun, not weighing myself down with responsibilities and heavy things like falling for a guy I can never have.

A woman barrels through the door right as I'm finishing cooking eggs and toast for all of us. She nods at Nikolai and heads into the house, a vacuum in one hand and a bucket in the other.

"Who's that?" I ask, sitting down and pointing to the plates. Ayana digs in and Nikolai sits across from her, his own plate stacked with more eggs and toast than I can fathom one person can eat.

"I scheduled the housekeeper to come today. She normally

only comes once a month since I am usually by myself or traveling."

I finish chewing the bite in my mouth. "Oh, I was going to do laundry and run the vacuum around today."

Nikolai puts down his fork and gives me a serious look. "You do the sheets every other day. Your job is to be with Ayana, not clean this house. I should have hired her to come more often right from the beginning. I am sorry."

My cheeks heat. I flick a glance at Ayana, seeing that she's occupied with the iPad Nikolai lets her have for exactly one hour a day. I lean closer to him and lower my voice. "That's just from the hormonal night sweats. You didn't need to pay for her to be here more often. I can do my own sheets."

He frowns, eyebrows drawn together. "Night sweats even with the air conditioning going full blast?"

I shrug, used to this particular symptom. My doctor in Wisconsin assured me it was normal, especially considering the stress of the last few years. "Yeah. It's not really something that you can stop, even with an arctic blast. I sweat like a sinner in church almost every night. The AC is nice, but it doesn't stop the sweats. Old lady hormones are just hormoning."

He's still frowning as he shakes his head. "This is not right. Women should not have to go through this."

I grin. He's not wrong. "That's why we're the tougher of the two sexes."

"Agreed." He digs back into his breakfast while I try not to swoon over the fact he noticed my frequent trips to the laundry room and scheduled his housekeeper to take over.

"Hey, I talked to . . . the guy fixing my condo." I flap my hand in the air, searching for a word I can't seem to grasp. The guy with the toolbelt telling everyone else what to do. Damn this perimenopausal brain! "They should be done in the next few days. I'll be out of your hair before you know it." I keep that smile on my face, even as my heart sinks at the idea of not seeing Nikolai every day.

He puts his fork down again, looking puzzled as he says, "I like taking care of you. You are not . . . in my hair, as you say."

"Dad?" Ayana pipes up and we both swing our gazes over to her. She's looking at both of us, iPad forgotten, the corners of her lips turned down. "I don't want to leave."

Nikolai looks like he's been punched in the gut. Ayana knows she goes back to her mother's house tomorrow. Nikolai shoves his chair back and comes around to the other side to pull Ayana into a tight hug. "Your mother and I are working out a plan so that I can see you more often. I promise you. No more months in between visits."

My heart aches, seeing the two of them together. Then Ayana turns her sweet face in my direction, her blue eyes filled with tears. "But what about Chloe?"

I reach over and stroke her arm where she's still wrapped in a hug with her father. "I'll see you all the time at hockey practice, sweetie. And if your father is okay with it, we can do a few ice cream dates after practice, so we have a chance to talk."

She beams, tears forgotten. "Please, Dad?"

"We'll see about that. Ice cream is not good for you," Nikolai grumbles.

I snort and Ayana laughs. We both know we'll be going on those ice cream dates. He can't say no to us when we combine forces. I help clean up from breakfast, and when the guardian ad litem arrives a couple hours later, the place is spotless, Ayana is happily drawing at the kitchen table, and there's no way this woman can find fault in Nikolai's parenting. Especially when Ayana interrupts the interview to tell the woman about the horrible confetti cake we attempted to make a few nights ago and how we'd get kicked off *Bake Off* for baking such a sad-looking cake. No one can resist that little girl's giggle.

The woman leaves, but only after informing Nikolai she'll have a glowing review to give the judge. His shoulders drop away from his ears as he closes the door behind her. I put a hand on the middle of his back, so happy for him I could burst. He stiffens at my touch.

"You did it," I say quietly.

Nikolai spins around and glances at Ayana trying to sit on Paul's back while he dodges her advances and then looks up at me. "No, *we* did it."

He gives me one of his rare, unguarded smiles and that's when I know for sure. I've completely fallen in love with the grumpy goalie.

Chapter Twenty-Six

Niko

"You're late," Peyton announces upon opening her front door. Despite her downturned mouth, she looks flawless in a pink sundress and slicked-back ponytail, a full face of makeup on even though she is home alone on a Saturday morning.

"It is nice to see you too," I reply, hefting Ayana's bags up the steps. I drop them just inside the door before retreating to the edge of the porch.

My ex peers past me, her brow knitting. "Where is she?"

"In the car, saying goodbye to her dog." Paul started training last week, and Ayana is taking it quite seriously. The dog must now sit before he is allowed through any doorway by his tiny taskmaster.

Peyton folds her arms and frowns up at me. "I'm not getting a dog, you know."

"I did not ask you to."

She scoffs, flipping her ponytail. "Right. You're just the fun parent now who buys her puppies."

Since the last thing I want is an argument, I turn away, intent on retrieving our daughter from the vehicle.

"It's not all fun and games all the time, Niko. Parenting is hard work. Thankless work."

I pause, turning back to Peyton. "Yes. I am aware."

She sniffs. "You've got a nanny to do the work for you."

I take a breath and hold it for a few seconds to keep myself from losing my temper. "The nanny is for when I am working."

"I always schedule *my* work around Ayana's schedule. She needs a parent, not a nanny," she insists, a decidedly unsubtle note of superiority in her tone.

Despite my best efforts, my voice rises in response. "And *I* need to work so none of us are homeless and you and Ayana can enjoy a nice life." She knows as well as I do that her lifestyle would be substantially different without my money.

"We both know she should be with me." Her voice is little more than a hiss.

Now we are getting to the crux of the matter.

I sigh, sinking my hands into the pockets of my jeans as the sun relentlessly beats down on my head and shoulders. "I disagree. And so does the judge."

"We'll see."

"It is done, Peyton. The representative submitted her report and has approved of the home I can provide. The judge will grant joint custody."

I almost feel sympathy at her stricken expression, but she has gone to such lengths to keep my daughter from me that I cannot quite get there. Without another word, I walk to the Rover and hold Paul back as Ayana slips out the door. Paul paws the window with the most pathetic expression he can muster.

"Don't forget to keep up the training, Dad." Ayana looks up at me, worry in her eyes.

"I give you my word." I place one hand over my heart and the other on her head, memorizing her features and trying to loosen the knot in my chest.

"Baby!" Peyton exclaims, bounding down the stone steps to intercept us on the walkway. She folds our daughter in a tight embrace. "Goodness, I missed you," she says into Ayana's hair.

"Did you know I'm on a real hockey team now?" Ayana asks, pulling from her mother's arms. "And the dog trainer says I'm an excellent trainer and should maybe consider making it my life's work."

I cannot help the quirk of my lips.

"Wow." I must give Peyton credit for not reacting with the disdain I know she is feeling inside.

Our daughter's next words, however, test Peyton's acting ability beyond its limits.

"And wait till you meet Chloe! She's not just a nanny; she's a killer hockey player too. She's my coach *and* she makes super yummy pancakes *and* she loves dogs. She's ah-mazing!" Ayana's gesticulations only add to her enthusiasm—and to the tic in Peyton's jaw.

"I see," is all she manages, but Ayana has already turned to hug me goodbye.

I crouch down, allowing her to throw her arms around my neck while I pull her to me. "Bye, Dad. I'll miss you tons."

"Goodbye, *zajushka*," I tell her as I stroke her fine hair. "I will see you very soon. I promise."

With that, she breaks free of my hold and races up the steps and into the house, calling behind her, "Take care of Paul and Chloe!"

I straighten and turn to leave, anxious to exit the scene before Peyton has a chance to deliver another speech. But it is impossible to miss my ex-wife's expression. It is one I have seen before, and it fills me with uneasiness because it is the kind she wears when she is preparing for battle. And that is the last thing any of us need.

My mood is foul the rest of the day, and I take it out on Mac, even though he has been doing his best to toe the line these past two weeks and put in the proper effort. When I shout at him for missing a puck even I would have had trouble intercepting, I know it is time to call it quits for the day.

I grind out a weak apology and stalk from the locker room in search of peace. When my mind immediately goes to Chloe, my steps quicken as if I might have the ability to outrun my own thoughts. It is no use.

She was gone when Ayana and I woke this morning, having left only a note for Ayana on the dining table. "See you soon! XOXO." It has not escaped my attention that she has been avoiding me ever since our encounter in her bathroom. The image of her naked body is burned into my brain, and I hope it never recedes. The woman tests my self-control like no one ever has, and it brings me a level of discomfort and confusion I do not often experience.

I am used to always being in control, and Chloe makes me feel as if I am driving while blindfolded. My skin feels too tight for my body as I pull from the parking lot and tear down the street, nearly running a red light as my mind races. Fuck. I need to pull myself together.

When I arrive home, Chloe's Bronco is in the driveway, but the house is empty. It is quieter than I remember, Ayana and Chloe's voices having filled it for the last two weeks. The only sounds are Paul's nails on the tile and the dull hum of the air conditioner. When I look for another note from Chloe, this time for me, I do not find one.

"You're sure you flipped the fuse off, right?" Benny asks through my earbud.

"Of course," I mumble around the small flashlight clenched between my teeth.

Benny's family owns a construction supply company, so he was the first person I thought to call for help with my little home improvement project.

"Once you remove the plate, you should see wires with plastic connectors." He pauses. "Tell me again why you can't just wait till Monday and get a handyman to install it."

I finish unscrewing the plate and drop it to the mattress beneath my socked feet before pulling the flashlight from my mouth. "Because it has to be tonight." That is all the explanation he needs.

While I have much experience with farm chores and physical labor, installing a ceiling fan is beyond my scope of expertise. Still, I am determined to complete this project before Chloe returns from wherever she might be tonight.

My restlessness from the earlier silence and the absence of my two companions meant that I had to find another purpose for my hands and mind. Before I knew it, I found myself at the local hardware store purchasing a ceiling fan for the guest room. Chloe's room. I had not thought any further than procuring it when I realized I should probably call for help before electrocuting myself.

"Okay, okay," Benny says. "Tell me, am I going to be this grumpy when I become a dad?"

When I ignore his question, he continues with the next set of instructions. It takes over an hour to finish, during which Kaitlyn commandeers Benny's phone to pepper me with poorly disguised inquiries about Chloe and me. But I deflect them by asking about her pregnancy and sharing unflattering stories about her fiancé.

I am just clearing up the last of the mess when headlights flash through the draped window, telling me that either Chloe has returned or the Jehovah's Witness evangelists have started working nights.

While I do not know for certain where Chloe has been, I have not been able to ignore the likelihood that she was out on a date. My conflicting emotions on the matter are concerning, which is why I have steadfastly pushed them aside all evening.

The two distinct voices—one feminine and familiar and the other foreign and masculine—coming from the front porch have my pulse galloping, and I force myself to continue hauling the fan packaging to the garage. This is none of my business.

As I re-enter the house, the sound of the front door closing brings my spine stick straight. Did she invite him in? Is she taking him to her bedroom? Red clouds my vision at the thought, a mix of anger, denial, and self-loathing racing through me and lighting every muscle, bone, and string of sinew in my body. I am moving before I know it, my feet closing the distance to the front door.

And then . . . there she is. Alone and achingly beautiful in a red dress the same color as her trademark lipstick. I catch a glimpse of her lower lip trapped between her teeth before her mouth drops open and her startled eyes lift to my face. Whatever she sees there has her blue irises going liquid and her cheeks flushing with pink.

"How was your date?" My voice sounds foreign—a sharp strum on a cable stretched tight enough to snap.

A sense of intense dread washes over me as her eyes drop. I command myself to turn and leave her alone, but the soles of my feet have grown roots. After what feels like an entire season, she merely shrugs one shoulder before returning her eyes to mine, this time with one corner of her mouth lifted.

"Meh," is her answer, but it is followed by a yelp of surprise as I advance with undisguised intent, walking her backward until her shoulders hit the entryway wall and my lips slam down on hers.

Chapter Twenty-Seven

Chloe

I have exactly two-point-five seconds to feel relief that I let Tanner down gently tonight, insisting he would remain in the friendzone. He took it well, making me doubt myself for telling him no. On paper, he had all the things to make for a perfect date, and yet I felt nothing sitting across the table from him at dinner. I refuse to settle for anything less than fucking fireworks. Which is exactly what happens when Nikolai pounces.

His kiss is nothing like that night in Toronto. It blows that one right out of the water, like a tiny peck from a schoolboy compared to the hot, raging man now consuming me like I might be the key to his survival. His hands tilt my head where he wants me, his tongue and lips taking control of the kiss without even a hint of seeking permission. Thing is, I gave him permission months ago. He just hadn't acted on it. Until now.

My hands fly to his muscled waist, fisting the material there while I try to keep up. His teeth nip at my bottom lip before his tongue drags across the abused skin. The hands that held me in place and probably made an absolute wreck of my hair now slide down to my hips and hoist me up. I gasp and go to wrap my legs around his waist, but the dress hinders me. His growl of frustration rumbles my own chest. He sets me back down on my feet and doesn't hesitate.

"I apologize," he barks before grabbing both sides of the slit that shows off my left thigh every time I take a step. The man rips the material, a renting noise filling the silence between us. A draft hits the skin above my hip as I gape down at my dress, now exposing my matching red satin panties. He fucking ripped my dress apart.

Why is that so fucking hot?

He lunges again, his mouth coming down on mine while he hoists me up, my back sliding easily against the wall. This time, I get my legs around his waist and my arms around his neck. My high heels fall off and I can't be bothered. He presses me into the wall, an impressive erection digging into my core and making me light-headed. His hand leaves my hip to cup my breast through my dress. He wrenches his mouth away from me to stare down at the white flesh.

"Fucking hell, Chloe. How are you so beautiful?"

The question must be rhetorical because he doesn't wait for an answer. Roughly pulling down the top of my dress and bra in one tug, he exposes my breast and hisses. The same devastating combo of teeth, lips, and tongue are now on my breast, teasing my nipple and leaving red marks along the pale globe. I toss my head back—breathing so heavily I feel like I've been running—and promptly hit it against the wall.

Nikolai's face comes up, his eyes burning hot as he takes me in, hair a disaster, breast exposed, and my dress ripped to hell. He lets out a feral growl and pulls me off the wall. I tighten my arms around his neck and let him carry me through the house. Stalking is more like it. The man can move fast, something I've seen out on the ice, but never in this capacity. He carries me as if I weigh nothing. A mental image of Josh refusing to pick me up and carry me over the threshold of our house when we got married flashes through my brain and I push it away. He has no place here in this thing with me and Nikolai.

Nikolai stops short of his bed and runs his hand through my hair, looking at me with something I've never seen before. Gone is the familiar aggression from earlier, replaced by a look of caring so strong it makes my eyes water. He lowers me down gently to the edge of the bed. I'm so focused on keeping eye contact and memorizing this new expression, I can't take in the details of his bedroom. He kneels on the floor between my legs, his face now even with mine. His hands never leave my skin, just swooping up and over and around, like he can't stop touching me. It's enough to make me mewl like a cat.

"Chloe," he breathes, "I cannot deny you any longer. I should. I should push you away and keep you far from me." He bows his head over my lap.

I used to be a silent partner, letting my husband lead and stuffing down my concerns. I vowed after Josh's death not to live that way any longer. So I run both hands through Nikolai's hair and pull his head up sharply. His eyes hold a note of regret in those ocean blue depths, and I refuse to have any of that enter whatever this is between us.

"You and I both want this. Doesn't that matter more than everyone else? Why are we denying ourselves some fun?" I tug on his hair harder, hoping it'll make him listen. "I haven't had fun in a long time and I'd like to have it with you."

His eyes briefly shut, and he turns his head to kiss the inside of my wrist. "I cannot offer you a relationship, which is most certainly what you deserve."

I let out the saddest laugh I've ever heard. "I don't want a relationship. Had one of those and it ended horrifically." I lean in and place a kiss on both sides of his mouth, letting his whiskers scrape against my skin. "Can you just make me feel good, Nikolai? Just for tonight?"

We both still, my question hanging there between us. Then he lunges, his mouth fusing to mine, a promise of pleasure and nothing more between two people who care about each other but have no future. It's exactly what I set out to do when I moved to Tampa. Exactly what I wished for. Exactly what I need. All those feelings I thought I had for Nikolai? Misplaced sexual longing, clearly. Nothing in my past could prepare me for how badly I want Nikolai. This is new territory for me and it's clear I was confused.

Nikolai gets to his feet, the kiss going on and on until he breaks away, chest heaving. The room could be on fire and I wouldn't notice. He lets me go and takes a step back, his gaze burning into my skin. He lifts his shirt over his head and tosses it aside. That physique I got a glimpse of the other night is right in front of me. Except this time, his hands go to the buttons of his jeans as he works them open. My mouth goes dry, and my gaze tracks his progress. He shoves the material down and out springs the most perfect cock—long, thick, and perfectly veined. Instinctively, I reach for it.

"No," he commands and I freeze, greedy hand in the air. "I have been waiting months for this, and I have very specific things in mind. I hope you do not intend to sleep tonight, Chloe Cooper."

I swallow hard and gaze up at him, taking in the finest physique I've ever seen in person. The man should retire from hockey and become an underwear model. Pose nude for artists. Be the next inspiration for a sculpture. Hell, an Only Fans account would make him more money than hockey.

"Look now while you can," he threatens, holding perfectly still. My heart's beating so hard I'm not sure this is healthy.

Goddamn, he's even hotter when he's bossy. "Stand up and turn around."

I obey, though my legs are quaking so badly, I'm not sure I'll be able to stay on my feet for long if that's what he has planned for me. His hands gently glide the zipper down the back of my ruined dress, leaving a line of goosebumps in their wake. Rough fingers slide the straps off my shoulders and the dress falls to the ground. I've never been so thankful for my obsession with beautiful and expensive lingerie. It went unappreciated by Josh, but based on the deep growl coming from behind me, Nikolai is a man who appreciates the finer things.

He unclasps the bra and assists its fall to the floor. And then his touch is gone.

"You have tempted me every day," he mutters menacingly.

I'm trembling, just seconds away from begging him to touch me again. I look over my shoulder to gauge his next move. He has one giant hand wrapped around his cock, stroking it as he zeros his attention in on my backside. I'm about to turn, but he barks out another command.

"Get on the bed on all fours."

I swallow hard, not sure about putting myself into that type of compromising position. Maybe I could ask to turn off the bedside lamp first? I'm realizing quickly that everything I've participated in before could be classified as very, very vanilla.

"Now, Chloe."

I jump, realizing that Nikolai is in control here and I, for one, want to see what he does with it. I scramble onto the bed exactly as he instructed, but he barks at me to back up until my toes are hanging over the bed. He steps up right behind me, the heat of him searing my skin. My breaths are now audible gasps. His hand grips the material between my cheeks and rubs it ruthlessly back and forth over my wet flesh. It's vulgar and rough and so damn amazing I have to bite my lip to keep from crying out.

"How many times can you come in one night?" Another slide of that material across my aching clit. I release my lip to utter an incomprehensible *I don't know*. "Let us find out, yes?"

"Yes!" I gasp, proud of myself for getting a single word out of my mouth.

His chuckle is deep and low. The sound of material ripping has me squeezing my eyes shut. My pretty panties are gone, and I can't even be sad they met their demise. Not when Nikolai's knees hit the carpet behind me and his hands slide up my cheeks. He parts me, making me gasp and then nearly swallow my own tongue when he boldly licks me front to back. My arms buckle and it's my face jammed in the bed that's supporting my upper body now.

"Yes, *malish*, just like that." His tongue takes the same trip again, this time focusing on either end before a long, thick finger slides inside of me. His finger glides in and out, stretching me when he adds another digit. His tongue finds the puckered knot of muscle no one has entertained before, teasing a series of uncoordinated gasps out of me as my whole body begins to shake.

My heart is about to explode right out of my chest. I'm barely dragging air in and out and I can't seem to focus on anything but his tongue, his fingers, those hands holding me ruthlessly open for him. Every ribbon of desire in my gut turns to flames licking across my insides in an inferno that finally decimates.

I scream his name into the mattress and tremble so badly I lose all control over my muscles. His tongue and fingers keep going, torturing me, not giving me one second to ride the wave and come down gently. My guttural whimpers turn to a maniacal laugh. Here I wanted to turn off the lamp and now I'm face down, ass up, spread out for Nikolai's tongue to explore every nook and cranny.

The world flips around as I'm turned onto my back. Nikolai crawls up my body, his hard whiskered jaw wet, and his beautiful eyes a steely gray. He settles between my thighs, his erection wedged between us. I reach one arm up, barely able to feel the limb, and dive my fingers into his hair.

"Are you trying to kill me?" I ask in all seriousness. A bubble of insane laughter escapes my throat yet again.

His answering smile is that of a wolf, about to eat his prey. "The night has just begun, *malish*," He rolls to his back beside me, leaving me without the blanket of his heat. "Come sit on me so I can look at your beautiful body while I'm inside you."

I look up at the ceiling and have an out-of-body experience. Here it is, everything I wanted when I moved to Tampa to start my life over again. A hot, gorgeous man who wants nothing from me but my body. And yet . . . I'm scared.

Rolling over, I nestle into Nikolai's side, not on top of him like he firmly suggested. "Are you sure about that? I mean, wouldn't a little missionary be fun instead?"

He lifts his head, looking so pissed off I shrink back. "Are you fucking with me?"

"Umm." Is this a trick question? A language barrier issue?

"I'm trying to fuck you, yes. But not fuck *with* you."

Nikolai grinds his teeth together, reaches for me, and sprawls me on top of him before cupping my face and forcing me to look at him. "You have the most gorgeous body I have ever seen and you do not want me to look at it? Why are you so cruel, Chloe?"

My jaw drops open and I have no words. Which is fine, because he's not done.

"Ride my cock right now or I will get a belt."

Now I'm truly gaping, which I'm sure is very attractive. "A belt?" I squeak. "To tie me to the bed?" I'm so out of my comfort zone it's not even funny. That phrase about being careful what you wish for floats through my addled brain.

Nikolai only frowns harder. "No. So I can use it on your beautiful ass for talking badly about the body I desire."

"Hey!" I sputter, though the idea of me draped across his lap receiving my punishment forms like an X-rated movie in my brain, and I find I like it.

He lifts an eyebrow in challenge. I narrow my eyes at him, push off his chest, and shift backward until I feel that cock digging into my backside. "Fuck your belt, Nikolai Drugov."

It's time to put my money where my mouth is and live my life to the fullest. I have a hot, willing man in bed with me, a man millions of women would do shady things to be with. If he wants me to ride him like a Russian stallion, I'm going to fucking do it. Because if I don't, I'll be so disappointed with myself. And life's too short for regrets.

I hold out my hand, happy to note it's no longer trembling. "Hand me a condom, cowboy."

Chapter Twenty-Eight

Niko

I seldom think of myself as a stupid man, but as the word "mine" echoes off the walls of my skull, I must acknowledge that I am the worst kind of idiot. And I do not fucking care. Not right now when Chloe looms over me, rumpled and warm, her lips bruised from my kisses and her chin pink with beard burn.

I allow her to roll the condom over my cock as her soft thighs straddle my hips and her gorgeous breasts bob before me for the taking. A perfect handful each, just as I prefer them. It takes a lot to fill hands my size.

It is not as if I have been celibate since Peyton, but I have certainly been careful—and picky, ignoring the advances of puck bunnies and preferring instead to bed women who have no knowledge of my profession or, often, my name. It is better that way.

But this—being with Chloe—brings a sort of intimacy I have no experience with, no reference point with which to compare it. Yes, Peyton and I were married, but I am unsure we ever even *liked* one another. We married because she was pregnant. No other reason, nor did she appear to require one.

But Chloe is my friend. We share genuine affection, which makes fucking her not only indescribably stupid but dangerously complicated. I told her I cannot offer a relationship, and she agreed this is only about scratching an itch, but I cannot afford any confusion before I take her body.

So, despite ninety-nine percent of the blood in my veins currently residing in my cock, I manage to rein in the remaining one percent to shore up a handful of brain cells and pause. "Chloe," I draw her attention, my voice ragged.

She looks up from my straining dick, which is now half covered in latex, to meet my gaze. Fiery lust fills the blue of her irises, her pupils wide and her chest heaving. "What?" Her voice is breathy when she stills her hands.

"I want to make sure we . . . both truly understand what this is . . . and what it is not." I am unsure which of us needs the reminder.

She grins then, leaning forward to drop a quick kiss on my lips before straightening again. "What do I keep telling you?" She doesn't pause before answering her own question. "You need to lighten up, big guy."

Since there is only one way to interpret her words, I release that last 1 percent to do its worst while Chloe resumes her task. I vow to make her pant my name as many times as possible before dawn—and real life—break in.

As soon as I am sheathed, she rises to her knees, stroking my cock before positioning the head at her entrance.

"Stop," I command, causing her eyes to flash back to mine. "You will go slow. I will not have you hurting yourself, *malish*." I am big—proportional to the rest of my body, which makes me more than some women can take.

She draws in a breath and lowers herself until just the head of my cock is seated in her heat. She groans. "I'm not sure if I can go slow." When she hastily rises and drops her pelvis farther this time, I lock my jaw and brace her hips with both hands to halt her movements.

"You *will*."

The steel in my tone has her nodding and finally obeying. Her next movement is slow and controlled as she takes more of me, causing us both to groan. She is impossibly tight and wet around my cock, and I regret the need for a condom. I want to be coated in her juices and spill my cum into her like the beast I am.

As with all things in my life, I take fucking very seriously. If anything is worth my attention, it gets my entire attention and effort. It has proven to be too much for some women, but everyone has their own preferences. Mine lean toward women who like being controlled in the bedroom and allow me to make their pleasure my objective.

"Good god." Chloe's head falls back on her next downward slide. "'Big Guy' is beyond fitting as a nickname." One more rise and fall, and I am finally seated fully inside her, tight in her body's grip. She brings her head up, a half laugh escaping her throat. "I'm a little concerned you might puncture a lung."

I frown at her, my hands freezing on their path to her breasts. "Are you in pain?"

This time, her laugh is followed by a groan, and I move to pull her off me. She bats my hands away and reseats herself, sheathing me to the root.

"Don't you dare! I was joking." When she groans this time, I recognize it as pleasure instead of pain.

My hands fall to the sheet under me, my frown intensifying. "You think this is funny?"

When her only response is a wide grin, I decide Chloe Cooper is in need of a lesson she will not soon forget. Before she can so much as blink, I flip her to her back and drive my cock inside her until she gasps. Her thighs hug my hips as she moans, "More."

I need no further invitation. My strokes are measured but strong. But when she winds her arms around me, her hands beginning to explore my back and shoulders, I halt all movement. Chloe whimpers in protest.

"Hands above your head," I instruct. "I want you focusing on my cock taking your pretty pussy and nothing else."

Her immediate compliance has the beast inside me purring with contentment. "Good girl," I murmur before resuming my thrusts into her wet heat. Her mewls and moans are too much, so I take her mouth with mine and we mimic our bodies' movements with our tongues, delving and retreating.

When I feel the first flutters of her inner muscles around my cock, I tear my mouth from hers and shift to my knees. Gripping one creamy thigh in each hand, I jerk her into me as I thrust forward, my eyes trained on her pink, swollen pussy taking the length of my cock over and over.

"Nikolai." The word is a plea, but I do not relent in my motions, driving into her until she spasms wildly around me. Her back arches off the bed and her head digs into the mattress as she whimpers my name. Every muscle in her body is drawn tight as I continue to fuck her through her orgasm.

Sweat drips from my forehead into my eyes, and I swipe it away as the familiar rush of adrenaline races across my back, and my balls draw almost painfully tight. Chloe is mewling beneath me, her arms still above her head like the good girl she is.

I readjust my grip on her thighs, our skin slick with perspiration as I piston faster, the loud, repeated slap of my pelvis against her luscious ass and thighs reverberating around the room.

Then my vision clouds with white, and I'm coming hard and long, never letting up my pace until the last shockwave rushes down my spine and I am utterly drained. My body collapses to the bed, but I am careful to land just beside Chloe, pulling her limp body with me so we remain connected.

Ragged breaths spill from my lungs as Chloe's face collides with my shoulder and she quietly pants what sounds like a mantra. "Holy shit. Holy shit. Holy shit."

I slide an arm around her waist, drawing her even closer. "Are you all right?" I manage to ask over the heaving of my chest.

"With utmost sincerity, I can promise you I have never been better."

I can feel her lips curving against my skin, and a sense of profound satisfaction settles deep within my chest.

"I will need a few minutes to recover, I am afraid."

This time she barks out a laugh, and it is only then that I realize this might be the first time there has been laughter in my bed. To my mind, humor and fucking are the most improbable of bedfellows. But to think of Chloe without a ready smile on her lips or a chuckle in her throat is even more incongruous.

When my breathing returns to normal, I reluctantly pull out of her, securing the condom as I do. "Stay here," I instruct before climbing out of bed to dispose of the rubber in my bathroom.

When I return with a warm washcloth in hand, it is to find Chloe reclining with a sheet pulled up to her neck. My nostrils flare as I bend and yank the sheet down, tearing the entire thing from the bed and tossing it to the floor in one motion.

Chloe gasps and brings a hand to her breasts, but I only respond with an order. "Thighs apart, *malish*. Now."

Instead of complying, Chloe narrows her eyes and asks, "You keep saying that. What does it mean?"

Without answering, I sit on the bed and run a hand gently up one of her legs. When she finally allows me to guide her thighs apart, I say, "It is a . . . what is the word? A name you call someone special."

Her face softens at that. "An endearment."

"Yes, an endearment," I confirm before lifting the washcloth to her mound.

"There's really no need," Chloe says as I lay the cloth over the pink skin. "We used a condom."

"It is for soreness," I explain, concentrating on my task.

"Oh." She allows herself to relax back into the mattress. "Thanks." Her tone is almost shy.

But I am afraid I have veered into territory that is only shared by people with a different kind of intimacy between them, so I add, "I am nowhere near finished with you tonight, and I need you to keep up."

I cannot help but chuckle when her responding gulp is audible.

Two hours—and two orgasms—later, Chloe is having difficulty keeping her eyes open. "So, where did you learn English?" she asks over a yawn.

I bring my folded arm behind my head to prop it up while she burrows into my chest. It feels too damn good having her soft curves relaxed against my body, skin to skin. "I moved to Canada to play when I was twenty years old. The only English words I knew were 'hamburger' and 'hockey.'"

"Well," Chloe murmurs, "That's really all a guy needs when you think about it."

My lips tip. "I suppose. But I soon learned enough from my teammates and from watching old television programs at night. *Laverne and Shirley* and *Happy Days* were my favorites."

She lifts her head to smile drowsily at me. "I am such a

sucker for anything fifties and sixties, in case you can't tell from my personal style."

"Ah. I knew there was a reason I liked all of your tops."

She dips her chin into my chest again and laughs. "Yeah, I'm sure that's the only reason."

I drag a finger over her bare shoulder and smile to myself. "My teammates waited an entire season before telling me no one has used the words 'nifty' or 'shucks' in forty years. I was beginning to wonder how my luck with women was so awful."

Her body shakes with her silent laughter.

"To this day, I have never figured out what a *shlemiel* or a *schlimazel* are," I confess, referencing the words used in the theme song for one of the shows.

"Me neither," Chloe responds, following it with another giant yawn.

We are both quiet for a few minutes while I absently caress the soft skin of her shoulder. When her breathing begins to even and slow, I am faced with a conundrum. As good as it feels lying here with Chloe, sleeping in the same bed is a mistake. However, there is no way I would ask her to leave, so I resolve to sleep in Ayana's room or on the couch since I long ago turned the fourth bedroom into a home gym.

"I am going to shower," I whisper before carefully disentangling myself and shifting sideways to the edge of bed.

"Hmm," Chloe hums, eyes closed and body limp under the sheet we retrieved from the floor. She is so fucking beautiful. Her eyes blink open once, then twice, and when she sees me standing beside the bed, she jerks up to prop herself on an elbow. "Oh! Sorry. I fell asleep." Her unfocused eyes dart around the carpeted floor. "I'll grab my clothes and go."

I narrow my eyes and return to the bed on hands and knees, not stopping until she is trapped under me, wide eyes taking in my stern expression.

"You will not."

"Nikolai," she protests. "We already agreed this is just sex. I don't need to sleep in your bed."

I bend closer until I feel the brush of her breath on my cheek. "You are right, *malish*," I whisper. "It is only fucking. But when you are in my bed, that entire gorgeous body— including your sweet pussy—belongs to me. And I am telling you to close your eyes and go back to sleep."

I don't wait for any response. Instead, I close the small gap and kiss her hard and deep before taking my half-hard cock to the bathroom for a long shower. When I emerge thirty minutes later, I find Chloe sprawled out naked on my bed, sheet thrown to the floor once more. Any urge to smile at the sight, however, is tempered by the uneasiness that progressively grew and settled as I showered.

So, I pad quietly from the room in search of a place to pretend to sleep until morning.

Chapter Twenty-Nine

Chloe

My eyes flicker open to see the barest hint of sunlight coming through the closed blinds across the room. I immediately look to my right, to the empty side of this king bed that smells of Nikolai and sex. Not even an indentation is left to indicate that Nikolai came back to bed with me at some point. I sit upright, clutching a sheet to my bare breasts, suddenly feeling awkward and out of place. This is Nikolai's room. His bed. I shouldn't be here. Clearly. The man couldn't even bring himself to sleep next to me. I cringe, thinking of him being irritated that I essentially kicked him out of his own bed, even with that last line he gave me about owning certain parts of my anatomy.

I scramble to my feet and tuck the sheet around me like I'm attending the world's lamest toga party for one and gaze down at the perfect imprint of my body on his sheets. A sweat outline.

"Fucking great," I mutter, leaning down to rip the fitted

sheet off the bed. I'll have to do Nikolai's sheets before I leave for the ice rink. At least there's one good outcome of him not sleeping with me last night. I didn't night sweat all over him.

I march out of the room, arms full of bed linens and also trying to keep the sheet around me tucked under my arm. I don't hear Nikolai in the house, which isn't surprising. He's probably training with the goalies or off on a run. With my up close and personal perusal of his body last night, I can easily believe the man is most definitely working out any moment he isn't asleep.

Throwing the bedding into the washing machine, I close it and throw in some detergent, reaching up into the cabinet to grab a clean pool towel. Before it's fully wrapped around my body, Nikolai raps his knuckles against the doorway, startling me. I make sure both boobs are covered and turn his direction, a smile pasted on my face.

"Hey. I thought you were working out."

What does one do with their hands the morning after one-sided incredible, life changing sex and they're barely covered in a towel? I settle for one hand on the washing machine and one hand on my hip. Hey, look at me. All casual and shit when what I want to do is run from the room and hide. Nikolai looks better than ever, if a little sleepy with the puffy eyes and unruly hair. The shorts are riding low on his lean hips and his chest is bare. He's unfairly handsome whereas I probably look like a sweat-soaked troll.

"More sheets?" he asks, voice rough and rumbly and so damn delicious I forget for a second that he never came back to bed.

I clear my throat and focus on keeping things friendly between us. That's what I agreed to, right?

"Yeah. It's a known thing with perimenopause. Nothing to worry about. Just an annoyance."

He frowns, crossing his beefy arms over his chest. "What is this perimenopause? You are too young for this, yes?"

"Well, I'm forty-two and this stage of life can last up to ten years, so no, not too young. It's just most women don't talk about it, which is a shame. I could have really used a heads up." I tighten the towel around me. "It started a little before Josh passed away. Given our battle with his cancer, I was concerned that maybe I was sick too. Several blood tests later and the doctors informed me I was merely dealing with hormone issues. No big deal."

Nikolai, still frowning, steps into the laundry room and pulls my hands from the towel to hold in his. "Do not do that."

"Do what?" Don't sleep in your bed? Got it. Won't do that again, believe me.

"Do not downplay something that affects you. This has been a shift in your life, yes?" At my nod, he continues. "Then it is worthy of talking about. And worthy of me listening."

My heart, the organ I locked away behind a thick wall of easy breezy friendship and nothing more, thumps in my chest. I squeeze his hands and tell my eyeballs to cooperate. Crying will not be tolerated.

"Thanks," I say thickly.

He gives my hands a tug and suddenly he's kissing me, his broad shoulders blocking out the garish overhead lights and creating a cocoon of just him and me. He releases my hands and cups my face, deepening the kiss. And then he's gone, letting me go and inching backward.

"I must go. See you later tonight?"

I nod, head spinning, unsure if he wants me here or what we're doing with each other. He leaves and I hide like a scaredy cat in the laundry room until I hear the garage door open, his car fire up, and the garage door close once again. I push out a long breath and rush to my room, hurrying to get ready. It's only when I come out of the shower that I see it.

A brand new ceiling fan. Installed in my room. Along with a remote next to my bed.

My eyes squeeze shut and I curse Nikolai in my head. He is not making this easy. He's doing all the things that would make a woman fall for him. A woman like me.

I pull out my phone and shoot off a text.

> Me: Did you install a ceiling fan in my room?

> Nikolai: We have already established that these night sweats are a problem. Your comfort matters.

It's a simple statement and yet more profound than anything anyone has said to me in decades. I flop back on my bed and groan up at the ceiling fan. Dammit. Why is he so sweet? Josh didn't do considerate things like that. I'd have to remind him about our anniversary or pick out the clothes he should wear when we went to a fancy restaurant. He was a good man, don't get me wrong, but sweet and attentive was not in his wheelhouse.

"Don't even think about it," I tell my heart out loud. She pounds against my ribs anyway.

> Me: Thank you.

I have time to meet up with Dad before my first league practice starts. Or I would if I could find him. I've been bumbling around the practice facility for fifteen minutes looking for him and so far, he's evaded me. Imagining both of us circling this place and never finding each other, I decide to think like a lost kid at a grocery store and stay in one place. I plop my ass down in the chair in his office and wait him out. He shows up ten minutes later, his hair looking like he hit a windtunnel on the way in. He nearly takes out the door with a well-placed kick when he sees me in his office.

"Chloe?"

I stand and put my hand on his arm to steady him. The man is fit, but also getting older. I don't need him falling. "Hey, Dad. Glad you remember me."

He gives me a deadpan look and closes the door before having a seat behind his desk. "To what do I owe this visit?"

"Were you at lunch?"

He clears his throat and starts opening and closing drawers. "Nope, just making it in today. Did you wait long?"

I know there's a moment in every child's life when the tables turn and suddenly you're the mature one and they're the ones who need supervision, but I thought I had longer before that moment arrived for me. Dad's acting suspicious as hell. Then again, I guess we both have a little secret we're hiding.

"Ten minutes or so. Just thought I'd swing by and see how the interviews are going for your replacement."

He settles into his chair, looking more like himself now that we're back on a topic he eats, sleeps, and breathes. "Good, good. I'm lucky management includes me in everything still. Wants my opinion of each candidate. I need someone who will keep the culture of the team front and center. If the team is in turmoil, you can kiss that Stanley Cup run goodbye."

"The Storm Chasers seem to get along pretty well, don't they?"

He chuckles. "There've been a few over the years who threatened the vibes, but we've got a solid team now. Though it'll change when Niko retires next year." He leans forward, hands clasped on the desk. "How are things going with him and his daughter, by the way? He keeping his hands to himself?"

My cheeks, the goddamn traitors they are, nearly give me away. "Yes, Dad. Jeez. I'm forty-two, not a teenager you need to protect with a shotgun."

He studies me for a moment and then nods, sitting back. "I know, pumpkin. But in my mind, you'll always need protecting. Besides, after you made me Google The Villages, my mind has been opened to sexual activity long after retirement age."

I wince. "Okay. New topic, please."

He chuckles. "Ready for your first practice? I've been hearing great things about your open houses. I'll check things out in between packing up my office."

I sit up straighter. "Yeah, I'm really excited to get to be back in front of kids. I don't want to teach full time, but hockey lessons will keep me tied into the youth of the nation."

Dad dips his head. "Bet."

We both crack up at the slang and I stand. "Okay, well, this has been enlightening. See you later?"

Dad gets up too and comes around the desk to hug me. "Yeah, actually, I was hoping to take you to dinner soon. Let me know what days you're available?"

I agree and head down to the rink to get my skates on, wondering if that was a casual invite or if he has someone he wants to introduce me to at a restaurant where I can't pitch a fit over a new woman in his life. There's no way I'd have a problem with him dating. I know exactly what it feels like to be alone, and I don't want that for my father now that he'll have more free time on his hands. A little voice in the back of my head screams that I should come clean with him about Nikolai too, but she shuts up as the first kid arrives for practice.

Working my way through the new arrivals, I've talked to

eight concerned parents and tied six pairs of skates for kids who aren't sure they got it right when a little voice steals my attention. "Chloe!"

I turn, nearly falling backward in my crouch as Ayana barrels into me. I hug her back, steady myself, and then get to my feet. "You made it!"

"Introduce me, Ayana," interrupts her mom.

I look up and hold out my hand, refusing to acknowledge that the woman looks like she stepped away from a fashion shoot to drop her daughter off. "Chloe Cooper." I don't bother to mention she already knows who I am. I was at the court hearing and we both know it.

She grasps the tips of my fingers in a weak handshake. "Peyton Drugov, Ayana's mother."

The smile I give her is as fake as the one she gives me. Hearing Nikolai's last name attached to hers is enough to turn my stomach. Matt, the assistant coach I hired, blows his whistle, interrupting us and saving me from small talk I just don't have in me right now.

"Everyone line up on the ice once you have your skates on! Coach Chloe is going to show us how to skate with our sticks."

"Got your skates handled?" I ask Ayana, ignoring her mother entirely.

"Her father has already shown her how to lace them," Peyton says, emphasizing *her father*.

My smile cranks up. "Great! Then I'll leave you to it." I walk away and head for the ice. I have a practice to run, not time for some pissing match with Nikolai's ex-wife.

Given that this is our first practice, I still give each kid a pool noodle, not an actual hockey stick to hold. Still, many of them use it as a sword or put it on top of their heads like a unicorn horn. By the time we have a moving line of hockey players actually holding the noodles like a stick, I glance up to see Nikolai has joined the stands with the other parents. Peyton is trying to talk to him, her arm pasted to his leg as she leans into his personal space.

Not my monkey, not my circus, I repeat to myself, over and over.

Another glance shows Nikolai's gaze trained on me and Ayana. Back and forth, checking on us both while Peyton chats away. When we move into another drill, I hazard another glance in the stands. Peyton has her arms crossed over her chest and a scowl aimed directly at me.

Chapter Thirty

Niko

"Dad!" Ayana shouts as she staggers on her skates over the rubber floor toward me. She trips at the last second, but I easily catch her, making her giggle. "Did you see me out there?"

"You are almost ready to try out for the Storm Chasers," I say, unbuckling her helmet and pulling it from her head. In reality, the kids all spent more time falling than skating, but there were no tears, so I assume Chloe would consider that a win.

"Bathtime when we get home," Peyton says from beside me. "You're a sweaty mess."

"I know." Our daughter grins in delight, showing off the new gap in her teeth. The tooth mouse came to visit last week when she was with Chloe and me, and Ayana relished the opportunity to introduce her nanny to the tradition. The look on Chloe's face when Ayana said she needed to leave her tooth under the bathtub had both of us laughing.

"Are you ready for your first day of school tomorrow?" I ask, ruffling her hair so it releases from its sweat-matted form. It is hard to believe she is starting second grade already.

"Yup. I'm wearing my Storm Chasers jersey."

"No, you're not," Peyton interjects, taking Ayana's helmet from my hands as if I were about to smuggle it out of the facility. "I got you that cute purple sundress, remember?"

Ayana frowns up at her. "But now that I'm a hockey player, I gotta dress the part," my daughter protests.

Peyton glares at me as if I forced Ayana to prefer a jersey over a dress. I vowed long ago to stop trying to understand the woman. She showed up today severely overdressed for a hockey arena in a dress and heels and proceeded to talk my ear off the entire practice. Topics ranged from her latest modeling job for a local flooring company to her disdain for men who wear cargo shorts but are not, in fact, carpenters. I did my best to tune her out, which was not all that hard when I had Chloe's ass to stare at and my daughter's skating to watch. Not to mention keeping an eye on this new coach, Matt something or other. His hand lingered a bit too long on Chloe's arm than was strictly necessary to get her attention earlier.

I should not have kissed Chloe in the laundry room this morning, but it is difficult to regret. I realize now that we need to set some strict boundaries and adhere to them.

As if reading my mind, Peyton's eyes shift to the rink door where Chloe stands on skates, chatting with Benny's Little, Eli, and a woman who must be his mother.

Ayana's gaze follows Peyton's, and she pushes off me to pick her way toward Chloe on her blades. "I'm gonna say bye to Chloe. Be right back."

Peyton releases a beleaguered sigh. "The famous *Chloe*. I don't know, but I imagined her somehow being . . . skinnier."

A headache starts behind my eyes, and it is not from the puck I took to the head during today's training. I wear a helmet for a reason. Peyton is full of shit. Although she and Chloe did not formally meet at the courthouse, Peyton got an eyeful of her that day. Unless she was glaring too hard to focus.

Peyton has always been overly occupied with her body and looks, often making negative comments about herself in a bid to win my protestations and subsequent compliments. I do not know how much of her insecurity is manufactured for attention, but she incessantly complained about her height and was resentful that she could never be a "real" model at five feet and four inches. Cursed by Mother Nature to be beautiful but not tall.

And she is beautiful. But not as beautiful as Chloe. I keep that thought to myself.

Since hanging around here listening to Peyton's passive-aggressive chatter ranks on my list of hated pastimes just above sticking my dick in a beehive, I say goodbye to my daughter and wish her good luck at school in the morning. I do not speak to Chloe, but she catches the heated look I send her way, if her blush is anything to go by. It takes concerted effort not to picture her naked body beneath me in bed last night. This is not the time or place for a boner. But there are so many things I still want to do with that body.

When I notice Eli's mother glancing back and forth between a blushing Chloe and me, however, I realize my mistake. I need to be careful. Time for that boundaries conversation.

On my way home, I stop at the home goods store to buy six new sets of sheets, telling myself it is only due to my sense of practicality. To distract myself from the lie, I sit in my parked car and call Safiya back in Kazakhstan, even though it is late for her.

"I might have been asleep, you know," she greets in Russian.

"When have you ever gone to bed before midnight?"

"Last month. I had a cold." She pauses. "What is wrong? You never call. You only text."

She does not say it to make me feel guilty, she is merely stating a fact. I have never been one for talking unless there is a clear purpose. I do not understand the concept of small talk. In fact, I find it utterly exhausting trying to think up words just to fill some silence. What is wrong with silence?

I tap my hand on the steering wheel and squint out at the sunny afternoon sky. "Nothing. How is the weather there?"

"You called to talk to me about the weather?" Her tone is incredulous. See, I told you I was worthless at small talk.

"How are Mother and Father?" I ask instead. Our parents do not believe in burdening other people with their problems, so it is worthless to ask them directly. When my father had a heart attack three years ago, I did not find out until two months later. Similarly, my mother once broke her foot and did not speak a word of it to anyone for over a week. Our father assumed she had had a rock in her shoe. For a week.

Safiya is the only person who will be straight with me. Sometimes I think she even enjoys delivering bad news. She has always been a drama queen.

"The same as always. I went over for dinner the other night. They told me not to bring anything, so when I showed up with a bottle of decent wine, I lied and said I found it on the sidewalk." She laughs, and I cannot decide if she is joking or not. "Mikhail stopped by, and you should have heard Father waxing on about you and the name you have made for yourself. Blah, blah, blah. I might have thrown up a little."

I shake my head to myself and pull my sunglasses from the visor. Mikhail is the nearest neighbor, and he prides himself on making every conversation a competition.

"They should have talked about their daughter, the artist," I reply. Safiya is an accomplished painter, even if her audience is very niche. Not everyone appreciates paintings of men dressed and made up to look like Cher or Diana Ross. But she has exhibited in several countries across Europe and been commissioned to do portraits. She earns enough to pay most of her bills, although her taste tends not to align with her income very often, which is where I come in. But Safiya looks after our loved ones while I play hockey on the other side of the world, so it is no sacrifice to send money to them. It is my duty, and I am happy to do it.

"Oh, Mother did. Do not worry, Niko. But, of course, Mikhail made a smart comment saying anyone can be an artist when their brother pays for the best school on the continent."

I frown at the nearly empty parking lot. "The man is full of shit. Mikhail is neither fish nor meat," I tell her, knowing our neighbor has few skills of his own to brag of.

"You think I care what Mikhail thinks?" my sister chirps. I can picture the smirk on her face. Safiya is my opposite in many ways, but we both share a healthy degree of confidence earned by our mutual inability to give up on anything. "How is my adorable niece?" she asks.

I have not shared about the latest custody progress, worried I might jinx it if I celebrate before the judge's official order comes through. Nor have I shared about my impending retirement. Some things are better communicated in person. When Peyton and I divorced, I flew home to break the news face-to-face, knowing my parents would be devastated and disappointed. They do not approve of divorce as a concept, so I shouldered a considerable degree of shame, even if I knew divorce was the only option at that point.

So, I tell my sister about Ayana's lost teeth and her new hockey program. She is delighted when I share Ayana's planned outfit for the morning.

Safiya knows me well enough not to ask about any prospective relationships on my end, but she lets it slip that she is seeing someone new. She caught her last boyfriend cheating on her and broke up with him. The only thing that kept me from flying home to punch the asshole in the face was Safiya flying here to see me immediately after the breakup. I did not want to miss her visit, so I stayed put. That does not mean I did not call an old teammate from my youth league and ask him to drive the hour to the boyfriend's apartment to pay him a visit. Safiya never needs to know that. Instead, she can keep believing the cheating asswipe ran into a door.

"Does this one treat you with respect? Does he hold doors for you and pay for dinner?" I force myself to loosen my grip on the steering wheel when I realize my knuckles have gone white.

"Yes, big brother," she answers with an exasperated sigh. "Do not worry. I can take care of myself." I want to tell her she should not have to, but she is likely to lecture me if I do. Instead, I tell her I am wiring her money to buy her and our mother plane tickets to see our aunt in Spain.

Once I have received Safiya's assurance that Katya is doing well, we say our goodbyes. I drive home and lug the heavy shopping bag of bedding into the house before attending to Paul. Chloe is not here yet, and I remind myself that she will soon be back in her duplex and it will be only me in this big house once again. I used to relish the privacy and silence. Now, I fear a return to it might just suffocate me.

Chapter Thirty-One

Chloe

I hang up with the contractor from my duplex, thoroughly frustrated and wondering how they can be so dang wrong with their estimate of completion. The only professional that gets more things wrong is a weatherman. My home was supposed to be ready tomorrow, but he's informed me that now I'm looking at middle of next week. Pushing open Nikolai's front door, Paul's excited whine greets me. His tail sweeps across the wood floor, but he stays seated.

"What a good boy you are," I coo, crouching down and dumping off my duffle bag to pet the cutie. "Those obedience lessons are paying off, aren't they?"

The high-pitched voice does him in and he lunges, knocking me backward. I laugh, rolling with it and getting a face full of dog tongue as I sprawl out on the floor. Seconds later Nikolai appears above me, lifting the excited pupper off me and offering a hand.

Not exactly the way I wanted to greet Nikolai after our night together. Dog slobber and on my ass. I let him help me up though, and he shakes his head.

"Let me put Paul outside." He disappears before I can tell him it's fine. The dog didn't hurt me. He was just excited. I take the opportunity to head for the kitchen where I splash water on my face and wash my hands. Nikolai finds me there a few minutes later, his arms crossed over his chest. Big surprise, he's frowning.

"Everything all right, big guy?" I revert to the teasing that hallmarked all our interactions before our night together. It's a defense mechanism, and I know it, but I'm grasping at straws here to keep my heart from getting into the mix of things.

"Practice went well," he says. Which does not explain the frown. I dip my head and put a hand on my hip. He steps farther into the kitchen and I can't help myself. I discreetly inhale, getting a whiff of that scent of his. Is it cologne? Body wash? A fucking pheromone designed to bring women to their knees?

"Matt seemed . . . helpful."

He doesn't elaborate and my mind whirls, trying to figure out what he's not saying. "Uh, yeah. He's great. I'm glad I hired him. He's good with the kids and will be absolutely necessary when we split the league into age groups."

"We must talk," he says abruptly, dropping his arms and clenching his fists.

I shoot him a smile he most certainly doesn't return. "Aren't we talking right now?"

"Chloe," he growls.

"Nikolai," I growl right back in a lowered voice that sounds nothing like him.

And suddenly he's not across the room, he's right in front of me, a single hand gripping my face while his body presses me into the counter behind me. "You are driving me crazy," he admits, dropping his head to lean his forehead against mine, eyes squeezed tightly shut.

My hands land on his hips, disobeying me by fumbling under his shirt and sliding against the warm skin at his waist. "How so?" I ask, voice coming out shaky.

His eyes fly open and all two hundred plus pounds of him is pressed against me, angry at me for some reason. Even though my breathing kicks up, I don't feel afraid. He flexes his hips against my belly. Aha. Not angry. Turned on.

"I see you with other men and it makes me insane. I want you to touch *me*. Smile at *me*. You teased Matt about his spin away at the end of practice and I realized I want all of your teasing too. Aimed at me and me only. I want to own that mouth of yours."

My face is on fire. I've never been talked to this way, and I fucking love it. The mouth he wants so badly can barely form words. "It's yours."

And it's true. As much as I wanted this year to be about fun and exploration and nothing serious, I have zero interest in sharing anything of myself with any other man. Foolishly, I tried. And it was an utter failure.

Nikolai inhales, his eyes sliding shut once more. He looks pained, like every muscle is clenched tight while he tries to get himself under control. Then his eyes flick open and his blue gaze sears into my soul.

"Show me."

He moves back an inch, his hands leaving my face to put pressure on my shoulders. My eyes go wide and my mouth waters. I'm so wet I have a Slip 'n Slide party in my pants. I drop to my knees, steadying myself with my hands on his muscled thighs. He exhales, taking me in on the kitchen floor in front of him and he smiles. It's not a happy smile. It's a wolfish smile that makes me rub my thighs together even as they tremble.

His hands fly to his pants, unzipping and shoving them down over his hips. His cock is out and hard and already dripping. He fists the base of himself and cups his other hand under my chin, drawing my gaze back up to his face.

"If you need me to stop, put your hands up in the air. Otherwise, hands on my legs." I nod, more turned on than I've ever been in my life. "Hold on, *malish*. I am going to fuck that smart mouth."

He runs the tip of himself across my lips, his taste blooming as I dart my tongue out to lick the moisture away. A hum of approval hits my ears. His fingers slide into my hair, fisting it around his hand, and then he plunges inside ruthlessly and without further warning. It takes all of my concentration not to gag when he hits the back of my throat. He withdraws, giving me a precious few seconds to inhale oxygen. Then he takes control of my head completely, thrusting back inside over and over again. My lips ache at the stretch and there's no time for me to do anything but hold on.

Spit lines his cock, helping to glide him in and out, and soon it's dribbling down my chin too. Tears prick at my eyes as I struggle to breathe through my nose, but I keep my gaze trained on his face. I've never seen a more beautiful sight than Nikolai with his jaw clenched hard and his gaze trained on my mouth. My throat relaxes, wanting to give him everything he needs in this moment, and he takes advantage, drilling down past my gag reflex and groaning at the depth I take him.

"Fuck," he breathes, pulling almost all the way out and staring down at my lips wrapped around him like I'm some sort of princess of blow jobs.

A single tear slips down my cheek and I wish I could brush it away, but I don't dare take my hands off his rock-solid thighs. He plunges back inside, my nose hitting his pelvis as I gag over the thick pipe currently occupying my throat. His muscles go impossibly harder and then he's grunting. His cock jumps in my mouth and warmth floods down my throat. I suck air in and out of my nostrils, willing myself to relax and take it. He doesn't ease up until the jerks have stopped, assuming that I can handle him. And I can.

Tears stream down my cheeks now and I'm not even sure why. Nikolai slides completely out of my mouth and releases my hair, tucking himself back into his jeans. He doesn't bother to zip them up before he's reaching down and swinging me up into his arms. I suck in great gulps of oxygen and wrap my arms around his neck as I lay my head on his shoulder. He carries me to his bedroom, laying me down and smoothing my hair away from my forehead. My shoes are next to receive his attention and the sheets are drawn over me. I close my eyes and try to regain the energy I just lost doing something I want to try again. I've participated in blow jobs before, of course, but never like this. Never where I wasn't the one in control. Everything I set out to do by moving here and creating a new life is happening. I know now what I was missing before.

Nikolai is back with a washcloth, gently gliding it over my face before he tosses it aside and hands me a glass of water. He sits on the edge of the bed and monitors me drinking it. For not wanting me in his bed, he sure does put me here a lot.

"Is that your idea of having a talk?" I ask wryly, putting the glass down on the bedside table and breaking the silence.

His lips hook to the side in an embarrassed grin. "I see I did not succeed in fucking the smart comments from that mouth."

I shake my head. "I don't think that's possible."

His eyes are doing that smoldering thing again. "I would like to keep trying."

I put my hand on his leg. "Me too."

"I did not hurt you?"

"Nope."

He studies me, as if looking for a lie, but not finding one, he climbs over me and onto the bed. He rests his back against the headboard and pulls me into his side. His feet and legs extend over a foot longer than mine do, making me feel like I really am from a long line of short people. I rest my head against his shoulder and breathe, wishing we could have done this last night too. You know, if he hadn't run from the room and never returned.

When I feel him finally relax against me, I bring up what might have caused his territorial behavior in the kitchen. "You know, I don't flirt with Matt. Or anyone else."

The thumb that was casually stroking over the cap of my shoulder stills. "Yes. My brain knows this."

I huff a laugh. "But the rest of you doesn't?"

"Exactly." He goes back to stroking my shoulder. "I did not know this about me."

I tilt my head to find him frowning in concentration. "I think everyone gets a bit jealous at times. I didn't particularly like seeing Peyton all over you today either."

His gaze flies to mine, startled. "She means nothing beyond being Ayana's mother."

"My brain knows this."

We share a smile, understanding each other, even if we don't understand what we're doing here in Nikolai's bed when we said we wouldn't. I go back to resting my head against his shoulder and just breathe in the moment, not sure if I'll get another with him like this.

"How did you know she wasn't right for you?" I finally ask, wanting to understand the dynamic between him and his ex before I have to face her again at another practice.

His hand tightens on my shoulder. "When I walked in on her with her acting coach in my bed."

I bare my teeth. "Yikes. Yeah, that'll do it."

"It was more than that, of course. Our problems started long before or she never would have wound up there in the first place. We are very different. Not even a baby could bring us together. I know the divorce was the right thing to do, but it is still my greatest failure."

"Ugh," I moan. "The F word. I have danced around feeling like a failure for more time than I'd like to admit."

"You?" Nikolai scoffs, bending his knee to tap the side of his foot against mine. "You have never been a failure. You are an accomplished woman with many talents."

"Thank you, but when you're in the trenches of trying to keep your spouse from dying a terrible death, you feel like a failure on a daily basis." I lick my lips, finally feeling ready to explain more and knowing Nikolai will listen intently. "Two months before Josh was diagnosed, I visited an attorney. I was thinking of filing for divorce. We'd slid into being friends years prior and there was no great passion left between us. I was approaching forty and kept wondering if that was all that's left in this life. Then, of course, he was diagnosed and I felt like I couldn't divorce him when he was facing the fight of his life, you know? I vowed to stuff down my issues and take care of him. But I failed at that too because he died. I couldn't save him. During that time I also couldn't bring myself to love him like he deserved. And I never got to speak my truth either. I failed myself."

"Chloe," Nikolai says quietly, sliding down the bed and taking me with him. He rolls onto his side and props his head on his hand, stroking my face with his fingertips. "You did the most honorable thing a person can do. That can never be viewed as failure. And now, you speak your truth every day. I did mention you have a smart mouth, no?"

I grin, loving that he can bring that out in me, even in the middle of a vulnerable conversation. "I'm working on it."

His fingers still, but his eyes blaze. "How about I help you lose these clothes and I can show you what *my* mouth can do?"

"Yes, please."

His answering groan is music to my ears.

Chapter Thirty-Two

Niko

"You should marry Chloe."

The napkin reaches my mouth barely in time to catch the water I just choked on at Ayana's words. It takes close to a minute to stop coughing and compose myself. We're drawing the attention of nearby diners, but that is the least of my concerns. Nor is it Ayana's, based on the grin she is wearing.

"Why would you say such a thing?" I finally manage to ask.

When I agreed to dinner out after dance practice, I did not know it would include relationship advice from a seven-year-old.

She lays her triangle of grilled cheese back on her plate and dusts her hands off as if preparing for a presentation. "Well, why not? Brook's dad just got married, and her mom's been married to her other mom since she was like three. You and Mom aren't married anymore either, so . . ." She trails off as if this is basic logic and I am unbearably slow.

I push my half-eaten sandwich aside and rest my elbows on the table. "And that is nice for them, Ayana. But Chloe and I are *not* a couple."

"But you could be."

"No, we . . . this is not your concern." I shake my head, wondering why I am trying to reason about adult relationships with a child whose future plan includes marrying her dog. "Chloe is your hockey coach, and she is a very nice person."

Ayana is undeterred. She begins ticking off her fingers, one by one. "And she's pretty, she's great with Paul, she's funny, she likes *Bake Off*, she makes the best quesadillas, she finds puzzle pieces faster than anybody, she's an awesome skater, she knows vanilla ice cream is a waste of time, she wears cool clothes . . . oh, and she smells good."

Fuck. Of course, all of those things are true—as well as many other tempting traits I have come to know. But Ayana must not let her mind go there. A man other than me will ultimately be the one enjoying and appreciating all that is Chloe.

"Chloe is a friend, Ayana. Like Brook is your friend." It is all she can ever be, despite our current arrangement. But we are only having fun—letting off steam. The fact that I cannot stop thinking about her lips around my cock and my hands fisting in her hair is only the result of a cock's universal ability to rule the thoughts of whichever man it is attached to.

"I might marry Brook. I mean, we like all the same stuff."

My brain is beginning to hurt. "I thought you were marrying Paul?"

"I haven't decided yet." She shrugs and picks up her sandwich again before taking a man-sized bite. My lips quirk at the sight, despite the turmoil she has just instigated.

We must move on from this topic, the sooner the better. But it is concerning that my behavior has perhaps prompted such notions about Chloe and me. We have been so careful, though, especially since that day at the ice rink with Eli's mother last week.

Yes, we did end up sleeping in the same bed the last few nights, but not intentionally. I am out of practice, so properly fucking Chloe and keeping her sated takes a toll on my energy. The first time it happened, I had just closed my eyes for a moment, fully intent on moving to the couch as soon as I caught my breath. The next thing I knew, the sun was streaming through the gap in the blinds, and Chloe's warm body was splayed across my chest, my hand cupped around one of her ass cheeks. There is a lot to be said for convenience.

We have not discussed it since that first night—and we never did have that conversation about the importance of keeping this between us—but we both know this is a temporary arrangement—a "situationship," if I understand Roadie's use of the term correctly—which is unlikely. There are enough English words to remember already; I do not understand the need to invent more.

Jealousy has risen its ugly head, which still baffles me since Chloe is not mine anywhere but in the bedroom. But our physical connection is so strong, perhaps I should not be overly surprised at my baser instincts overpowering reason.

The bottom line is that we are friends who are sexually compatible, but neither of us is looking for a relationship— despite what my daughter might wish.

I pull my plate in front of me once more and pick up my sandwich as I eye my daughter. "Well, considering that you will not be allowed to date until you are thirty years old, I would say you have time to decide."

She rolls her eyes and wraps both hands around her glass of milk. We chat about school, Paul, and our family in Kazahkstan through the rest of the meal, and then I return Ayana to her mother's house in time for bed.

Peyton declines to come out for a chat, a stark turnaround

from her behavior at Ayana's hockey practice when she couldn't seem to stop talking. I suspect she has learned the hard truth from her lawyer, and her act at the rink was a last-ditch effort to charm me into . . . who knows what.

"Have a good day at school tomorrow," I tell Ayana as I hug her goodbye on the porch. Her tiny body feels so fragile sometimes, I am afraid I will break her. But my daughter is strong, I remind myself. "Listen to your teachers, yes?" I release her.

"I will," she promises before opening the door. "Give Paul a pat for me."

"I will," I return the promise.

A smile curves my lips when I pull into my garage to see Chloe's Bronco safely tucked into the third bay. It made no sense for her to continue parking in the driveway when the weather was so hot, despite her insistence that it was no big deal. All it took was temporarily denying her orgasm by pulling my fingers from her pretty pussy to get her to accept the extra garage door opener.

As soon as I open the door, Paul greets me with paws to my thighs and a wagging tail. "Off," I command, and he obeys with no fuss, deciding to run circles around me instead. "Your mistress says hello," I tell him with a scratch behind his ears.

"Hey!" Chloe appears around the corner from the kitchen, a patch of white on her cheek and her hair tied up with another of her kerchiefs. More white covers the front of her shirt, some of it dusted along her exposed collarbone. She looks good enough to eat. She ducks back into the kitchen, and I follow to see what she is up to.

"Coaching has already driven you to cocaine?" I quip as I turn the corner and stop short. Every surface is covered in cookies, muffins, pans, trays, flour, and lord knows what else.

"He tells jokes," she says, transferring cookies from a baking sheet to a plate. "How was dinner with your ballerina?"

"Good," I answer absently, my eyes still taking in the disaster surrounding us. "She wants you to send my mother your pancake recipe since you all appear to share the same sweet tooth." Chloe has confided secrets and stories from her past, and her vulnerability has compelled me to share some of my own. She now knows about the farm I grew up on, about Safiya's unconventional career, and also the importance of Ivan's role in my success. She cried when I revealed he sold his car without telling me in order to fund the travels that got me noticed by scouts. I decided then that sharing time was over and replaced her tears with orgasms.

"I'm relieved to hear you're the black sheep of the family when it comes to sugar," she responds before spotting my expression and biting her lip. Her gaze follows mine around the kitchen. "Uh, yeah. I guess I got a little carried away."

I approach and gently wipe the flour from her cheek with the pad of my thumb. I don't miss Chloe's intake of breath or the tightening of her nipples through the thin fabric of her top. She is so responsive, she makes it impossible not to touch her.

"I just . . ." She pauses, her breath whispering over my wrist. "I wanted to do something to thank you for . . . everything." When I lean in and nuzzle the skin under her ear, her head drops back, but her words continue in a breathy tumble, their meaning becoming almost nonsensical. "But it's hard baking for a guy who doesn't eat sweets, so I tried to find a recipe for . . . *oh god*," she moans when I nip her earlobe and lave it with my tongue. "F-for healthy muffins," she continues, her body beginning to tremble when my hands slide along her hips to the hem of her skirt. "So I decided to say screw it and made my favorite blueberry ones instead."

My tongue finds her pulse point as her fingertips skate up my abs to my chest. "But then I remembered somebody telling me to use applesauce instead of . . ." I run the knuckles of one hand up her thigh to find her panties already damp. "Oh god . . . b-butter, so I tried three different recipes for cookies and . . ." I push the gusset aside and plunge one finger deep. "*Omigod* . . . they all tasted . . . terrible." She's panting now, and I would laugh at her determination to complete this detailed account of whatever destroyed my kitchen, but my cock is too painfully hard.

"So, you are making me terrible cookies to thank me for what?" I ask into her throat as I back her into the counter for leverage. She digs her nails into my pecs when I thrust another finger into her pussy.

"F-for letting me stay for so long." Her breath hitches on the last word as my thumb finds her clit. She moans before saying, "My duplex is ready."

My fingers still inside her, and I pull my head back to look down at her. Flushed cheeks, damp lips, half-lidded eyes. She is a dream come true. "Why did you stop?" Her voice is husky.

I open my mouth to answer, not having the first clue what words will come out, but my phone rings from my back pocket. My mind still swirling, I absently pull it from my pants with my free hand, and we both look down at the screen.

Jane.

I move to set the device on the counter, but Chloe grabs it and pulls away, causing my fingers to slide out of her. "It's Jane. You have to answer." She shoves the phone at me, pressing the accept call button.

I have not even had the chance to put the phone to my ear or say hello when Jane's voice comes over the line, loud enough for both of us to hear.

"Guess what I have in my hand?"

I awkwardly shift the phone to my ear, but she does not wait for my reply. "The judge's final order!"

Chloe gasps and I stumble forward, dropping one hand to the counter to brace my body.

"Niko?" Jane asks.

"I am here." My voice sounds foreign. There is something stuck in my throat.

A warm hand rests on my back, stroking up and down my spine as Jane continues at a breakneck pace, "Everything has been filed. And I already submitted our proposed custody schedule covering now through the hockey season. We'll create a different one to start next July—with the assumption that you'll be busy winning the Stanley Cup in June, of course," she continues, but I only hear bits and pieces of it. My mind is too focused on the miracle that I finally have my Ayana back. "Things will be easier once you retire, but we've outlined plenty of time for you two between now and then—starting with weekends and two weeks at your house beginning the first of the month!"

That gets my full attention, and I straighten. Now that I have dates and this is all a reality, I must find childcare. And it cannot be Chloe anymore.

As if hearing my thoughts, her arms come around my waist from behind and she squeezes me tight, her cheek resting against my back.

"Listen to me talking your ear off." Jane laughs. "Peyton has another week to respond with changes, but we were generous with the schedule—and alterations can easily be made as we go. We just have to make sure we keep following official procedures." She finally exhales and pauses. "But, Niko?"

"Yes. I am here," I repeat, seemingly unable to produce any other words.

"You're done proving yourself." Jane's voice has gone gentle, but still loud enough for Chloe to hear based on the prolonged squeeze she delivers.

Part of me wants to laugh at my lawyer's words. When is a

man ever done proving his worth? But I understand her meaning.

"You're her dad, and you finally get to enjoy it."

"Thank you, Jane. Truly." My voice sounds a little more like my own now.

"You're welcome." I can hear her fingernails begin to clack on her keyboard. "I'll let you go, but I'll be in touch. Crack open a bottle of champagne, okay?"

She hangs up, and my phone hand drops to the counter, the device staring blandly up at me as if it did not just change my life forever.

I finally have the right to be my daughter's father in a full and meaningful way, just as I have always fought for. And there is no way in hell I am going to fuck it up.

"I'm so happy for you, Nikolai," Chloe says on another squeeze, but I don't turn to her yet and I don't say a word. Because the one word we both know is coming is the one I am not ready to say.

Goodbye.

Chapter Thirty-Three

Chloe

I press my nose against the glass and mimic a fish opening and closing its mouth. Sushi is not impressed. In fact, she swims away from me, a corner of her bright turquoise tail the only thing visible outside the underwater castle where she hides.

"Oh, you like the construction workers better now? So much for female . . . what's the word?" My breath fogs the glass and I stand up, stretching my back and hoping the word will come to me before I grow another gray hair. "Oh! Solidarity! Believe me. I saved your life not bringing you into the house with Paul. He would have had you for a snack on day one."

I've only been home one night in my duplex and already everything feels wrong. My mattress isn't as comfortable as Nikolai's. My fish seems pissed off I left her with someone else for a few weeks, even though I came over every day to feed her. My plants have been rearranged in the wrong spots. My refrigerator is pristine instead of covered with dirty fingerprints and colored drawings from Ayana.

Pacing my living space, I think about what those two might have been up to today. Nikolai was able to negotiate another afternoon with Ayana before their parenting plan schedule kicks in. Paul must be in heaven with that little girl home and joining him in straight chaos. I rub my chest bone and realize I'm jealous of a grown man having time with his own daughter.

"Ugh!" I flop down on the sofa in an overly dramatic fashion.

My stomach rumbles but I ignore it. Who can eat dinner when they're in the middle of an existential breakdown? I came to Tampa to get away from all the people who looked at me with pity in their eyes. I came to start a new life, one that's formed with my truth at the center and fun holding up the edges. And what did I do? Fall in love with an unavailable single dad who refuses to even consider that we could have a relationship, so here I am pretending I'm not feeling what I'm actually feeling. Again. This is basically my old marriage on repeat.

Disgusted with myself, I roll off the sofa and head for my bedroom. I'd rather go to sleep at nine at night than sit here and feel sorry for myself. Come tomorrow, I'm turning over a new leaf. No more sad sack moping and gazing over at Nikolai like he might be my knight in shining armor. Nope. No siree. I'm saving my own goddamn self this time. I'll throw myself into my league and build a life just for me. Surely there are other hot men in this city that can get me over Nikolai. Right?

The doorbell rings right after I slide into my favorite pair of sweats. The kind you wear for maximal moping and ice cream binging. Pretty sure that brown stain on one thigh is from a night of rocky road rage eating. The look on Nikolai's face yesterday when he said goodbye tells me he meant more than just goodbye for that day. I'll need more than a tiny pint, so I'm hoping the gallon I vaguely recall buying before the flood is still in the freezer.

I swing open the door and stagger back a step when my knight stands before me, a brown paper grocery bag in hand.

"Hallo, Chloe. I thought you might need a house heating gift."

"House warming?" I murmur, then swing the door open farther. Because right now? I have zero defenses against this man. If he's here, I'm letting him in.

He steps inside and looks me up and down. I don't even feel self-conscious in my drab attire. Not when his eyes flare like that. Like he has x-ray vision and doesn't even see the stained cotton.

"What did you bring?" I ask after I close the door, trying to appear unaffected by his late-night visit.

He reaches into the bag with a smile tugging on his stoic lips and pulls out a gallon of chocolate ice cream. "I also bought the whipped cream you spray from a can." His smile takes on a wicked slant. "I thought I could feed you and then you can return the favor."

Images of naked bodies, sticky with whipped cream and melted ice cream instantly come to mind. Good thing I already decided to wait until tomorrow to turn over a new leaf.

Because tonight I'm going to allow myself to indulge.

The man is diabolical. And sweet. A deadly combination.

First, he strips me naked right there in my living room, then backs me into the bedroom where he pushes me onto the bed and whips off his belt to tie my wrists to my bedpost. My lungs are heaving before he's even touched me.

"Hey. What about that ice cream?" I pant, not actually giving a damn about it.

Nikolai holds up one thick finger. "I give you what you want when I hear a please."

Oh, so that's how it's going to go tonight. Nervous energy and the carnal knowledge of this man's ability to please me beyond my wildest dreams have my heart beating wildly. "May I please have some ice cream from my naked server?"

His answering grin makes that stupid organ in my chest beat out a rhythm of love and affection. A rhythm I know he won't allow himself to feel in return. I shush the beat and focus on each inch of tan skin that slowly emerges as Nikolai strips for me. He's hard already, his cock standing proudly. My mouth waters as I think of how it can gag me with its girth and length.

"Nah ah, *malish*. You do not get this cock yet. First, you eat."

He bends down and grabs the tub of ice cream, a silver spoon also emerging from that brown bag of his. He pops the top off, puts one knee on the side of the bed, and spoon feeds me chocolate ice cream, bite after decadent bite. The dessert is cold, a relief from the heat streaking across my skin and in my core from just looking at him. When I can't take another bite, mostly due to the restlessness between my legs and not from actually being full, Nikolai sets the ice cream on my bedside table and sits back to look his fill, taking in the length of me from my red painted toes to the dark curls on my head.

"I have more for you in this bag. Would you like to see?"

Expecting whipped cream, I nod, shifting my wrists to keep feeling in my hands as they're suspended above my head.

Nikolai reaches down and comes back up with something clutched in his palm.

"Do you trust me, *malish*?"

I nod without thought. I do trust Nikolai. I trust him to take exquisite care of me while also breaking my heart. His fingers unfurl and a small silver knob of some sort lays in his palm. The end of it is a beautiful ruby gem. Nervousness replaces a portion of the eagerness.

"What is that?" My voice is a whisper.

"It is for you to wear. I want to fill all your holes and see a ruby the shade of your lips winking at me. Will you let me?"

I have too good of an imagination to be left wondering which hole he intends to fill with that steel plug. I've never done anything like that. Then again, isn't that what I intend for my life now? To try new things? I lick my lips and nod.

Nikolai pounces, positioning himself between my thighs and burying his face. His tongue laves my clit while his teeth graze it next. His chin gets in on the action and pretty soon I'm a quivering, wet mess. I'm chanting his name and begging for release, but he won't give it to me. He backs off every time I get close. The third time he drives me right to the edge, the cool touch of steel hits my flesh. I gasp.

"Relax, *malish*," he whispers, gliding it up and around the wetness left from his tongue and my desire. Then he slides it to the knot of muscle no one has breached before, and it slips inside me. The feeling is foreign, bizarre. And oh, so hot.

"Nikolai," I cry, hips squirming for more of him, but he evades me. He sits back on his haunches between my thighs, hands now holding my knees out to the side, baring me completely.

"*Izyskannyy*," he breathes, voice breaking.

"Please."

Just one word. One plea in the form of a moan and the man moves, positioning himself at my entrance and slowly sliding his thick cock inside of me. His elbows land on either side of my head and he gazes down at me, our noses touching.

"If I hurt you, just say stop and I will stop."

I feel impossibly full and he's not even halfway in. My eyes want to cross but I hold my gaze on him, watching the wonder in his face as he slides forward another inch. I dip my chin in a nod to continue and he gives me another inch. He shudders, eyes closing and forehead touching mine for a moment. Then he lifts his head and slides all the way home, scanning me for discomfort. He won't find it, however. I feel stretched. Full. Tight as a bow. Ready to shatter if he so much as breathes too deeply.

"Good?"

So, so good. So fucking good the pleasure feels a bit like pain. I'm poised on the edge of something so big I'm sure it'll take me under when it sweeps me away and I don't fucking care if I die. Nikolai doesn't move. He just stares deep into my eyes until I give him another affirmative nod. Sweat dots his skin and that vein on his temple pulses wildly, yet he doesn't let himself unleash. He pulls his hips back ever so gently and stars dance across my vision. I had no idea sex could feel like this, could overwhelm one's senses and reduce them to a lump of nerve endings pulsing with the need for more.

"Please, Nikolai."

Finally he unleashes, slamming home over and over again until everything explodes in a pleasure so great I'm not sure I'm still a fully formed human. My mouth starts chanting his name and cursing gods I never knew existed. He slams his lips to mine, tongue in my mouth, stealing my breath. I'm somewhere else, floating in a plane where only pleasure exists and silly things like oxygen don't matter. He barks a Russian word into my mouth and I'm aware he's shaking above me, but I'm still free falling.

Long moments later, Nikolai rolls to his side, twisting me

with him, the two of us still connected. My eyes are closed and I briefly wonder if I'm still here on this earth. He huffs a laugh and the vibration sets off another orgasm. A small one this time. My eyes fly open and I whimper as I shake. He stares down at me in wonder before stealing another kiss. Every bit of energy flees my body as the waves recede, leaving me a limp noodle of pleased female.

"I take it you liked my housewarming present?" Nikolai's rumble of a voice holds a note of humor.

Without opening my eyes, I respond. "Please tell me you don't take butt plugs to everyone's housewarming parties."

His laughter stirs my eyes back open. He's handsome every second of every day, but his face in laughter is something I can't miss. He unties my wrists and massages my arms before stroking strands of hair off my face as we settle into cuddling. I can feel him debating whether to leave or stay. I close my eyes and hope for both. Staying would make my stupid heart fall harder, but I can't wish him gone. If I had my way, he'd never leave my side. I'm on the verge of sleep when the doorbell rings again.

Nikolai jolts his head up, muscles tensing. "Are you expecting someone?"

I shake my head and pull him back down. "No. Ignore it. Probably a door-to-door salesman."

"At midnight?"

I frown. He has a point. That would be quite odd. The doorbell rings again and I groan. "I should probably get that before they wake up my neighbor."

Nikolai lets me go and I roll out of bed, shifting awkwardly with the toy still wedged tightly in my ass and legs that don't seem to want to hold me upright. "Can I walk with this thing?"

A full-of-himself-and-his-sexual-prowess smile is the only answer I get. I roll my eyes as I pull on a robe and tie it tightly around my waist. My hair probably looks like I got struck by lightning, but there's nothing I can do about it and it's the least of my problems right now. Hopefully I can get rid of my midnight visitor quickly.

I pop the door open an inch with a remark about going away on my lips. Instead, I gape at the person on my welcome mat.

"Dad?"

He gives me a sheepish smile. "Do you mind if we chat, pumpkin?"

Kill me now. I swallow hard, trying to remain calm even as my cheeks flame bright. "Now?"

He shrugs and sends that easygoing lopsided smile my way. "I really need to get something off my chest."

So I do what any daughter would do when faced with her contrite father. I let him in and walk over to the couch, acutely aware of the steel toy still in place and the man hiding from his coach in my bedroom.

Chapter Thirty-Four

Niko

"Fuck" I mutter to myself as I cower like a child behind the laundry room door. The last time I hid from a girl's father, I was sixteen with barely a hair on my chin or balls. Kiara was fifteen, and her parents forbade her from dating hockey players, telling her all they wanted was to get in girls' pants. They weren't wrong. Nine out of ten thoughts were focused on that very thing back then.

Not unlike now, except my current preoccupation is centered on one particular woman's pants. And her father is not some unknown entity; he is my coach and mentor.

From my vantage point, I see Chloe lead her father to the couch where she gestures for him to sit. He settles with his back to me, the thinning patch at the crown of his head reflecting the overhead light, while his daughter remains standing in her silky robe. It is one I have not seen before, and it has me wondering if there are more sexy night clothes she has been hiding. I followed Chloe when she went to answer the door, part of me wanting to get another look at her body in that robe and another part knowing few good things result from a midnight caller. But as soon as I heard Coach's voice, I ducked into the closest room like a fucking coward.

And now my heart beats heavy in my chest as I wait to hear what was so urgent it couldn't hold until morning. I worry my worst fear is about to come true, and Coach is here to tell Chloe he knows what I've done and how I've taken advantage of her.

Fuck. How have I allowed my moral compass to spin so out of control?

"What are you doing out so late?" Chloe asks, worrying the sash of her robe with restless fingers. She has the same fear, it is clear. "Has retirement made you a night owl?"

Coach chuckles uncomfortably. "Uh, something like that." He clears his throat. "I need to tell you something."

Now is the time. I need to man up and go to Chloe's side. What kind of weakling am I to leave her to bear this alone? I draw in a deep breath and straighten as I reach for the door handle to swing it wide. There is no time to regret not dressing in more than my boxers.

"I've been seeing someone for a while, and we're in love." The words spill from Coach's lips in a rush, and my hand freezes on the handle as my eyes dart back to Chloe.

Eyes wide and lips in a surprised O, she drops down to the couch as if her legs have given out on her. No sooner does her ass hit the cushion, however, and she is back on her feet with a strangled "*Argh!* Oh god!" I am alarmed for only a split second before remembering the ruby plug in her ass. If this situation were not so fraught, I would probably laugh.

Coach drops his face into his hands. "I knew it was too soon! I'm so sorry, pumpkin. I just hated all this sneaking around, and Sharon said it was time to come clean and that you'd probably be happy. I told her it's only been a little over a year since you lost Josh, and shoving our relationship in your face would hurt you."

"Dad!" Chloe has to shout to get her father's attention.

"What?" He drops his hands and looks up at her again. Her expression has shifted from surprise to a gentle smile. Of course it has. This is Chloe we are talking about, and someone she loves is in need of her understanding and comfort.

She steps toward him and lowers to the couch beside him so slowly and carefully, glaciers have moved at a faster clip. The effort she puts into keeping her expression steady is written all over her tense posture. Yet, when her butt finally settles, she still lets out a tiny squeak.

"You okay, pumpkin?" Coach asks, concern in his voice. "Are you hurt?"

Her smile is more forced this time. "No! I . . . uh . . . took a spill on the ice the other day." She pats her hip with a fake chuckle. "Not as young as I used to be, you know."

"Chloe, I—"

She cuts her father off, reaching out to take his hand. "Dad, I can't even begin to tell you how happy I am for you and . . . Sharon, is it?"

"Yes. Sharon. But—"

"No buts. You deserve to be happy and be in love. I think it's fantastic!" Her other hand joins the first, and she bounces their clasped hands against his knee for emphasis.

"Really?" Relief seeps into Coach's voice.

"Really."

He shakes his head. "It's been so hard for you since Josh passed that I've been feeling like the biggest asshole in the world being so happy when my daughter is suffering so much."

"Dad," Chloe says, shifting closer and letting out another surprised squeak.

"Maybe you should get that hip looked at by a doctor."

Coach leans in with an extended hand, causing Chloe to back up again. This time the squeak is more of a yelp.

"Nope! All good!" Her tone borders on panic, and Coach takes the hint, settling back into the cushion with stiff shoulders, clearly still on alert.

Chloe exhales before drawing a deep breath in through her nose and squaring her shoulders and chin. "What I was going to say is that life doesn't work like that, Dad. Things don't happen in perfect sequence like we might plan. Josh wasn't supposed to die at forty-one, you and Mom weren't supposed to fall out of love, I wasn't supposed to restart my life halfway through, the Gophers weren't supposed to beat the Badgers last fall. Shit happens."

"I'm pretty sure Ghandi said something similar," Coach quips.

Chloe grins and leans forward again with the utmost care. "The important thing is that we get back on our feet and keep going. It's why I moved here. It's why I refuse to regret anything anymore. Frankly, I'm surprised it took you so long to find somebody else."

Coach sighs, and I know he's looking at his daughter with both pride and love. It is how I would look at Ayana in such a moment. "It's my greatest hope that one day you'll be ready to move on and find someone else too."

Chloe's smile is teary this time. "I *am* ready, Dad."

For some reason, the hairs on the back of my neck stand at attention.

"What do you mean?" her father asks.

"I lost Josh long before the day he died. I've had a lot of time to look back on my life with him, on all the memories—some of them good and some of them . . . not."

"I don't understand. I thought you were happy with Josh."

"I was. A lot of the time. But . . . we married young, and we grew apart, just like a lot of other couples."

"I didn't know that." Coach shakes his head again, regret plain in his tone.

"I didn't exactly advertise it."

Coach coughs out a mirthless laugh. "Sounds kind of like your mother and me."

"I don't know that I'd go *that* far." Chloe returns his laugh. "Josh didn't max out our credit cards on a shopping spree on the Home Shopping Network." I can't see Coach's expression, but Chloe's responding laugh—this one pure amusement—clues me in. "Still too soon? It's been thirty years, Dad."

"Let's not talk about your mom. I'd rather get back to you."

Chloe's eyebrows spike, and her lips spread into one of her brilliant smiles. "And *I'd* rather hear about Sharon. How did you meet? What is she like? Is she the one you kept sneaking off to call at Roman and Olivia's wedding?"

Coach begins to fill Chloe in on all the details about the woman in his life, but I mostly tune him out. My mind is stuck on only one thing. Something I have known all along and have cavalierly brushed aside for my own convenience and pleasure.

Chloe has suffered greatly in her life, and she deserves a happy ending, starting right now—an ending that includes a man who will make her the center of his universe. One who is like her: open, kind-hearted, decent, easygoing, full of joy and free of messy baggage. One who does not take advantage of her giving nature and distract her from her goals and wishes.

For all I know, Tanner could have been that man, had I exercised even a modicum of self-control and refrained from flirting so shamelessly with her–from fueling our chemistry with stolen kisses and heated looks. She abandoned a perfectly good candidate to indulge in this dalliance to nowhere with me, wasting precious time she should have used more wisely.

I knew it all along, yet I have persisted in my selfishness, not only using Chloe but betraying the trust of a man I revere and respect above all others. Since Ivan died, Coach has filled his shoes in so many ways, and my recent behavior is a slap to both of their faces. My stomach lurches as I imagine what Ivan would think if he could see me now. I recall with disgust the weakness I demonstrated earlier tonight when faced with the prospect of an empty house. How I fooled myself into thinking it was Chloe's happiness driving me to knock on her door with ice cream and sex toys.

"So, what about you?" Coach asks, drawing my attention back to their conversation. "Anyone interesting in your life?"

Chloe's expression turns coy, heat rising to her cheeks, and I feel the blood begin to drain from my own. I might need to sit on the floor. "Perhaps," she responds, her tone purposely evasive.

I mutter another curse under my breath.

Coach pauses a few moments before saying, "You really have moved on, haven't you?"

A smile is her only answer, and it has me battling with myself again. Should I make my presence known and confess everything to Coach so he can deliver the beating I deserve? Should I make it clear that nothing will ever happen again between Chloe and me? Should I tell her to call Tanner and try again?

Yes. I should do all of those things. But I do none of them as I watch Chloe escort her father back to the door and bid him goodnight.

I emerge from the laundry room and lean against the wall, my head dropping back and my eyes falling shut.

"Holy shit, that was close!"

My eyes fly open at Chloe's exclamation to see her with a hand to her ample chest over the red silk of her robe.

When I don't respond, she comes closer, a grin on her lips. "Here's a sentence I never thought I'd hear myself say: Next time the doorbell rings, I should really take out my butt plug before answering." Her eyes sparkle with amusement for several seconds before she realizes I am not mirroring her expression. "What's wrong?"

I straighten from the wall to fully face her. "That never should have happened." My tone is harsher than I intended, but I cannot remember a time when I was angrier with myself.

She rests a hand on my bare bicep, defaulting to her compassionate nature as always. "Nothing happened. He had no idea you were here."

I bring both hands to my head, spearing frustrated fingers through my hair and dislodging her hand from my arm in the process. "I should not have been here! I should not be here *now*!"

Chloe's chin jerks back. "Why not?"

I draw a cleansing breath through my nostrils in an attempt to calm myself. "You know why."

This time, her eyes drop to her bare feet for a few silent beats before she shakes her head. "I've got to admit, Nikolai, the reason has become a bit fuzzy for me."

"What does this mean? Fuzzy."

Her brow knits as she lifts her head to look at me again. "Fuzzy? You know . . . unclear, cloudy . . ."

I shake my head with impatience. "Yes, I know what it means. I was asking for an explanation of your statement."

"Oh." Her expression relaxes, and I do my best to keep her beauty from distracting me. "What I mean is . . . it's been *weeks*." Her silk-covered shoulders lift in a shrug. "I already feel like we're in a relationship, so it makes perfect sense to me that you'd be at my place. In my bed. Just like it makes perfect sense that we have nothing to be ashamed of—nothing to hide. Especially now that you officially have shared custody of Ayana."

My lips tighten in a straight line as my jaw ticks. What have I done?

"In fact," she continues, "if I had my way, I would have dragged you out of the bedroom and onto the couch with me so you could have witnessed my 'emotions-are-for-suckers' dad prattling on and on about being head over heels in love with an interior designer named Sharon."

"I heard," I manage through my tight lips, unsure why I am commenting at all.

There goes her chin again, this time accompanied by crossed arms. "And you don't approve?"

"I don't give a fuck about Coach's love life," I bite out.

"Wow." Her expression is pained, and I have the sudden urge to put my head through the wall.

"That is not what I meant." My hands go back to my hair. "Fuck! I meant he can do what he wants. It is not my business."

Chloe tilts her head. "Yeah. Just like *our* relationship is none of *his* business."

"We are not in a relationship, Chloe," I proclaim over the shards of broken glass in my throat. "I told you from the beginning I could not do that for so many reasons, and you agreed!"

"Yes, but that was then." Her nostrils flare as a sheen of tears forms over her blue eyes. "Before."

Everything in me warns me not to ask, but I do anyway. "Before what?"

"Before I fell in love with you." Her voice cracks on the last words, but the tears remain trapped in her eyes without falling.

We stare at one another for several long moments. With

each passing second that I don't move or respond, Chloe's eyes lose more luster and her lips fall into a downward curve. And like the asshole I am, I wait until her eyelids fall shut before retreating to her room to get dressed and then let myself out her door for the last time.

My only solace is in knowing she will thank me one day for setting her free.

Chapter Thirty-Five

Chloe

"I know I said I'd rather take a puck to the head than mope around anymore, but this hurts like a motherfucker." My ass is flat on the ice, but I could use the ice on my unprotected boob.

Bobby sits down right next to me, hands frantically waving in front of me like he wants to make things right but isn't sure how to go about it when it's that particular body part.

"Druggy is gonna hand me my ass at our team meeting with the new coach," he mutters.

I rub my breast and breathe through the pain. That puck to the chest is going to leave a bruise, but what did I expect playing a friendly pick-up game with a professional athlete nearly half my age? I'm lucky I don't need a full body cast.

Bobby has definitely become a friend since I moved here. Once we got past his constant flirting, that is. He called me up this morning after two weeks of me dressing in all black and scaring my hockey league kids with my intensity. Ayana slipped me a piece of paper earlier this week with an overly sunshiney note about watching *Bake Off* together sometime soon and I had to hand over practice to Bobby and Matt while I sobbed in the bathroom. I think my less-than-stellar mood was fairly obvious.

Let's be real. I'm a fucking mess and I'm just about done with it.

"Druggy doesn't give a shit what happens to me." And it's true. He walked out my door that night, never to be seen again. He's clearly trying to avoid me, somehow never at the rink anytime I'm slated to be here.

Bobby snorts, getting to his feet and offering me his hand. I take it, letting him help me up, but he doesn't let go. "Oh, yeah? Want to run a little experiment?"

His blue eyes are twinkling, and even in my foul mood I can't ignore the power of Bobby's mischievous grin. I nod. What the hell? Why not?

His hand tightens and he pulls me close, running his fingers through my hair and pushing the strands behind my shoulder. He leans in and looks like he's about to sniff my neck.

"What the hell?" I mutter, looking at him like he's lost his damn mind.

"Shh, just go with it, Coop." He snickers, but lowers his head anyway and licks my neck.

"Hey!" I cry, pushing him back the same time there's a growl from the side of the rink.

"What the fuck, Roadie?"

We both turn to see Nikolai standing like an avenging Slavik warrior, ready to spill blood and burn villages. His fists clench tight at his side and his eyebrows are officially a unibrow. If he doesn't cool that glower, his sweats are in danger of burning clean off him.

"Told ya," Bobby whispers with an obnoxious wink. He releases me and dares to give Nikolai a grin. "Hey, Druggy. Nice to see you."

"Get your ass off that ice before I drag you away."

"I'm outta here!" Bobby holds up his hands in peace and wisely skates off the ice in the opposite direction. He runs right into the mom of one of my students as she looks for a spot for her son to put on his skates. I roll my eyes, but I can't seem to turn away from Nikolai long enough to make sure Bobby apologizes.

Nikolai's standing there, fuming like an angry bull. I drink him in and realize seeing him again hurts worse than that puck to my breast. I fell in love with the guy, told him so, got rejected, and now I might have to see him on the regular. Jesus. Talk about fucking up my move to a new state right out of the gate. Mom and Dad were right all along. Have to steer clear of those hockey boys.

"Do not even think about that," Nikolai commands.

I frown, clearly lost. "Think about what? Hockey boys?"

His frown deepens. I didn't think it was possible. He points his finger at me in warning and stalks off without saying a word. I watch him go, telling myself this will be the last time I watch him walk away from me. We're clearly done and I need to let him go. The locker room door swings shut behind him, and I let out the breath I'm holding.

"Coach!" Little voices sound behind me and I paste on a smile, telling myself to get my shit together and give these kids the kind of fun lesson they deserve. I can lick my wounds later. So that's what I do. I pour everything I have into these kids and focus on building my life the way I always planned.

Later, I tell myself I have one more night of moping before I put that shit to bed.

Nikolai ruined ice cream for me so I stick to the ultra-processed brownies from a box, knowing he'd never allow such terrible nutrition past his lips. I'm four brownies and two glasses of wine into the night and feeling like I might have hurt myself by consuming this for dinner when my doorbell rings. I groan, having no intention of answering it. I'm done with doorbells. Done with tall, Russian-speaking men with magic dicks and big, stubborn hearts. Done with single dads whose kids make you fall in love with them too.

"Chloe? Can we talk? It's Kaitlyn." A muffled female voice through my front door has the wine glass freezing against my lips.

Basic etiquette has me groaning again. I can't just ignore a pregnant woman at my door. Putting the wine glass down, I get to my feet and head for the door. I swing it open and lean against the doorframe. Yes, I answered the door, but I'm not giving the body language of someone who wants an extended visit.

Kaitlyn, perfectly tall and gorgeous and successful, holds up a bottle of wine above her very pregnant belly. "I can't drink it and Banks is trying some no carb diet to keep the old man pounds off. Can I come in?"

"How did you know wine was the magic password?" I give her a wry grin and step back to let her in. We settle on the couch and I pour her wine into my glass. The bottle looks way more expensive than the cheap grocery store brand I had on hand.

She leans her head back on the couch and rubs her belly. "Do you mind?" She gestures to the coffee table and I wave a hand. She kicks off her heels and props her feet up, wiggling her toes. "Damn, no one told me you lose your ankles when pregnant. I knew my waistline would go, but ankles too?"

I take a sip of wine and immediately close my eyes to savor the rich flavor bursting across my tongue. Now I feel bad for not wanting company.

"I know we haven't really reached that level of friendship

where we visit each other unannounced, so let me get to the point." She barrels ahead in true Kaitlyn fashion. "Banks sent me."

My eyes fly open. "Why?"

"The boys are worried about you." Kaitlyn zeros in on me with those brown eyes that don't miss a thing. "They had a meeting after Niko left the rink."

My jaw drops open. That just might be the sweetest, most embarrassing thing I've ever heard. "Like, all of them?"

Kaitlyn smiles. "Yep, the whole team. They're all worried about you. Said you haven't been your normal spicy self and they think Niko is to blame. Which is why I'm here. If there's anyone who understands the fuckery of dating a hockey player, it's me." She tips her head back and forth. "And Olivia, I suppose. Roman wasn't exactly easy either."

My hands are shaking at the implication, so I put the wine glass down on the coffee table. I spin toward Kaitlyn and lean forward. "Does *everyone* know about Nikolai and me?" Honestly, I don't care if they do, but I know Nikolai would care. Very much.

She rolls her eyes. "It's kind of obvious. The two of you look at each other and panties spontaneously combust in a five-mile radius." Then she frowns. "Until recently. The boys say Niko's been an absolute beast. Made MacDougal cry the other day."

I wince. That sounds on brand for Nikolai. I reach for the wine and fill my glass to the brim before sitting back and unloading the entire story on Kaitlyn. By the time I wind down, my glass is empty and she's fanning her face.

"I need to get home to my fiancé. Fun fact: libido cranks up again third trimester."

I force a smile, happy for my friend, but heart aching from retelling our story, knowing that's all I have left of Nikolai.

"Well, thanks for swinging by. The wine and company were fantastic."

Kaitlyn waves her hand away from her face. "Oh, I'm not leaving yet. I gotta know how this ends."

I shrug, feeling the buzz of the wine now and enjoying the way it blunts the ache in my chest. "I wish I knew, but I have a feeling it ends with nights like this. Wine, sugar, and crying myself to sleep until I'm over him."

"Oh, honey. No. Absolutely not." She shakes her head so hard her hair starts tumbling out of the messy bun on top of her head. "That man is in love with you."

The words hit like an arrow lancing my chest. It's hard to breathe around it, but I force myself to respond. "No, he actually isn't. And I need to accept that and move on."

Kaitlyn reaches over and squeezes my hand, surprisingly hard for a woman putting all her resources into growing another human being. "That's just it, babe. The boys are convinced he's in love with you. He actually laughed at one of Bobby's jokes in the locker room three weeks ago. You know, when things were still good between you. And that's also why he's been such a beast now that you've been apart."

Her words spark some stupid flame of hope, but I squash it. Quick. "Listen, I settled in a relationship before and I refuse to do that again. My late husband and I were good friends, and that was nice, but I need more. I want someone who loves me passionately. This is supposed to be my second chance at life and love. I won't settle again."

"You definitely shouldn't!" Kaitlyn agrees, patting my hands. "But these men . . ." She shakes her head and huffs out a breath. "They're not much brighter than their hockey sticks when it comes to love. You have to shove them into a wall to get their attention."

Reaching over, I pull her into a hug. "Thanks for trying to help, but I don't want to shove anyone anywhere. He's gotta figure this one out on his own." I'm still hurting, but I can feel the resolve settling in my bones. I know what kind of man I want and if Nikolai can't be that man, then I need to move on. "I won't settle, Kaitlyn."

She gives me a sad smile but nods this time. "I understand. For his sake, I hope he pulls his head out of his ass. He's about to lose a queen among women. Now help me up, would you?" She flails her hands in the air and I laugh. It takes a count of three and a generous tug upward, but she makes it off the couch and onto her feet. I walk her out and lock the door behind her.

Nothing is actually better, but I *feel* better. As I collect my glass and pan of brownies, taking them into the kitchen for a round in the dishwasher, I think about how I've been through the stages of grief before. This time feels different though. Back then, I was exhausted, relieved, and then feeling guilty for being relieved after Josh died. I'd been hopeful for a better life, one built on my terms. This time around, I just feel sad. Sad for all we could have been but will never be because of Nikolai's misplaced sense of honor. Or maybe I'm delusional and he just didn't love me enough to work through the blended family issues and telling my father about us. And I guess I'll never know. Nikolai has never been one to communicate much, even on a good day.

Slipping into a pajama set that makes me feel like a sleek and sexy woman, I know I'll wake up in the middle of the night and have to change them. I dump a few extra flakes in Sushi's tank. She gulps them down and stares at me through the glass. At least she's not hiding from me any longer.

"Just you and me and waking up soaking wet, Sushi." Her mouth opens and closes. I grimace. "Yeah, I know. That sounded weird. I blame the wine."

I slide into bed and close my eyes, refusing to acknowledge how much I miss Nikolai's strong arms wrapped around me.

Chapter Thirty-Six

Niko

Three hours earlier

The new coach is a hardass—good. That is exactly what this team needs: discipline, purpose, and accountability. Roman ran a tight ship as captain, and Dan-O does his best to fill Roman's shoes and keep everyone's feet to the fire. But from everything I have seen, heard, and read these past few months —as well as throughout the meeting that just adjourned— Coach Andre Marsh will deliver a firm brand of leadership even Ivan would approve of.

Ivan was the original hardass of hockey back home, and I would not have had it any other way. He always said, "A player without an impossible challenge before him has no reason to rise." That was just one of the many nuggets of wisdom he enjoyed dispensing. "Do or do not. There is no try" was another favorite, which, to his dying day, he insists he coined long before Yoda came around.

When Coach Bowman and the franchise heads officially introduced Coach March at our team meeting tonight, mixed emotions flashed over Coach Bowman's face. It is the end of a chapter. The man has dedicated such an enormous part of his life to the Storm Chasers, he deserves to enjoy a long retirement with a new focus. His impact on all our lives cannot be understated, and we owe him much gratitude. Me, especially.

Benny embraces Coach Bowman just inside the door while I stand back and watch my fellow teammates. Dan-O and Money are deep in conversation with Coach Marsh while the younger players exchange back slaps and laughs, many having not seen each other since early June.

When Benny backs away, I believe I detect a wayward tear in the corner of his eye. The man only gets sappier the further Kaitlyn's pregnancy progresses. By the time she gives birth, he will be a blubbering mess. Cappy quickly takes Benny's place in front of Coach Bowman as Benny flicks a hand across his eyes while glancing around to make sure nobody notices.

His gaze catches on mine, and he freezes before shrugging and loping over my way.

"What can I say? I'm gonna miss the guy."

My only response is a grunt, a perfect reflection of my dark mood. I was nearly late to the meeting after entering the practice facility earlier to see Roadie and Chloe embracing on the ice. I stalked into the locker room after Roadie, intent on ripping his head off and shoving it up his impertinent ass. But he must not be as stupid as I believed him to be because he had already made himself scarce.

By the time he slipped into the media room, the team meeting had already begun, and I did not want my first impression on my new coach to include a homicide.

It is my sincerest hope that Chloe is not allowing Roadie to waste her time. The last thing she deserves is a partner whose idea of a good time includes lighting his farts on fire and picking fights with opposing teams' rookies.

While it is none of my business, of course, I feel protective of Chloe. If I am being honest, I feel a variety of things for Chloe, none of which I can ever entertain again, however. I have already done too much damage.

In the absence of a real reply, Benny feels compelled to continue this conversation alone. "I see it's still grumpy season."

My glare only makes him grin.

"You don't happen to have any coal lying around the house, do you?" he asks.

"Have you taken a puck to the skull?" What else could explain his arbitrary question?

He continues as if I have not spoken. "'Cause you could have a pile of diamonds in a matter of days if you tucked a few lumps of coal in those clenched fists."

My jaw tightens as I frown at him and force my hands to relax at my sides.

Benny points at my face with another grin. "Or between your molars."

"Leave me," I dismiss Benny, not in the mood for his jokes.

"Wish I could," he says, although he does not sound very regretful. "But you're a ticking time bomb, Druggy, and I'm not the only one who's noticed."

At his comment, I dart my gaze around the room. He is correct. Several pairs of eyes flash away, their owners doing a shitty job of hiding their curiosity.

Shit.

"Explain," I demand.

Benny sighs and settles against the wall next to me. "Dude, you have been a complete bear these last couple weeks, snapping at everyone like a wild hyena and stalking around the place like you're plotting a decidedly violent coup."

Instead of allowing his words to sink in, I retort, "Which is it? Am I a bear or a hyena? I cannot be both."

"How about a jackass?"

My glare intensifies, but behind my eyes, my mind is working over his earlier statement. "It is the custody issue—that is where the dog is buried."

Benny's eyes bulge. "You killed your dog!? I knew you were in a mood, but what the fuck, man?!"

I respond with growing impatience, "It is an expression, you moron."

"Why are Russian expressions so terrifying?" He looks like he's sweating.

I consider reminding him of the English phrase, *There is more than one way to skin a cat*, but I refrain. "My mood, as you put it, is from the custody fight," I lie as I return us to the topic. "I will temper my behavior when training camp begins next week."

"Custody, my ass. You think our women don't talk?"

My pulse jumps. "What women?" Could he possibly suspect?

"Kaitlyn, Olivia, Sara, *Chloe*." His emphasis on the last name is so exaggerated it's almost comical—and it causes my heart to thump wildly in my ribcage.

"Explain," I repeat my earlier command as beads of sweat begin pricking at my temples.

Benny shakes his head with something too closely resembling pity for my liking. "Man, everybody knows you won your case. Chloe told us." He drops a hand on my shoulder. "And we're damn happy for you. You deserve to have equal time with your little whippersnapper."

Okay. I suppose it makes sense that she might have shared the news. Those of my teammates who remained in Tampa this offseason knew she was Ayana's nanny.

"Thank you," I manage, still wary.

He waves me off, intent on whatever point he is trying to make. "So, don't you think it's odd that a man who just won an agonizing two-year battle would immediately turn around and act as if he just found out he accidentally married his sister?"

"Do not think about my sister." My response is more reflexive than anything.

Benny rolls his eyes and sighs. "You know, Druggy, you need to wake up and stop getting in your own way." When I don't respond, he pats my shoulder again. "Just think about it." Then he walks away to join the conversation with Coach Marsh.

I return my focus to Coach Bowman, who is laughing at something Forns said. Benny obviously suspects something, even if he did not come right out and say it. Does Coach suspect as well? I wonder again if I should come clean, even though there is no longer anything going on between his daughter and me. It is the honorable thing to do.

As if sensing my thoughts, Coach turns his head and locks gazes with me. His laugh peters out as he holds my eyes. I cannot discern his expression. It almost resembles sadness mixed with a dose of that compassion his daughter is so good at. But I must be mistaken. Perhaps he is secretly plotting my painful death by torture.

But that would not be his way. This is a man who, despite no longer being employed by the team, continues to monitor my progress with Cappy and Mac as if his own future depends on the outcome. He is a man of great integrity, and he will always have my respect. I only endeavor to deserve his in return going forward.

I muster a ghost of a smile and nod at him, hoping the gesture communicates what I want it to. Coach returns a similarly weak smile and nods back before his attention is seized by Roadie coming in hot for a hug that borders on inappropriate.

That boy needs a lesson, but I am suddenly not in the mood to be the teacher.

"Hello, Paul," I greet the dog before setting my keys on the entry table. He has grown quickly since his first days with us as a pup. He obediently sits, tail wagging against the wood floor as I scratch behind his ears.

"Dad!" Ayana tears around the corner, still wearing the Storm Chasers sweatshirt she donned for practice earlier. I brought her to the rink, but her babysitter picked her up and delivered her home since my team meeting ran longer than the practice.

My mind goes back to Chloe standing defiantly on her skates and giving me that challenging look. I have avoided her as much as possible, for both our sakes. I never intended to hurt her, and I still do not entirely understand how things went so far off the rails.

She only thinks she loves me, though. It is in her nature to become attached to people and focus only on their good qualities—and, in my case, invent some that do not actually exist. Chloe does not know me. We have—*had*—sexual chemistry, and she is perhaps the most decent human being I have met. That is the long and short of it.

She will get over this misplaced preoccupation and realize I am not worth her time or thought. Hell, based on the interaction with Roadie I witnessed, perhaps she already has.

"Kara and I made you a present," Ayana announces.

"A present? What did I do to deserve this?" If anything, my recent mood has earned me punishment, not gifts.

"Duh. You're my dad." Ayana says this as though it is an irrefutable rule of the universe.

I follow her to the living room, where Kara rests on the couch, scrolling through her phone. Kara is Dan-O's baby sister who just graduated from college and hasn't found the right job yet. Since she had great references and I know her brother—and she passed the background check as well as social media vetting for red-flag behavior—she has been watching Ayana here and there when our schedules require it. I am still interviewing for a long-term nanny, but no one has been the right fit thus far.

Peyton has been surprisingly cooperative about the custody calendar, and Ayana and I are currently in the middle of a two-week stretch together. We have already established a routine that has been my only source of joy since that last night at Chloe's condo.

We wake up early each morning, and I cook breakfast while Ayana gets ready for school and feeds Paul. Then we take him for a walk before I shower and get ready. Ayana insists on using that time to practice her kitchen skills and pack lunches for both of us. I do not have the heart to tell her that Mac and Cappy often eat mine—especially when she packs her lopsided peanut butter and jelly sandwiches. I do not understand Americans' obsession with a substance that seems to have no purpose other than sealing one's tongue to the roof of his mouth. Still, I will never tell her to stop making them.

I drop her off at school and either go for my workout or meet up with Mac and Cappy for drills or more training. I leave the rink just in time to pick Ayana up after school, and we work on her homework or a puzzle together while sharing a snack. It is the cozy life I have longed for with my daughter, but I cannot escape the feeling that something is missing. I refuse to think too hard about it because this is what I have strived for all this time, and I will not be ungrateful for any of it.

"Hey, Mr. Drugov." Kara looks up from her phone to greet me. She has the same light hair as Dan-O, but has luckily inherited everything else from their mother. I nod my hello, and she continues, "I didn't know Ayana was such a talented artist."

I glance down at my daughter, who is beaming at her sitter. I run my hand over her head, ruffling her fine blond tresses. "You must get that from your *tetya* Safiya."

Ayana's eyes widen. "Oh yeah. I forgot to tell you my aunt is a painter. People pay her for her pictures and everything," she informs Kara.

"Cool." Kara stands, setting her phone on the coffee table before lifting a small gift bag from beside it. "You should do the honors," she says to Ayana. My daughter rushes over to snatch the bag and then skips back to me.

"Open it!" she invites, extending the paper bag.

I take it with a smile and gently lift the tissue paper hiding its contents. Ayana takes the paper and bounces on her toes with a wide grin as she waits for me to withdraw the gift.

My breath catches when I remove it from the bag, finding that my daughter has painted and decorated a small picture frame holding a snapshot of Chloe and me. I recognize it from a night the three of us took Paul for a walk and he began jumping and barking at fireworks lighting the sky from a nearby park. The sounds coming from the dog kept escalating until he was belting out extended yearning howls that had all three of us bent over laughing. I did not even know Ayana had her phone with her that night, much less took a photo.

Chloe, looking gorgeous as always, is leaning into me with

a hand to my chest and I . . . I am *gazing* down at her—there is no other word for it—with naked affection and an expression of pure happiness. An evening with just my daughter, her howling dog, and the most beautiful, sweet, and charming woman on earth. In other words . . . my wildest dream come true–even though I never meant to dream it in the first place.

Chapter Thirty-Seven

Chloe

"Can I ask you a quick question?" asks Molly, one of the moms who come to collect their kiddos after practice. She's dressed in a gorgeous suit, and despite being a beautiful woman, looks like she's had a rough day.

I put my bag back on the bench and give her a warm smile, pushing down the panic that if I stay any longer, I risk running into Nikolai. Considering I've held fast to my vow to move on and quit moping after I had that wine-fueled night with Kaitlyn, I can't chance a run-in this soon.

But Molly is wringing her hands and the tug on my heart has me forgetting about Nikolai. She leans in and drops her voice. "Matthew's has been acting out recently. He'd kill me for telling you this, but he pushed another kid off the lunch table the other day and got suspended."

"Oh, no," I breathe. I saw a lot of kids with behavioral problems when I was a teacher. It almost always stemmed from an issue at home or bullying going on. But Matthew is such a nice boy, if a little quiet, from what I've seen in our practices. "What can I do?"

She glances over her shoulder and continues, seeing Matthew still putting his shoes on with another kid from practice. "Could you keep an eye on him? If he causes problems, I want to know about it as soon as possible. Single mom guilt over here. I worry I'm dropping the ball."

I put my hand on her shoulder. "I promise to keep a close eye."

Molly's shoulders drop in relief. "Thank you so much. I wasn't sure who to ask."

"This is why I started coaching, actually. I wanted to reach kids like I used to as a teacher without all the grading papers. Here's my number. You can text me anytime with concerns." We exchange numbers and then Matthew walks up to his mom, seeming to hide behind his floppy hair.

"Hey Coach. Jack keeps getting blisters. Can you see if his skates are jacked up?"

"Sure." I give Molly what I hope is an encouraging smile and head over to offer my support. By the time I restring the laces on Jack's skates, his father has arrived. I also notice Bobby hovering nearby for no apparent reason. There's a flush on Molly's face, like she noticed Bobby's attention too, but is too shy to do anything about it.

"Ready to go, Matthew?" Molly swings her keyring around and around her finger.

I look past her to see Bobby staring at her ass with the kind of appreciation little kids give a three-scoop cone of ice cream. I give him laser eyes that clearly say, *stop the ogling, dumbass.* He must feel it because he snaps to attention and walks off. I shake my head and say goodbye, mentally adding "check on Matthew" to my list of things to do. And having a chat with Bobby about staying away from my students' moms.

Back at home, Sushi ignores me, giving an extra shake of

her tail as she swims away from me into her castle. Sassy little thing. I don't blame her though. Sometimes a girl just feels like hiding away from the world for a while.

"I'm not moping," I tell her tail defiantly as I slide into my favorite baggy sweatshirt and spandex. "I'm just getting comfortable."

The doorbell rings and I freeze. Sushi pops her head out of the castle. "What is up with people just coming over whenever they feel like it? Is this a southern thing?" I wrinkle my nose. "Florida's not really southern though, right?"

Sushi opens and closes her mouth as I exit the bedroom to answer the door. I feel like I deserve a glass of wine for not immediately thinking it might be Nikolai coming to beg for my forgiveness. My heart is finally realizing that ship has sailed.

"Chloe, darling!"

Mom stands on my doorstep, her gold sandals brighter than my porch light.

"Mom? What are you doing here?" I step back and she comes in, enveloping me in a hug and kissing my cheek. Her why-spray-a-little-when-you-can-spray-a-lot perfume makes my eyes water.

"What? I can only come over when you have plants you need me to water?"

Ah, there it is. The mom guilt. "You know you're welcome any time." I sit on the couch and she joins me. She's looking like she spent the day at a tennis lesson ogling her instructor instead of playing tennis. "Cute skirt."

Mom preens. "Thank you. Jeff took me shopping yesterday. Said I have great legs and should show them off."

I think back over the long list of prior husbands and boyfriends, but can't place a Jeff. "Well, that's nice. You should always rock those legs, no matter what age."

Mom's smile fades. "Chloe, darling, what's going on?"

The question sets me on edge, but I lean back into the

couch cushion like my life lately has been nothing but sunshine and roses. "What do you mean?"

She sighs, spinning to tuck a leg under her, and reaches over to squeeze my hands. "This is your mother, Chloe Cooper. Cut the bullshit."

I pull back my head. "Jeez, Mom."

She gives me a look only your own mother can pull off. It melts away all the excuses on the tip of my tongue and leaves me feeling five years old with my hand stuck in the cookie jar. I huff and accept my fate. "Fine. I fell in love with the wrong man. And now I'm getting over him and moving on with my life."

"Oh honey. If there's one woman who can understand falling in love with the wrong man, it's me. I've fallen in love with all of them." She laughs softly. "So tell me what this man has that Tanner doesn't, because that man is . . ." She trails off, eyes glazing over.

"Mom! Tanner is way too young for you!"

Her smile is pure feminine confidence that I can only hope to have a fraction of one day. "There's no such thing, darling." I roll my eyes, used to Mom's antics with men. She takes pity on me and moves the conversation along. "Seriously, though. Tanner is everything a woman is looking for, but he didn't do it for you. Tell me why."

My chest aches, thinking of all the reasons Nikolai is far superior. Not in looks, or manners, or even demeanor. It's all the things that matter on a deeper level. "This other man made my heart flutter with the way he looked at me so intensely. Like he wanted to hear every word I said because each word mattered. Like he'd do anything to make my life easier, even if it was an inconvenience for him." My eyes fill with tears and there's nothing I can do to stop it. "He made me feel beautiful."

Mom squeezes my hands tightly, her voice soft but firm. "Then why aren't you with *him*?"

And there it is. The deep wound in my chest that I've tried to ignore. A tear slips down my cheek. "He's got a child. And a career. And an overly complicated sense of duty to . . . well, everyone. Those have to be his priorities. What I want doesn't matter."

"Oh, Chloe, darling, what you want always matters. And if that man has any sense in his head, he'll see that. He'll come back and put you right at the top of his priority list like you deserve."

I shake my head, thinking of Dad's sacrifice throughout my childhood. He never remarried after he and Mom divorced. Later, once I was an adult, I overheard him telling someone he'd done that on purpose. He put me first and I'd never felt so loved as I did in that moment. I was also incredibly sad for my dad. That he'd lived life alone.

Mom lets go of my hands and sinks back into the couch cushions. "Your father and I were so different. Opposites, really. It was a wonder our marriage lasted as long as it did. He was so focused and I was a scatterbrain with a thousand things going on at once." She chuckles, then sobers quickly. "He ended up alone and I ended up with a drawer full of engagement rings. I'd like to think the best route might be something in the middle."

I feign shock. "Are you suggesting moderation?"

She bats away my sarcasm. "Don't disrespect your mother, darling. I have embarrassing baby pictures that can suddenly resurface, you know. I'm being serious. Single parents aren't relegated to a life alone, you know. You can be a good parent and also be in a long-term relationship."

"Tell that to him," I shoot back. "Also, since we're having this bonding moment, I think I should tell you that Dad's in love."

Her features soften. "I'm really happy to hear that." She looks away and seems lost in thought. After a few moments, she turns back to me. "Enough about these men. How about we sit here and mope together? If my daughter's hurting, I'm hurting. Come 'ere."

She lifts her arm and waves me in. I let myself lean her direction, tentatively resting my head on her shoulder. For a woman who cares a great deal about keeping her body fat low, she gives good cuddle. When she begins to play with my hair and tell me stories from when I was growing up, I officially give in. Apparently, there is no age limit on accepting snuggle time from your mom.

My eyelids are drooping when my phone rings. Mom leans forward, taking me with her before snatching the phone off the coffee table and handing it to me. Ayana's name lights up the screen. Putting it to my ear, I lose the sleepiness in an instant. Ayana only has a phone for emergencies.

"Chloe?" Ayana's voice comes through the phone loud and clear. Also clear? The wobble that has my insides clenching.

I jump to my feet in alarm. "What's wrong?"

"Can you come over? I'm home all alone and I'm scared."

My mind spins, even as I'm already flying to the front door where I shove my feet into the first pair of flip flops I find. What the fuck? Shouldn't Ayana be with the new nanny? And where the hell is Nikolai?

"I'm on my way, sweetheart. Stay inside and don't answer the door. I'll be there in ten." I hang up.

"Mom, I'm sorry but I've got to cut this short." The door swings shut before I even hear her answer.

Chapter Thirty-Eight

Niko

Two hours earlier

My phone rings right in the middle of post-hockey-practice math homework. When I see who is calling, I leave Ayana and Paul in the dining room and head out to the lanai for some privacy.

"Hello, *moy khoroshiy*." Katya's warm greeting hits my ears and I feel like I am twelve again, visiting Ivan and Katya's home for the first time.

"Katya. It is so good to hear your voice."

"You act as if we have not spoken in years," she says with amusement.

"I know. I . . ." I trail off, not sure what to say now that I have her on the phone.

Ever since Ayana presented me with that photo the other day, my mind has been swirling with all manner of regret and second guessing. I have spent so much time staring at it, I have every detail memorized. It now rests under all the contents of my sock drawer to keep me from obsessing over it any longer.

In a moment of weakness yesterday, I called Katya, almost relieved when I got her voicemail since I had yet to form a concrete reason for calling. As it turns out, I am no better off a day later.

Katya waits for me to continue, and when I do not, she sighs. "Talk to me, Niko. You do not sound like yourself. What is troubling you?"

"Nothing," I lie, deciding she does not need to be burdened with my problems. "I was only calling to check on you." I turn back to the glass door to see Ayana perched on her knees on a dining chair, tongue clenched between her teeth in concentration as she leans over her math homework.

"Ivan always said you were a bad liar because you did not have enough practice at it."

I cough out a rough chuckle. "I am not so sure about that. Perhaps he was just easy to fool."

Katya laughs, the sound lilting and bright. She sounds like her old self, which is relieving. "That is a good one, Niko." She is right, of course. Ivan was as sharp as they come. Sobering, she continues, "Out with it. And I want the truth this time. Allow me to help you for once."

"You and Ivan have both helped me more than enough," I remind her.

"Oh, Ivan wanted your success more than you did, I would wager. You should have seen him preening around town bragging about you."

"Ivan did not preen," I insist, picturing my old coach, lines etched into his stern face and his posture permanently set in battle mode.

"Stop evading, Niko. I keep telling you it was just a rough few days and you do not need to worry. My neighbors and Safiya check on me so often my doormat is worn thin."

"I am glad."

"You are a good boy."

I cannot remember the last time anyone but Katya referred to me as a boy, and it takes me back to early days.

"I am not so sure about that." My eyes drop to my bare feet on the stamped concrete surrounding the pool. Here goes nothing. "I am struggling with a . . . situation." My voice sounds strangled, even to my own ears. "I think I made a mistake."

I hear a sharp gasp from the other end of the line and wonder for a split second if Katya has injured herself. My concern is invalidated when she exclaims, "It is a woman!"

"What?! How did you . . . I never said–" I sputter, my eyes flashing back to Ayana behind the glass. But she remains at the table, oblivious of my conversation with Katya.

"Nothing makes a man sound so confounded and desperate as love."

My voice drops to a whisper for some reason. "I certainly never said anything about love!" Although that very sentiment is written all over that photograph, despite all my efforts to deny it.

"So, who is she?" Katya ignores my protests and forges ahead. "Has she met Ayana yet?"

Since she clearly cannot be dissuaded, I exhale loudly and give in, getting straight to the heart of the matter. "She is Coach Bowman's daughter."

I half expect Katya to lose her shit and fall over laughing at the irony, however, she does nothing of the sort. Instead, she is silent for so long, I wonder if our connection has been broken.

"Katya?"

"My darling boy," is all she says.

"I crossed a line and tried to go back . . . but now I fear there *is* no going back." My eyes close, the heavy weight of disappointing either of my mentors resettling on my shoulders like a familiar cloak.

Katya sighs. "You have spent so much of your life repaying imaginary debts, Niko. But you are your own man—a good man—and the best way to honor those you hold in high esteem is to allow yourself to be happy. And to share that happiness, instead of miring yourself in that strict sense of duty you cling to." As if reading my thoughts, she continues, "If Ivan and I had been blessed with a daughter, I cannot think of anyone we would trust her with more than you."

"Katya." My voice is suddenly hoarse.

"Was Coach Bowman's daughter happy when she was with you?"

"I think so," I admit before anticipating her next question. "And I *know* I was happy with her."

"Then honor everyone—including her and yourself—by living your life to its fullest. You only live once, my boy."

Her words conjure more images of Ivan. He certainly lived his life to its fullest, that cannot be denied. And then another coach's face takes Ivan's place in my mind as adrenaline begins filtering into my bloodstream.

"Katya, I need to go."

She must like something in my tone because her response is, "Bring her to visit next time you come home, yes?"

Instead of confirming or denying, I thank Katya and hang up. It is time to get a sitter for Ayana and get my ass across town.

Forty minutes later, I am knocking on Coach Bowman's front door.

He takes one look at my expression and swings the door wide to usher me in with an inexplicable, "I've been waiting for this visit." My confused expression goes unacknowledged as Coach leads me to his study and goes straight for the liquor cart. "Vodka?"

I nod absently, one hand going to the back of my neck and the other diving into my pocket as Coach pours our drinks. I wonder for a moment if Chloe has confided in him, but it matters little. I am here to say something I should have said weeks ago, so I forge ahead, intent on explaining myself and coming clean.

Instead, however, I simply declare, "Love is mean. You may fall in love with a goat."

The hand holding Coach's glass of bourbon freezes halfway to his mouth. "Excuse me?"

I shake my head, realizing I have cocked things up with another of my Russian idioms that does not translate quite as well as I had hoped. This situation calls for straight honesty, however, not metaphors or flowery speech.

"I am in love with your daughter."

The bourbon glass finishes its journey to Coach's mouth while his eyes stare into mine. He pulls in a sip and holds it before swallowing and lowering the glass. "I know." He hands me a crystal glass with my vodka, and I pull my hand from my pocket to accept it with wide eyes.

"You know?"

Coach gestures for me to sit in one of the matching wing-back chairs while he takes the other. "Everyone knows."

Fuck. How is this possible? I did not know myself until a few days ago.

I realize then that one corner of Coach's mouth is quirking. He is . . . amused? "I am sorry, sir, but why are you not angry with me right now?"

"Why should I be angry that you love my daughter?"

My eyes widen again as I sputter, "You have been . . ." I clear my throat, something suddenly clogging my words. ". . . like a father to me. I owe you so much. Chloe is your daughter—"

He cuts me off, all traces of amusement gone now. "Niko, I'm honored that you think of me that way, and I can tell you the feeling is mutual. But Chloe is forty-two and knows her own mind. As far as I can tell, she can decide for herself who she dates or falls in love with."

At its core, this makes sense, but there are extenuating circumstances. The adrenaline that began flowing after my talk with Katya surges again, and I spear frustrated fingers through my hair. "I fear Chloe would be wasting her time with me, sir. I have Ayana. I have family to care for. I have another year of hockey and then who knows what else. I tried to break things off before it progressed to something more serious."

When I see his responding frown, I hurry to explain myself before I dig this hole any deeper. "Chloe deserves to find someone she can have a real relationship with. She deserves better than me. She deserves someone like her—someone kind and optimistic and compassionate who can and will always put her first and lift her up."

"And you're nothing like that?" Coach Bowman asks, leaning forward in his chair. "Then why would she be interested in you in the first place?"

"Circumstances, perhaps?" I shake my head. "It was supposed to be . . ." I search for a word that would not embarrass either Chloe or Coach, but all I come up with is, "Casual. She does not know me."

"Right. Casual," he repeats, a definite tic in his jaw—not that I can blame him. "But *you* know *her*?"

"Yes. She is all the things I said, and more." I exhale, picturing Chloe's face covered with flour. "She laughs at herself and brings joy with her wherever she goes, even when she is faced with a challenge or forgetting why she walked into a room." I lift my eyes to Coach's face, searching for words that could adequately describe his daughter and knowing I will never find enough to do the job. So, I settle for, "She looks at life like a ripe piece of fruit to be devoured and savored at the same time. And she makes everyone around her do the same."

Coach nods. "So, during this *casual* thing, you spent all this time with her and know so much about her—not only who she is on the outside, but you know her heart. And you don't think she knows exactly who *you* are too?"

I set my untouched vodka on the edge of Coach's enormous wood desk and clasp my hands together. "Sir, I did not mean to be disrespectful when I said it was casual. I just mean . . . well . . . she probably only *thinks* she loves me. But she cannot. Should not."

But he shocks me by bursting into laughter in the next moment. When my frown intensifies, he oddly says, "I promise you'll think it's funny one day too."

I open my mouth to ask him what the hell he is talking about but he beats me to it. "Niko, I know few men as good as you. My father, my college coach, and maybe Roman when he's not buffing his fingernails. You have honor, integrity, and a sense of loyalty I've never witnessed in another man."

That object clogs my throat again, and I find I cannot speak. So, instead, I shift forward uncomfortably in my chair, resting my elbows on my knees.

"All of this is to say that If you're who my daughter wants, then I can only think of one reason you and Chloe shouldn't be together in a way that's *not* casual."

I nod, knowing exactly what he means. "My obligations that would prevent me from giving her all the attention and focus she deserves. My . . . surliness. My controlling nature. My dishonesty with you." I take a breath to continue since the list is endless, but Coach throws out his palm and sets his own glass on the desk.

"Stop. The only reason you shouldn't be together is if you don't love her with all your heart. If that's the case, I'll respectfully ask you to step aside."

I swallow thickly past the lump in my throat, heat suffusing my chest and belly and my pulse quickening. But the heat is not from anger or anxiety or self-loathing . . . it is from the overwhelming emotion filling me at just the prospect of being free to love and care for someone simply because she makes me happy. To love . . . Chloe.

Still. "But, Coach, I . . . she deserves . . . more.

His lips tug in a half smile. "Why don't you let my daughter decide what she deserves? In case you haven't noticed, she's not only bright, she's independent as hell."

"But Ayana," I begin again before shaking my head to better organize my words. "Ayana will always come first, and that is not fair to Chloe."

"Just like Chloe always came first for me when she was a child. But children eventually grow up—usually before their dads are ready. Besides, the Chloe I know would be suffocated by a guy who hovered over her day and night and had no other interests or obligations. Frankly, that sounds a little creepy, if you don't mind me saying so."

Before I can even begin thinking of a reply, he waves me off again with a short laugh. "I'm joking. But have you seen Chloe and Ayana together? They're two peas in a pod. In fact, you may have to fight your daughter for Chloe's attention in the end." A grin tugs at my lips even as I will it away, along with the burgeoning hope working its way through my chest. "Speaking of Ayana," Coach says with a lift of his eyebrows. "You think you're doing right by that girl walking around like a miserable lone wolf?"

My eyes narrow at his characterization, and I finally reach for my vodka and take a sip. The sharp liquor sears my throat. "Benny called me a bear. And a hyena. It seems I must add wolf to the list."

Coach chuckles knowingly and retrieves his glass as well. "Listen, Niko, I know I've never talked much about my personal life, and now I regret it. Because you could learn from my mistakes." He takes a small sip and swallows. "Dawn and I dragged out our marriage way longer than we should have, thinking we were doing right by Chloe in staying together. Then Dawn jumped right into an ill-conceived marriage while I remained single and threw myself into work and Chloe's hockey. Before I knew it, she was off to college and got hitched right after that. Dawn and I both messed up. Kids need examples of balance and healthy relationships so they can find both for themselves later on."

One of the reasons Peyton and I divorced was that I did not want Ayana to grow up with parents who were constantly at odds with each other. But I had not thought further than that.

"In the end, all we taught Chloe about relationships is that they're painful and not all that rewarding. I suspect she settled when she and Josh got married. Thinking back, I wonder if she just threw up her hands and thought, 'Well, he asked, so I guess this is what people do.'"

I do not like hearing this—or hearing that my behavior may be negatively affecting Ayana—and my responding frown indicates as much.

"I'm not saying he wasn't a decent guy. He was. I just

think he wasn't the *right* guy." He sends me a pointed look that is impossible to misinterpret.

"And you think . . ." I can't finish the question, I am so taken aback.

Coach nods. "If you want to be."

I study his face for a few moments before dropping my eyes shut. A flood of emotion fills my entire body as memories from the last several months wash over me. When my eyes open again, there is nothing but conviction in my voice.

"I do. More than anything."

"Then what are you waiting for?"

Chapter Thirty-Nine

Chloe

The house is dark when I pull up, which has me concerned. I barely get my car in park in the driveway before I'm running to the front door and ringing the doorbell cam.

"Ayana! It's Chloe! Are you home?"

The door swings open to reveal a young woman and Ayana, both with smiles on their faces. Paul runs up to knock me over with a headbutt. I scratch behind his ears and stumble over my words, not quite sure what's happening. "Ayana? Is . . . everything okay?"

"Hi, I'm Kara, babysitter for Ayana. We have a confession." The girl nudges Ayana with her elbow.

Ayana jumps into action, taking my hand and pulling me into the house. Paul's nails click on the floor behind us. "I kiiiind of told a lie when I was on the phone with you."

I dig my heels in and put my hands on my hips, heart rate finally coming down from the stratosphere. "There are no 'kind of lies.' Only flat out lies."

Ayana's shoulders shift up to her ears and her smile is more sheepish now. "Yeah . . . so I lied to get you here."

"I told her it was a bad idea to lie," Kara chimes in, earning a glare from Ayana.

I put my hands up and they both hush. "Is Nikolai here?"

"No," they answer in unison.

"That's why I wanted you here," Ayana goes on. "We don't have much time."

She takes my hand again and pulls me into the living room and down on the couch with her. I let her, wanting to get to the bottom of what's going on. Paul curls up at my feet and I realize I've even missed the dog. Now that I know Nikolai isn't here, I hope I won't have to run into him if I get out of here quickly enough.

"I miss you, Chloe." Ayana looks at Kara. "No offense." Kara waves off her concern.

"I miss you too, Ayana, but you can't lie about an emergency just to see me. If you talk to your dad, I'm sure we can come up with times we can hang out."

"Okay, but that's not why I had to get you here."

I try not to let the exasperation into my voice. "Then why am I here?"

Ayana spreads her arms out to the sides. "Because Dad's in love with you. Duh!"

I'm shaking my head before she even finishes that sentence. "No, honey. He's not." My heart aches with the admission, but the sooner I disabuse her of this notion, the better off she'll be.

Ayana jumps to her feet and begins to pace the floor, looking agitated. "Yes, he is! I know what love looks like. He's happy and smiley when you're around and grumpy and mean when you're gone. He works out all the time now that you don't live here. And he keeps your photo in his sock drawer!"

That last one has my attention. "Sock drawer?"

"Yes!" Ayana exclaims, like this explains everything. "Dad always says you don't just fall in love with a goat."

I try to turn that one around in my brain, but come up with more confusion.

"He just means that you choose who you fall in love with and I think he's right. He chose you to fall in love with, but he's too stubborn to admit it. So, you have to be here and get him to listen."

That heartache I've been nursing turns into a whole rib cage of pain. "Oh, honey. It's not that simple." I grasp her hands and pull her back onto the couch with me. "Two people can care for each other and still not be right for a relationship."

"That's stupid!" Ayana cries.

"Yes. That is stupid," comes a deep rumble from behind me.

"Dad!" Ayana shoots to her feet and pulls Nikolai into the room, just to shove him down next to me on the couch. "So glad you're here. Kara and I have to take Paul for a walk."

"Now?" Kara asks, checking her phone for the time. Ayana hisses and Kara jumps up, clearly remembering some scheme they worked out ahead of time.

My heart, the stubborn organ that can't seem to get up to pace with reality, is thumping against my chest at the sight of Nikolai. The eyes that I've seen go ice cold are crackling with warmth. His shoulders block out the world as he turns to me, creating a bubble of just him and me. His scent hits me and I swear every bone in my body aches from not being near him for several weeks.

The three get out the door with a whispered flurry of words and several barks from Paul to get a move on. When the door finally shuts behind them, Nikolai, who's been staring at me like he's drinking me in, finally speaks.

"She is right. Two people who care for each other is the basis of every solid relationship."

I nod, actually following along for the first time tonight. "I–I'm sorry to just show up here. Ayana called and insinuated she was alone. I came racing over, but I can go now."

Nikolai's hand shoots out to hold me in place. I freeze, absolutely unwilling to pull away from him. Not when my whole body is hyper focused on where his fingers are stroking my skin. "Please stay. There is much I need to say."

I may have started putting my own needs first with this move to Tampa, but I'm still me. When someone asks me for something, I tend to want to give it to them. And I really do want to hear what Nikolai has to say, even if it tears my heart in pieces. Again.

"Okay," I croak.

Nikolai doesn't release me, but he does nod. I can't tell if he's frowning because he's mad I'm here or if this is just his resting frown face. "Last time we were together you told me something that I have not been able to get out of my mind."

I hide behind my eyelids and wish for a hole to crawl into. Nikolai squeezes my hand and my eyes flutter open.

"I walked out like a coward and I owe you an apology for that."

I shake my head. "No apology needed."

"Yes, Chloe. Only an idiot would walk away from you sharing your heart. I am that idiot. You do not owe me anything, but I hope you will listen to what I have to say now."

I nod and he continues. I can barely breathe but promise myself one hell of a cocktail for surviving this humiliation.

"I thought I could not love you because my focus has always been my career and Ayana. Very important people in my life have shown me I am an idiot. What I taught Ayana is wrong. You cannot choose who you love or when it happens." He takes my hand and places it on his thigh, wrapping me in both hands. "I love you, Chloe Cooper."

My heart stills and I forget to breathe. I stare at him, waiting for the next part of that sentence. The "gotcha!" that surely is to come. The reasons for why we can never be together. Or that he is simply wrong for loving me.

But he doesn't continue. He just stares right back at me until we find ourselves in a staring contest.

"It is okay if you do not love me anymore. I have given you so many reasons to hate me, actually, but I wanted you to know that your love was returned. I was just too much of an–"

"Idiot?" I supply for him, finally finding my voice.

He dips his head. "Yes. Idiot."

"Wait." I screw up my face, trying to decipher this conversation. "Are you saying you still love me? Or you *used* to love me?"

He brings my hand up to his lips and presses the back of my hand to his mouth. Just a flutter of a kiss, but it sends off a riot of butterflies in my stomach. "I am in love with you now and I imagine I always will be. As much as I did not want to admit it before, I can see that I cannot stop it now."

I gape at him, somewhere in the back of my brain laughing at myself for my imitation of Sushi. "Okay, but what's the catch?"

Nikolai's eyebrows draw together. "The catch?"

I pull my hand from his before I beg him to let me move back in. "Yes. You love me, but . . . what? We can't be together because . . . Ayana? Your career? Your family? Explain it to me like I'm seven."

"I am like a goat looking at a watch." Nikolai shakes his head in disgust. What is with this family and the goat references? "I am good at hockey, but not much else, it seems. Chloe, I love you and I want to be with you. There are priorities in my life, yes. But I want you to be one of them. I am learning that life is not all or nothing."

I jump to my feet, suddenly so nervous I need to move or I

fear I might fall apart. "You love me and want to be with me. That's what you're saying."

He stands too, looking so unlike his take-charge self, under different circumstances I'd laugh. "Yes. That is all correct."

My lips understand first, slowly tilting up on the sides into the widest, cheesiest grin that ever grinned. "Well, I love you too. Still."

Nikolai's hands come up to land on my hips, pulling me into his chest. Every muscle in my body relaxes against him, like they'd just been waiting to be connected with this man all these weeks.

"Then be with me. Please. I am not good with words, but I will show you every day that you are loved."

I'm nodding automatically. He's not great with words, but damn is he good with his hands and his thoughtfulness. And I'm far too in love with him to not give him a second chance. "Consider me with you. Done."

He shakes his head, a lopsided smile finally replacing the frown. "No, *malish*. Never done." And then he dips his head and kisses me.

Niko

"I thought she'd never fall asleep," Chloe whispers as I press into her back, my hands circling her waist and my lips coming to rest on the side of her neck. She shivers, and I turn us both toward the hallway on the opposite end of the house—the one with the guest room.

It has been two hours since I came home to find Chloe's Bronco in my driveway and her sitting on my couch. At first, I thought my eyes were playing tricks on me. My intention had been to come home and talk to Ayana first before driving over to Chloe's duplex to confess my feelings—and idiocy. But fate —and my daughter's meddling—had led her to me instead.

"We must be quiet," I murmur into her neck before tasting the skin with the tip of my tongue. Sweet, just as I remember. I cannot believe I have her with me again, and this time, I get to call her mine.

"I'm not sure if I can." Chloe groans and almost trips, so I hoist her up in my arms to carry her the rest of the way to the guest room. At the sudden movement, she yelps in surprise before slapping a hand over her mouth. "See, I told you," she whisper-hisses, so I give her lips another purpose by kissing her hard while I take us the rest of the way and lock the door behind us.

I waste no time depositing Chloe on the bed and divesting her of her tight shorts before climbing on after her. My mouth goes straight to the spot on her inner thigh that makes her squirm while my hands smooth up her thighs to cradle her soft hips. I am not disappointed when she gasps and wiggles under my hands. But when my lips trail farther up her inner thigh, she jerks her hips off the bed and I pull back to frown at her.

"Stay still. I am working here."

Chloe giggles and spears the fingers of one hand into my hair. "Your beard tickles."

"Hands over your head, *malish*."

Since laughter is not my goal at the moment, I pull her thighs roughly apart and drag the flat of my tongue up her inner thigh to her panties, covering the gusset with my hot mouth. Her laughter dies, replaced by another gasp as her fingers leave my hair and she does as I asked. That is more like it.

Chloe's panties are gone seconds later, and she is coming on my tongue within minutes. She is a feast for my eyes, laid out on the bed panting with her cheeks pink and her sex pinker, swollen and pulsing from my attentions.

"Now you can sit up." My voice is tight and low, my entire body tense with desire. I gently pull her to a seated position and remove her sweatshirt before resting back on my heels to gaze at her gorgeous body.

"So beautiful," I murmur, watching my finger trace along the edge of her bra, my touch causing her nipples to tighten under the lace.

Chloe's hand comes up to cup my cheek, and my eyes shift to meet hers. They are liquid pools of desire and emotion. "Nikolai." Her voice cracks.

We look at one another for a long moment before I lean forward and kiss her, hoping she can feel everything I mean the kiss to say. But it is not long before the kiss goes from reverent to frantic, each of us desperate to devour the other. I unclasp her bra while she lifts my shirt, and then I quickly shed the rest of my clothes until we are skin to skin. When her teeth graze my nipple, I hiss and press her back to the mattress so I can close my lips around one of her gorgeous breasts.

After tasting my fill, I stand by the bed and drag her hips so they are poised at the edge, giving me the perfect view of her flushed body. I quickly apply the condom I took from my room earlier and bring her legs up so one ankle rests on each of my shoulders. Then I finally press into her slick pussy, my eyes falling shut for a few seconds as I savor the feeling of being enveloped by her tight heat. Her hand at my hip has my eyelids lifting again.

"Hands above your head, *malish*," I remind her.

"But I want to touch you," she says, almost pouting.

"And you will. Later," I promise. But I want to focus on properly fucking her right now, and I want an unobstructed view of all of her while I do. To that end, I pull back and thrust into her again. She whimpers in response, and I begin to establish a rhythm, my eyes intent on her pussy taking my length over and over.

Chloe's back arches, moans falling from her lips as I continue powering into her, sweat soon dripping from my temples as I fight to keep a hold on myself. With each drive forward, my hips slap into her ass cheeks, filling the air with the primal sounds of our bodies connecting.

Her heels dig into my shoulders while my hands clasp her legs so hard I need to remind myself not to hurt her. I adjust her position to seat myself at a slightly different angle, and the woman begins speaking in tongues as her inner muscles contract and flutter around my cock. It is all I can take, and I curse myself as I piston in and out at a brutal pace, allowing my climax to overtake me as Chloe comes apart before me.

When we are both completely spent, I allow her legs to fall to the sides and I collapse on top of her, careful to put my weight on my forearms on the mattress to either side of her. Choe immediately wraps me in the cocoon of her soft thighs and warm arms, and I decide right then that this is where I want to stay for the rest of my life.

"But, *Da-ad*!" Ayana pleads, doing her best to sound as pathetic as possible.

"No buts!" I insist. "The punishment for lying is no television, and that includes baking shows."

We are on our way to youth hockey practice the next evening, and it feels fucking amazing to be able to reach over for Chloe's hand–or thigh–whenever I feel like it. There is no more hiding, and it is more liberating than I ever anticipated.

Chloe laughed when I said I wanted to drive them both to practice instead of meeting them at the facility, but I insisted. Her argument that I would be there already for goalie practice did not matter. I have a driving need to take care of both her and Ayana–and I do not think that will ever go away. Nor do I want it to. I just need to follow Coach and Katya's advice about balance and happiness going forward.

"Chloe?" Ayana tries my woman next.

Chloe throws her hands up. "Don't look at me, kid. I agree with your dad."

Ayana harrumphs from the back seat, and a glance in the rearview mirror shows her crossing her tiny arms over her chest. "I can't believe this is the thanks I get for planning your big HEA."

"HEA?" Chloe asks over her shoulder.

"Happily ever after," my daughter explains over her pout. "Kara is into romance books, and she says all great romances end with an HEA."

"Ah, well if Kara says so." I shake my head and Chloe snickers into her chest. Kara might be popular with Ayana, but I do not know that I will trust such an impulsive person with my daughter going forward–even if her scheme had its intended effect.

By the time we arrive, Ayana has moved on to other topics, specifically her teen idol, Tara Swanson, and how she is *dying* to go to one of her concerts with Chloe. I grab the gear bags from the back of my vehicle and follow the two females into the practice facility.

The first person I see after dropping the bags rinkside is Benny.

"I thought you left already?" He furrows his brow.

Without hesitation, I drop one hand on Ayana's shoulder and throw my other arm around Chloe, unintentionally startling her and causing her to fall into me.

"Take it easy there, brick house," she says with a laugh, but I only draw her closer as I keep Benny's eyes.

"I had to go get my girls."

He glances back and forth between Chloe and me before his lips spread in a shit-eating grin. "*Nice*! I'm gonna get so much hea–I mean, *hugging*!—when I tell Kaitlyn about this!"

"Banks!" Chloe scolds, but he is already striding for the

doors, so she twists in my arm to look up at me. "I have to get things ready for practice."

"That is why I am here," I tell her, stating what I believe to be obvious. "To help you with practice."

Her expression turns soft, but her eyes light with fire. "You can't fool me, Nicolai Drugov. You're a marshmallow under all that gruff."

"Go put your skates on before I do something about that look in your eyes," I whisper so that my daughter cannot hear.

Parents and children start to filter in as Chloe and I line up gear and place cones on the ice. Matt arrives and begins helping kids with their skates and helmets. When I hear a familiar voice call Ayana's name, I glance up to see Peyton hurrying over to hug Ayana where she balances on her skates by the bleachers.

Peyton called earlier today to tell me she would be here to watch our daughter practice. It is taking time for my ex-wife to get used to our daughter not being with her all the time. She has even expressed some empathy, saying she is getting a taste of what I have experienced over the years. While she has not gone so far as to apologize, it gives me hope for a smoother future co-parenting Ayana.

My Storm Chasers teammates, who were running drills before the kids took over the rink, duck their heads in to chat with a few parents and youngsters. The season is almost upon us, and I face it with so many mixed emotions. It is my final season and the conclusion to a major chapter in my life. But when I consider what I have waiting for me on the other side, it is impossible to have regrets.

"Come on out on the ice when you're ready, guys!" Chloe calls to the kids, some of whom are lurking just outside the rink, others already gliding across the ice.

"Do not forget your helmets!" I yell when one boy steps onto the ice with nothing covering his head. He quickly scampers off, tripping on the rubber mats as he hurries back toward the bleachers.

"Wow," Chloe says as she skates up beside me. "I don't think I've ever seen Evan move that fast. But maybe take it down just a notch, yeah?" She does a terrible job at hiding her smile, but all I can do is shrug in return.

I push off to help a group of struggling kids near one of the nets but plow to a stop when I see Roadie blazing across the ice toward Chloe, a mischievous smile on his lips. I reverse direction, pointing his way. "She is mine, Roadie, and do not ever forget it!"

Mine. The notion feels so natural and right, I do not even have the slightest temptation to punch Roadie in the balls for his stunt the other day.

Roadie throws his head back and laughs, gliding by Chloe without even pausing. "Relax, man! I wouldn't dream of it." He continues across the ice, only stopping when he reaches a boy around Eli's age on the other end.

My eyes find Chloe again as I close the distance between us, and her smile is more dazzling than I thought possible. "What?" I ask, reaching out to pull her toward me on her skates.

"Nothing at all," she responds as I bend my head to capture her lips in another of her addictive kisses, not caring one bit who might be watching.

Epilogue

Chloe

I almost can't believe this is my life. Then I remember that I paid my dues and worked for something better. This isn't dumb luck or the result of someone handing me everything. I moved my whole life to Tampa, went out on a limb and created my own hockey league, and let a man back into my heart. That takes courage, and I like to think that fate smiles upon the courageous. Or fate just really loves love.

I stand by the rink and stretch before my private lesson, moving through the dynamic warm-ups that have become imperative for me before I head out on the ice. Just demonstrating the drills in practice and skating around helping the kiddos has led to a few minor injuries on my part. Kaitlyn told me all about her shoulder issues when she hit perimenopause, so you bet your ass I'm stretching.

Nikolai comes with me to practice quite a bit now and supports my league every way he can. Just thinking about the last month while I stretch has me smiling like a fool. Nikolai's made an effort to prioritize our relationship and my career, and like everything he puts his mind to, it's all flourishing. I spend the night with him when Ayana is with her mom, but head home to my duplex when she's staying with Nikolai. The two deserve alone time together and I don't mind having some of my own space too. I lived with one man for two decades. I think a solid year of living on my own is a healthy way to start something new.

"I didn't start it!"

I hear muffled voices coming from the nearby offices. That sounds suspiciously like Bobby, pleading innocence after he's caused a ruckus.

"He's a rookie, Rhodes!" I wince, recognizing the new coach's voice. He sounds pissed. "You're a veteran player and you haze a new guy? What the fuck? Did you honestly think that would help the team gel right before the season gets going? Oh, I get it. You didn't think at all."

"Coach, I swear I was just joking around with Mac and he got his panties in a bunch about it. I absolutely did not intend to turn it into a fist fight."

My heart starts racing. Bobby always skated on thin ice when my dad was the coach, but the two had a bit of an understanding. Bobby toned down the fighting as much as he could, and Dad spent a lot of time coaching Bobby about behavior. Coach Marsh doesn't sound like he's as understanding. Which sucks, because despite all his goofy behavior, Bobby's a good guy and I like him.

"I can't fucking babysit you, Rhodes. Get your shit together now, or you'll find yourself riding out your contract on the bench."

A door slams and I jolt. I sit down on the bleachers and grab my skates, pretending like I haven't heard a thing.

"Fuck!"

My head snaps over to see Bobby exiting the front of the

coach's office, his hands in his hair. I look around, but don't see anyone else. Thankfully, the kiddo I have a private lesson with hasn't arrived yet to witness one of the Storm Chaser's star players cursing.

"You okay?" I call out.

Bobby drops his hands and looks over in my direction. He gives a head nod but doesn't answer. I look at my phone and see I have ten minutes. The poor guy looks more sad than angry, which accentuates his baby face. It tugs at my heart.

"Wanna talk about it?"

Bobby plods over and throws himself onto the bleacher next to me, his head tilted up to the rafters. "I don't suppose we can pretend you didn't hear that, can we?"

"I think people out on the street might have heard that," I say dryly, nudging his shoulder. "What'd you do this time?"

Bobby huffs and scrubs his hands over his face. "Teased Mac about the frilly towel he keeps in his locker. How was I supposed to know his mama sewed it for him right before she died? He shoved me and before I knew it, I was punching him in the face and rolling around the locker room floor."

I shake my head. "You gotta stop with the 'roids, my man. They'll shrink your nuts."

Bobby gives me a grimace that forces me to roll my lips inward to stop from laughing. "I don't take that shit, Chloe. My balls are far too important. I just don't know when to stop. Something physical happens and I lash out, taking things way too far."

I sit with that for a bit, wishing I was a psychologist and not just a hockey coach. I know Bobby has four brothers, but I don't know anything else about his childhood. "Think he'll bench you?"

Bobby shrugs like he doesn't care, but I can see how tense he is. "Nah. I'll clean up my act. How hard can it be, right?"

I finish lacing up my skates and stand. "Not that hard. Get

a house, maybe a dog or a cat, settle down with a partner who loves you like crazy. Might even invest in a sweater that buttons up the front. Like Mr. Rogers. Everyone trusted Mr. Rogers."

Bobby stares at me like I've grown another set of boobs and he's not sure if he's ecstatic or terrified. "That was all easy peasy until you got to the sweater. A manly man doesn't wear sweaters, Chloe."

I know he's just trying to lighten the mood with humor so I follow suit, even if it might be another knowledge bomb to his poor testosterone-soaked brain. "Actually, it might be a cardigan and a real man can rock a cardigan, no problem. Now, don't you have your first game tomorrow night? You should be getting home to eat your plain chicken breast and broccoli before crawling into bed–alone–so you get your beauty sleep."

Bobby stands and heaves a sigh. "I was going to meet the boys down at Gus's for a pre-game beer."

"Not if you're cleaning up your act, partner." I pat his shoulder and throw him a wink.

Bobby makes a face I saw all the time on my third graders, usually before I made them do their multiplication tables. "Fine." He huffs out of the rink as I shake my head.

I sure hope he gets his shit figured out. I'd hate to see him benched when Kaitlyn finally got him the long-term contract he's always wanted. I'd also hate to sit here a whole hour for a no-show. I check the time again and decide to leave at fifteen after if the kid hasn't shown up. There are eggs to be hard boiled so Nikolai is ready tomorrow with his game day routine. I can't wait to cheer him on from the stands. He even got me an official Drugov jersey to wear.

I step out onto the ice and practice some maneuvers on my own, figuring I might as well use my time wisely. Can't have these kids getting better than their coach. We've had such great interest in the league, Matt and I have decided to split the group into two. Ten and under will go in one group with Matt, and eleven and older will be with me.

A few minutes later, the sound of another pair of skates on the ice hits my ears. I twirl around and see Nikolai skating out toward me. His sandy hair has gotten longer, but he refuses to cut it, mostly because he says he likes it when I curl my fingers into it when he kisses me. He's in black sweatpants and a black T-shirt that hugs his muscles. I swear they've gotten bigger over the off season with him lifting so much.

"Hey!" I call out, delighted to see him, but also confused. "What are you doing here? I thought you had plans with Ayana?"

He stops right in front of me, his gaze drifting over me reverently before snagging on my signature red lips. "I do."

I blink, not understanding. A whispered "shh" comes from behind him. I look around his hulking body to see Ayana leading three older people and a young woman to the bleachers I just sat on with Bobby. My eyes nearly fall out of my head when I see Dad and my mom–together–pulling up the rear, a sight I haven't seen in decades. "Nikolai? What–"

He interrupts me, taking my hands in his and dropping down to one knee right there on the ice. My mouth drops open and everything around me fades as I stare into his icy blue eyes.

"Chloe, you and I have both been here before, so I will not try to say something eloquent. But I promise you that the life we will make together will be better than anything we could live apart. I want to spend the rest of my life making you smile. Watching you bake with my daughter. Seeing how you brighten up a room just by being there. I want to start every day by kissing you good morning and supporting whatever it is you choose to do. I simply love you and that will never stop." He reaches into the pocket of his sweatpants and pulls out a black velvet box, flipping open the lid and exposing the biggest diamond I've ever seen. My mouth's still hanging open and I can't seem to do anything about it.

"Ivan used to say, a husband without a wife is like a goose without water. I do not want to be a waterless goose any longer. Chloe Cooper, will you marry me?"

That does it. My mouth finally closes, only to stretch into a broad smile. My heart's pounding and even though, as Nikolai said, we've both been here before, this time feels right. Like Nikolai and Ayana were the missing pieces to light up my heart.

"Yes, I think I will," I say, nodding my head and feeling giddy with happiness. "I think we'll be very happy, two geese in water together."

Nikolai stands, his face transforming from a nervous frown to the kind of smile that still makes my stomach flip flop. My talented man pulls me to him and kisses me, then twirls us in a circle on the ice, never breaking the contact.

"Well? What'd she say?" Ayana's excited voice floats over the ice.

Nikolai finally breaks away, both of us smiling like idiots. He opens the box once again, pulls out the ring, and slides it on my finger. The square cut diamond catches every single light source in here and bounces it back in a kaleidoscope of color. I put my hand up in the air and holler back, "I said yes!"

We skate over to the side of the rink and I meet Nikolai's family with hugs all around. His mother, father, sister, and Katya follow us back to his house. Nikolai and Ayana come in my car. And my father and mother head over together as well. Perhaps thirty years divorced is the lucky number for finally getting along with your ex. Nikolai had food delivered, so we spend the whole evening talking, getting to know each other, and celebrating our engagement. His parents are delightful, and it warms my heart to see how much they love him. The whole night, Nikolai holds my hand or touches my waist, like he needs that constant contact to make this thing real. I'm only too happy to give it to him.

After everyone leaves for the night, Nikolai goes to Ayana's room to put her to bed. I sneak down the hallway and peer into her newly redecorated room. She's snug in her bed, covers up to her chin as Nikolai reads her their special book *Hush, Little Bunny*. He reads it every night and she never gets tired of it.

"If the other bunnies do not play fair, Daddy will growl at them like a bear," Nikolai reads, his voice dropped even lower as he acts out the book. Ayana giggles as my heart melts. If my ovaries were still fully functioning, they'd explode at the cuteness. It may be a line from a book, but I know the sentiment is real. Nikolai would do anything for his daughter and he'd do anything for me too.

When he slips out of the room some time later, I meet him in the hallway. I slide my hands up around his neck and into his hair. I'll forever be grateful I had the nerve to kiss the grumpy goalie in a bar in Toronto. When his lips meet mine, I know that everything we both went through in our prior lives to get to this exact moment was so, so worth it. I thought I couldn't count on anyone, that the only way to live for myself was to be alone, but Nikolai has proven me wrong. Everything is better together.

Scan the QR code to go to Marika's Amazon page!

Grab my FREE book!

<u>Steamy RomComs in Blueball:</u>

Grumpy the Bear - Blueball Band of Brothers #1

S'more Than a Feeling - Blueball Band of Brothers #2

Home is Where You Park It - Blueball Band of Brothers #3

Set My Heart Bonfire - Blueball Band of Brothers #4

Pining For You - Blueball Band of Brothers #5

* * *

<u>Wolfe Brothers - Blueball Spinoff Series</u>

A Package Deal

<u>All Steamy RomComs Set in Hell</u>:

Grumpy As Hell - Hellman Brothers #1

Bro Code Hell - Hellman Brothers #2

Friend Zone Hell - Hellman Brothers #3

Cougar From Hell - Hellman Brothers #4

Falling First Hell - Hellman Brothers #5

* * *

Ridin' Solo - Sisters From Hell #1

One Night Bride - Sisters From Hell #2

Smarty Pants - Sisters From Hell #3

Ex Best Thing - Sisters From Hell #4

* * *

Love Bank - Jobs From Hell #1

Uber Bossy - Jobs From Hell #2

Unfriend Me - Jobs From Hell #3

Side Hustle - Jobs From Hell #4

* * *

Backroom Boy - Standalone

<u>Steamy Small Town Christmas RomCom</u>:

Grumpy Little Christmas

<u>Steamy Small Town Summer RomCom</u>:

Salt Love

<u>Steamy Hockey RomCom</u>:

Hot Flashes and Hockey Slashes - Hot Flash Hookups #1

Mood Swings and Hockey Flings - Hot Flash Hookups #2

<u>Steamy RomComs</u>:

The Missing Ingredient - Reality of Love #1

Mom-Com - Reality of Love #2

Desperately Seeking Househusbands - Reality of Love #3

* * *

Happy New You - Standalone

<u>Steamy RomComs with Delancey Stewart</u>:

The Spare and the Single Mom

Head Over Cleats

Falling For Mr. Safety

<u>Sweet RomComs with Delancey Stewart</u>:

Texting With the Enemy - Digital Dating #1

While You Were Texting - Digital Dating #2

Save the Last Text - Digital Dating #3

How to Lose a Girl in 10 Texts - Digital Dating #4

<u>Sweet Romances</u>:

The Marriage Sham - Standalone

* * *

The Widower's Girlfriend-Faking It #1

Home Run Fiancé - Faking It #2

Guarding the Princess - Faking It #3

* * *

Lines We Cross - Nickel Bay Brothers #1

Perfectly Imperfect Us - Nickel Bay Brothers #2

<u>Steamy Beach Romance</u>:

1) Sweet Dreams - Beach Squad #1

2) Love on the Defense - Beach Squad #2

3) Barefoot Chaos - Beach Squad #3

* Novella - Handcuffed Hussy

4) Beach Babe Billionaire- Beach Squad #4

5) Brighter Than the Boss - Beach Squad #5

* Novella - Christmas Eve Do-Over

Ale's Fair in Love and War (*Love on Tap*, Book 1)

Smooth Hoperator (*Love on Tap*, Book 2)

Deja Brew All Over Again (*Love on Tap*, Book 3)

Stout of My League (*Love on Tap*, Book 4)

Asheville Collection (Standalone Stories from the *Love on Tap* World)

* * *

The Fix (*Carolina Connections*, Book 1)

The Spark (*Carolina Connections*, Book 2)

The Lucky One (*Carolina Connections*, Book 3)

The Game (*Carolina Connections*, Book 4)

The Way You Are (*Carolina Connections*, Book 5)

The Runaround (*Carolina Connections*, Book 6)

Carolina Connections Box Set 1

Carolina Connections Box Set 2

* * *

The Nerd Next Door (*Carolina Kisses*, Book 1)

New Jerk in Town (*Carolina Kisses*, Book 2)

The Last Good Liar (*Carolina Kisses*, Book 3)

* * *

Between a Rock and a Royal, *Kings of Carolina, #1*

Blue Bloods and Backroads, *Kings of Carolina, #2*

Stealing Kisses With a King, *Kings of Carolina, #3*

Kings of Carolina Box Set

* * *

Poppy & the Beast

Then Again

Full-On Clinger (FREE for a limited time)

About That

Nuts About You

Booby Trapped

Acknowledgments

Marika and Sylvie met years ago at a book signing, instantly hitting it off as they were both quite funny. Fast forward a few years and they were on the phone lamenting all the very real symptoms of peri menopause that were affecting their lives when they both had the grand idea that they wanted to write about it! The goal was to normalize conversation about the various side effects of the hormonal rollercoaster that is aging, while also reminding women of their inherent beauty no matter their age.

From Sylvie - Thanks to Sparky for his support and endless dick jokes. And thanks to my fabulous Venty for keeping me cool. Not sure which one of you I love more.

From Marika - A big huge thank you to my husband, not only for his understanding, but also his patience when I yell at him for having the audacity to fall asleep so fast when I can't anymore. And his chewing. Dear god, the man's chewing!

Thank you to fellow romance authors for their enthusiasm and support of this book. You make a girl feel less crazy.

Last but not least...a huge thank you to Nancy Smay at Evident Ink for making this book shine with your editing and proofreading services!

Marika Ray is a USA Today bestselling author, writing small town RomCom to make your heart explode and bring a smile to your face. All her books come with a money-back guarantee that you'll laugh at least once with every book.

Marika spends her time behind a computer crafting stories, walking along the beach, and making healthy food for her kids and husband whether they like it or not. Prior to writing novels, Marika held various jobs in the finance industry, with private start-up companies, and then in health & fitness. Cats may have nine lives, but Marika believes everyone should have nine careers to keep things spicy.

If you'd like to know more about Marika or the other novels she's currently writing, please find her in her private Reader Group.

If you want to take your stalking to the next level, here are other legal-ish places you can find Marika:

Join her Newsletter - http://bit.ly/MarikaRayNews

Amazon - https://www.amazon.com/author/marikaray

Goodreads - https://www.goodreads.com/author/show/16856659.Marika_Ray

Bookbub - https://www.bookbub.com/authors/marika-ray

TikTok - https://vm.tiktok.com/ZMJvnQ2Cv

Instagram - https://www.instagram/authormarikaray

Website - https://www.marikaray.com

About Sylvie Stewart

USA Today bestselling author Sylvie Stewart loves dad jokes, dirty rom-coms, country music, and baby skunks—preferably all at the same time. Most of her steamy contemporary and romantic comedy novels take place across her favorite state of North Carolina, and her characters never run out of snarky banter or snacks. When her laptop closes, Sylvie is a sucker for hugs from her twin boys and a good laugh with her hot-nerd hubby. If you love smart Southern gals, hot blue-collar guys, and snort-laughing with characters who feel like your best friends, Sylvie's your gal. Stay up to date on all things Sylvie! https://sylviestewartauthor.com

Join her Newsletter - http://bit.ly/s-s-nl

Facebook Reader Group - https://www.facebook.com/groups/743238732533487

Facebook Page – https://facebook.com/SylvieStewartAuthor

Instagram – https://instagram.com/sylviestewartauthor

BookBub – https://bookbub.com/authors/sylvie-stewart

Twitter – https://twitter.com/sylvie_stewart_

TikTok – https://tiktok.com/@authorsylviestewart

Pinterest – https://pinterest.com/sylviestewartauthor

Goodreads – https://goodreads.com/author/show/15303783.Sylvie_Stewart

YouTube – https://youtube.com/@sylviestewartauthor